SEVEN DEADLY SINS

Compiled & Edited by
Ben Thomas & D Kershaw

Paperback : ISBN 978-1-925809-51-0
Hardcover : ISBN 978-1-925809-52-7

Cover Design by Dawn Burdett
Book Formatting by Ben Thomas

Too many a Samsan lip your teeth indent:

Too many a Sybil girl you lure to make

The Great Refusal for a fireside sake:

And glamoured poet many a look has sent

Into those eyeballs bear-brown, somnolent,

Nor dreamed that devils in each muddy lake

Were sucking his devotion in to slake

The furrowed belly of your fanged content!

Religion's bane and Freedom's subtlest foe!

Behold the poppied freight your barges bring

The dim-lit souls that crave the prophet's gleam,

Or fettered people's writhing 'neath their woe--

Gossamer clips and thriftless harvesting

Of phantom flocks and shadowy tilth of dream!

Sloth **by Bernard O'Dowd, 1909**

Table of Contents

The Fallen Sloth of the Dragon

by Zoey Xolton

Lucifer watched the succubi bathing in the hot springs of Hell; all long hair, naked limbs and devious laughter, and yet he felt nothing. Swirling his goblet of blood, he took a deep draught before resting it upon the bannister. He sighed. He felt utterly lacklustre, like the fires of rebellion that had fuelled him for so many eons had dimmed back to an unenthusiastic simmer.

He lived for extremes, revelling in pride and lust, the sins that so offended God. It normally thrilled, filled and consumed him. He had thought he'd never have enough; that his intensity, drive and wanton desire for domination would carry him on endlessly—throughout all of time— until the Day of Reckoning and beyond.

Yet now, he felt listless, vague and without purpose. *For how long have I felt this way?* he wondered. Soft footfalls and the scent of decaying violets and spoiling peaches alerted him to Lilith's presence. She curtsied, eyes averted, before rising to stand by his side.

"You are not yourself, my lord." She observed.

Lucifer smirked wryly. "What makes you say such a thing?"

"I notice every nuance and change in your mood and mannerisms; I always have, ever since you rescued me from Eden."

Lucifer interrupted her, "You saved yourself, Lilith. I merely presented an opportunity."

The Queen of Hell smiled, revealing small fangs. Brushing dark tendrils of hair from her eyes, she continued. "Even so, I feel your detachment and apathy in the very air, my love. All of Hell is governed by your life force, and every single soul here can feel you, though some more distantly than others. Hell needs you to be present again, Lucifer. It is not the same when you are not at your best. The fires do not burn as bright and strong, the screams from the Pit are not as tortured, the sinners not as justly punished and the demons run amuck, testing boundaries beneath your very nose. Hell needs its master, Lucifer. We are all lost without you. We have no hope of soliciting enough souls and tipping the balance, to overthrow Heaven when the times comes, if you are not leading our armies with unbridled, brilliant, self-righteous wrath."

Lucifer drained his goblet before sliding it across the bannister to his queen.

Lilith caught it, watching as it refilled of its own volition.

"I feel bereft, Lilith. I do not know what has changed, if indeed, anything has."

"Perhaps you need stimulation, a new challenge?"

Lucifer cocked a brow in her direction. "What kind of stimulation?"

Lilith laughed, nudging her king with her shoulder before sobering once more. "You have not visited the realm of men yourself, in half a century," she began. "Perhaps it's time that the Great Antagonist walked among the flesh puppets of God once more? Too long have they been without genuine temptation. There has been no one to truly push them."

Lucifer bit his lip, deep in thought.

Lilith snaked her arm around his waist, snuggling into the feathery alcove of his wings. "It will be entertaining," she promised.

Lucifer pulled her close. "You have someone in mind?"

"Would I have suggested such a venture had I not?"

Lucifer sighed, lifting her face to his. Kissing her forehead, he smiled. "You never cease to please me, my love."

Lilith nestled her face into the palm of his hand, and looking up through her thick lashes, put on her most mock-innocent expression. "Come play with me?" she teased. With a devious grin she winked at him . Then in a whisper of swirling black and midnight purple mist, they were gone.

***

Lucifer and Lilith reappeared, side by side, upon an expansive pastoral estate. A large home, painstakingly built by hand with bricks of clay, sat like a jewel at its centre. With many rooms, arched doorways and a low, thatched roof harried down with mud, it housed a family with many loyal, hard-working servants.

The sun was but a sliver above the horizon and already the fields were being worked. Men and women, robed from head to foot, toiled early to avoid the blistering heat of the afternoon sun. Children herded fatted goats, while the men tilled, guiding the ox-drawn ploughs through the earth. The women watered, milked and harvested. Each soul had their task, and each seemed content in their duty to the master of the land.

"Who dwells here?" asked Lucifer of his scantily

clad companion.

Lilith leaned conspiratorially toward him, though they could not be seen or heard, unless they willed it. "This is the home of Elon. He shares his home with his wife and two sons."

"And who are we tempting from the Path of Righteousness?"

Lilith almost bounced with excitement, which Lucifer observed looked most satisfyingly obscene, considering her debauched attire, long wild locks and blazing eyes. "The youngest son, Nathaniel!" She could hardly contain herself. "He yearns to leave the farm and travel. He despises toil and would be free of it if he could. He feels his elder brother, Gideon, causes him to look poorly in the eyes of their father."

Lucifer nodded, impressed with her find. "Well done, my love. It seems like just the task to drag me from my indolence. I feel the pleasure and thrill of the challenge already."

Lilith grinned.

***

Nathaniel kicked the ox and threw down the plough. Storming from the field, he found a shady tree and sat down beneath it, fishing a wooden pipe and pouch of *kaneh bos* from his robes. Lighting up, he reclined and enjoyed his smoke.

"Would you mind?"

Nathaniel startled at the silver-blue-eyed stranger seated beside him.

Lucifer raised an expectant brow.

The farmer's youngest son cleared his throat. "Of course," he said finally, and passed the pipe and flint to his new companion.

"I have no need of your rocks," said Lucifer in his mortal guise.

"Then how will you—" Nathaniel started.

Lucifer's clicked his fingers and the *kaneh bos* glowed, the embers of the dried herb smoking. Lucifer inhaled deeply and with a satisfied smile, exhaled in the morning breeze.

Nathaniel swallowed hard. "Who are you? You are no man of God."

Lucifer smirked. "Are you, my friend? A man of God?"

"I try to be."

"Why?"

"My father is a man of faith and so is his household. I must obey my father's example."

"And yet, you stray."

Nathaniel opened his mouth to argue, but thought better of it. "My father's faith requires sacrifice, endless labour and abstinence from pleasurable pursuits. I cannot help but feel there might be other ways to live. I do not feel suited to the cage my God has provided. My brother toils day and night, resting only on the Sabbath. He is the apple of my father's eye. I know I displease him greatly."

"Then why continue on in this way?" asked the fallen angel. "You cannot be your brother. It seems foolish to flog the ox when it has fatigued. Why not walk your own path? Surely life is for living, for enjoying?"

Nathanial eyed Lucifer. "Who are you, that you would encourage me to turn from God and my father?"

"I think you know."

Nathaniel sat up straight, his reddened eyes wide. "You are he, the Deceiver—Satan!"

Lucifer shrugged, nonplussed. "I have many names and many faces."

"You would have me burn in the Abyss?"

"I would have you be free of a tyrant, Nathaniel. I live my way...perhaps you should live yours? In your case, there will be no consequence."

"All actions have consequences."

"Not this one, I can assure you. You long to beg your

father for your share of the inheritance? Ask it of him, and he will relent. He will give you what is yours, and you can be free. Travel, indulge your every wanton guilty pleasure, and when the wealth has run out, you can return home."

"In shame? To a father who will have disavowed me?"

"To a loving welcome, a *feast*. Your father will welcome you with open arms—his prodigal son, at last returned to him. It is sin without consequence, I have foreseen it."

Nathaniel stared.

Lucifer smiled. He could see the thoughts racing through Nathaniel's mind.

"And what do you stand to gain if I do as I please? Will my soul be forfeit?"

"Not at all. I am not here to bargain or take your soul by force. I am here…to present an alternative option. Continue to follow your God, or do not. Ultimately, it matters little to me. However, there is always room at the long table in my kingdom for those who embrace the darkness and revel in it. I never refuse a kindred soul."

***

Nathaniel left the farm behind, taking with him his father's best cart and horse. Lucifer had spoken truthfully; his father had parted with his share of the inheritance without question, believing it to be the will of God.

"I know not what path you must walk, my son, but I know it will one day lead back to me," he had said stoically.

And so, for months, the farmer's youngest son drank and whored himself, experiencing every perversion Sodom and Gomorrah had to offer—until at last his coin ran out, and his wineskin, dry. The twin cities of sin were unkind to the destitute. He had enjoyed taking from those who had only their flesh to sell in return for food and shelter; and now, he was faced with being one of them. *No,* he thought. *I have enjoyed myself, as I have always desired. I will not be a slave or indentured man. I will return home, and I will see at last if the Fallen One's word can be trusted.*

***

Elon wept as his youngest son approached, empty handed and spent, through the farm gate. The old man ran down the dirt path, arms stretched wide. "My son!" he cried, "you have returned to me!"

Nathaniel embraced his father.

"Woman!" he called over his shoulder, "have Gideon slaughter the fatted calf! This night we feast, for our son has returned, and our family is whole once more. God is good!"

Nathaniel smiled broadly, relieved as he rested his chin upon his old man's shoulder. He had been rewarded for his sloth. Beyond, immaterial to everyone else, Lucifer revealed himself, black wings outspread, silver-blue eyes bright with fire. He raised a knowing brow, a smirk upon his perfect angelic countenance. Beside him, a woman of inconceivably dark beauty appeared.

"Come share in the pleasures of Hell with us—when you are ready," she whispered, her soft, sultry voice carrying on the breeze to his ear.

Then they were gone, and his family ushered him inside for the celebrations. He smiled, a sinister delight brewing in his heart.

Death Care
by A.R Dean

Ruby Thomas has spent the past thirteen years at Creekside Daycare. It's the only job that she's been able to keep in her forty-seven years of life. When Ruby started, they considered her a top-notch employee but as she grew comfortable, she no longer felt a desire to impress. It was easy to blame the drinking or three failed marriages for Ruby's lack of enthusiasm for her job. Truth was she just didn't care anymore. She felt secure in her place.

Ruby was eventually placed in the back of the building with the pre-school aged students. Many of her co-workers joked that it was an out-of-sight, out-of-mind situation. In her years at the daycare, Ruby had gone through eighty-four classroom partners. Her inability to keep a co-teacher was probably one of the many reasons she had the smallest group of kids.

Ruby made no effort in her room. The Turtle Room as it was dubbed held no decorations or colour. While other teachers prided themselves on crafts and used those to colour up their space, Ruby didn't even have art supplies. They had run out years ago; Ruby didn't feel the need to order more.

The lack of supplies was one way Ruby was able to run off overly ambitious young ladies. The women who cared for their job never lasted a month. Ruby's lack of effort either drove them to quit or transfer rooms. It became worse if the partner followed Ruby's example. They always took their laziness a step further than Ruby, only to be caught.

Her work file was filled with staff complaints, child injuries and letters from angry parents. No matter what happened, Ruby slid past being able to continue her job. A few people thought it was Ruby's ability to charm that kept her at Creekside, but no one ever knew how someone like Ruby kept a job. She was never able to accept fault.

Knitting in her beanbag chair, she glanced around at the five children in front of the TV. Yawning, Ruby continued to fiddle with the blanket she was making while the princess sang on screen for her prince. Ruby snorted, remembering how all her prince charmings had become frogs. Ruby hated being married. The men expected her to hold a job and still take care of the house. Not one of her husbands understood how Ruby could allow her home to be filthy. They never liked the explanation that if she had to help pay for it then she didn't need to clean it.

The knock at her room door caused her to drop a stitch. "Damn," she muttered, pushing away the pile of yarn. "It's open."

Lisa shook her head as she entered. "Now Ruby, you know we are to keep the doors locked for the children's safety." Her supervisor's voice squeaking with cheerfulness.

"Guess I forgot."

"I see. Try harder to remember from now on," Lisa chirped at her. "Your new teaching partner starts today."

"Hurray?" Ruby shrugged, her long black locks fumbling over her shoulder.

"Ruby"—Lisa knelt down to pat the older woman's knee while she ignored the holes in her leggings—"this is your last chance for a partner. If this one fails to work out, the owner says they will take measures to replace you."

Ruby rolled her eyes. "I got that same threat two partners ago, Lisa."

"Do you even like working here?"

"It pays the bills," Ruby shrugged again.

"This isn't a threat, it's a promise. You drive off this one and you will be looking for another job. We've been friends a long time Ruby, but I can't keep covering for you." They both turned to the knock at the door. Clearing her throat, Lisa rose to introduce the new arrival. "Meet

Paula Gurch."

"Hi." Ruby waved from the bean bag a thin angry smile on her lips.

"Nice to meet you," the petite blonde responded. She was close to Ruby's age. It gave her hope that the woman wouldn't be as enthusiastic as the others.

"You two get acquainted. I'll be in my office if you need anything." Lisa gave a quick pat on Paula's shoulder as she walked away.

Paula had a large smile on her face as the door shut. At the retreating footsteps, her smile disappeared. "Ugh. Does she snort the chipper pills or just lace her coffee with them?"

Ruby's mouth dropped in surprise before twisting into a smile. "I know. People like her think you must be in a good mood to work with kids. All perky and happy."

Chuckling, Paula fell back on to the beanbag next to Ruby. "What are they doing?" She motioned to the kids zoned out in front of the movie.

"Mornings are video time. It allows me to get my knitting and crap done."

"Awesome! I was stuck in the Crab Room with Stella for training. Her mornings were crafts and stories. I hated it."

A boy turned to the two women. "I liked Miss

Stella's room."

"Shut up Tyler. Watch the movie."

"I'm Tyrell and we've seen this one already."

"Whatever," Ruby sneered, "Watch it or you don't get a snack." Tyrell sighed and turned back to the TV.

"What a brat. My kids would have been happier watching movies instead of books." Paula groaned.

"It's been a real pain in the ass since they disconnected the cable here."

Paula snickered, "I bet."

"So, what else do we do with them? I mean this room doesn't require diapers, does it? I don't do those." A grimace on Paula's face.

"God, no." Ruby gagged. "I'm not allowed in the Infant Room anymore. I refused to change the diapers and one of them got a rash."

"Is that why they gave you the older kids?"

"Yep. Pre-schoolers don't need as much hands-on attention. Leaves me free to do other things." Ruby picked up her knitting again. "After morning movies, I feed them lunch. They play outside and nap."

"What if they refuse to nap?"

Ruby reached over to her bag and pulled out a bottle of liquid sleep-aid. "Teacher's helper."

"Nice," Paula told her, impressed.

"If they wake up before their parents arrive, I put on another movie. Sometimes if I don't need a nap myself, I'll let them have free play with toys."

"Napping at work? Awesome."

"You bet. Plus, I know how to avoid recess duty so I can hang out here."

Paula glanced around the room, a huge grin on her face. "My husband made me get this job. He claimed that I couldn't be a stay at home mom now that my girls were in junior high. I really thought that I was going to hate it here."

"Now what do you think?"

"I think I'm not going to miss my soaps and I'll be getting paid to nap."

Ruby smiled over her knitting, "Paula I think we are going to be great friends."

Retrieving a silver flask from her purse along with her phone, Paula nodded to Ruby. "We are going to do just fine."

Together Ruby and Paula had become an unstoppable team of idleness. Ruby was right that she and Paula would become good friends. What time they didn't spend at work they spent at Ruby's apartment drinking. Paula's husband tried to talk to her about her drastic behaviour change, but it was shrugged off. He felt it best to ignore her and the toxic friendship she had made.

"Why do Mondays start so early?" Ruby groaned from her chair.

Paula laughed. "Because we drank away Sunday."

"That's right." Laughing, Ruby turned her attention to the kids quietly playing in the corner. "Hey kids!" They all startled at her harsh voice. "Clean up the crap, its movie time. Miss Ruby and Miss Paula need a break."

The children quickly ran about putting toys back on shelves before moving to the carpet in front of the TV. Paula glanced around the room cobwebs dangling from the ceiling. "I think we should have them dust if they have energy after nap."

They both jumped at the knock at the door. "Shit," Paula whispered.

"Come in," Ruby called.

Lisa shook her head as she entered the room. "Ruby, the door."

"Why are you here, Lisa?" Ruby asked, rubbing her eyes.

"I have had it brought to my attention that you two haven't done recess duty for over six months." Her lips pursed in a sour expression.

Ruby feigned horror. "That can't be right. I know we've switched around a couple of times, but I'm positive we've taken turns."

Lisa sighed, "No Ruby, you haven't. Trust me; I have checked the duty roster. There are also the complaints from the rest of the staff."

"No one told us they had complaints," Paula muttered nastily, "I like that they ran to you instead of talking to us."

"They told me that they had mentioned it to both of you."

"Nope. Sorry Lisa, I'd have remembered that." Ruby smiled. "I guess we will take our turn next week."

"Wrong. To make up for the past few months, you two will be on recess duty for the entire school for the next thirteen days."

"That's insane. We would be outside for two and a half hours straight," Paula protested.

"What about our room?" Ruby demanded.

"No worries. Chloe and Annabelle will take over while you're outside. Besides, moving around in the fresh air might do you both some good." Lisa's voice was so chipper the women worried for the windows. "I suggest you get your coats ladies, it's chilly today and the toddlers go out in ten minutes." Smiling, she left, locking the door behind her.

"What a shrew!" Paula hissed. "Can she do that? It's

February. Why do these kids need to go outside in February?"

"She thinks she is punishing us," Ruby said as she stood to retrieve her coat from the hook.

"Isn't she?" her friend whined.

"Not the way I do it." Ruby smiled handing over the other woman's coat.

"How do you do it?"

"The playground is on the other side of the parking lot next to the woods. We just need to park my car facing the playground so that we can keep an eye out for Lisa if she's checking on us. We would see her long before she'd see us."

"What about the kids?"

"What about them? There's a fence that surrounds the whole thing. We latch it and they're trapped there."

Paula gave Ruby a wicked grin. "We get to sit in the warm car while the brats freeze on the playground?"

"Exactly. We only need to get out when it's time to switch the classes around. Even better, we don't have to deal with our own room for almost two weeks."

"You're a genius."

"Not really. I just have worked here long enough to know how to work the system to my advantage."

They made sure to wave to Lisa in her office as they

collected the toddlers for recess. Once they were out the door, Ruby ran off to move her van so that they had a place to relax. Paula latched the gate, rushing to join Ruby in the warm vehicle. Pushing the fast food wrappers off the passenger seat, Paula climbed in. Her voice sounded concerned as she took a cigarette from the glove compartment. "Are you sure they can't get out? The playground is a little close to the bypass."

Shrugging, Ruby lit her own cigarette. "I mean at one point there was a hole in the fence next to the woods. It wasn't very big; I don't think kids can fit through it."

Paula lit her own cigarette. "Guess if the kids are stupid enough to get out, then they'd do it no matter where we are sitting."

"Exactly. I deserve to be warm," Ruby told her, settling into her seat while she flicked the ashes of her cigarette on to the van floor.

Three days passed without incident. The children played in the cold while Paula and Ruby relaxed in the van closest to the gate. "You make this job easy Ruby. When I trained with Stella, it was all nonstop."

"I know. I don't understand why these women try so hard. It's not like any of these kids are theirs."

"Right?" Paula cracked her neck before reclining the seat back. Ruby was digging through the trash in her backseat for another pack of cigarettes when they heard the screeching tires and honking horns. They glanced at each other with wide eyes.

"It's a highway. Accidents happen all the time," Ruby told her.

"Exactly." Paula nodded. "Maybe we check to make sure."

"Yeah. Can't hurt to check." They got out of the car, walking carefully to the gate. "How many are we supposed to have?"

"Ten."

"How many are there?"

"Nine," Paula gasped.

"Shit." Ruby walked quickly down the hill to the accident. Beside a truck was a sobbing woman. A few other motorists were out of the vehicles trying to help while others were on the phone. The truck was alone in the stretch of road, no other vehicle touching it. Ruby felt the dread unfurl in her chest as she bent to pick up a pink sneaker in the grass. Slowly, she made her way to the front of the truck. She gasped at the fluffy lavender coat under the passenger tire. Ruby knew that purple coat belonged to one of the toddlers on the playground. Ellie or Allie? Ruby couldn't be sure of the name.

The hysterical woman next to the truck crawled over

to grab Ruby's leg. She glanced down into the young woman's face, white with terror. "I didn't see her. I tried to honk." Shaking the woman away, she rushed kneeling over the child. The little girl's brown eyes were wide and vacant. With shaking fingers, she touched the girl's neck for a pulse. There wasn't one.

Paula had come up behind her puffing out of breath. "I got the others inside. You find the missing kid?"

Ruby stood grabbing Paula and jerking her back to the grass. "The kid's dead," she whispered harshly.

Paula glanced down at the body under the tyre before she started crying. "We will go to jail! We should have been watching them," Paula sobbed.

"Shut up! I know how to get us out of this."

"How?" Paula hiccupped.

"The hole in the fence. The gate wasn't open. She must have slipped out of it. It's not our fault they didn't fix it." Ruby shook Paula.

"We were in the car."

"How will they know? You won't tell them and neither will I. Those kids can't even use a toilet, let alone tell them we weren't on the playground. We say we turned our back on that side of the playground to break up a fight. She got out when our backs were turned." Ruby shook the sobbing Paula again. "Understand?"

"We were on the playground with them. It was an accident."

"Exactly." Ruby glanced up the hill where Lisa and the Toddler Room teacher, Megan, were running to them. "Keep crying."

Megan's voice was screeching the child's name over and over as she hurtled down the hill. "Addy!" Lisa stood in the grass; her hands covered her mouth in horror. Megan was kneeling over the body, rubbing the child's dirty hair. Ruby placed a hand on Megan's shoulder as the sounds of sirens came closer. Everyone there knew that help was coming too late.

"How did this happen?" Megan sobbed.

Ruby held back the urge to roll her eyes. She hated how Megan acted like these kids meant something. "I don't know."

Megan's body shook in a rage. "You needed to be watching them."

"We were."

Megan jumped up shoving Ruby back. "I doubt that. Everyone knows that you are lazy and worthless! I bet you were sleeping off another hangover!"

"Get your hands off me!" Ruby shoved back. "I don't care how upset you are!"

"Upset? You killed her! Your neglect killed her!"

Megan roared as she charged forward, taking Ruby to the ground. Megan had big fistfuls of hair as she bashed Ruby's head into the pavement. Grunting in pain, Ruby scratched to get the other woman off her. It wasn't until the cops pulled the two women apart did the fight finally end.

The media storm that followed had the attention of the whole country. Ruby was right that by sticking to their stories that the whole mess would be ruled accidental. They cleared Ruby and Paula of all wrongdoing. It didn't stop Creekside from shutting down.

Ruby and Paula received unemployment along with the disability. They had both claimed that the experience left them with PTSD. Ruby deactivated her social networking site because of the death threats but remained in her apartment. She finally got the life she'd always wanted. She was getting paid to do nothing. As she lay on her couch eating her takeout, she decided that the little girl had died for the best reason: Ruby's happiness.

The White Lady of Bachelor's Grove

by Sue-Marie St. Lee

Nina looked forward to 2003. Her hopes to be installed in Omega Kappa Xi were about to come true as she mingled in the sorority house until the call-to-order. "You'll be divided into groups of three," Marsha, the senior ranking member explained, "Each group has a designated abandoned home to scavenge for articles we hid. When I call your name, stand with your group." She gave each group a map to their separate destinations.

Nina felt happy that her group included Gayle, a fellow member of the chess team, and Sonya, her roommate and co-author of their campus newspaper column.

"Now, pick a notecard from your group's fishbowl. The object on your card is the hidden item you must find. After your group have found their treasures, return here for the night. Now, go!"

The three groups headed outdoors; some grumbled about the houses being haunted and the locations being too far away. Nina, Gayle and Sonya, already in Nina's Jeep, put the coordinates of their house into their navigation systems.

"Did you hear what those girls said about these places being haunted?" Sonya loved the supernatural, even claimed to be a *sensitive*.

Gayle laughed. "Are you kidding? What's there to be afraid of when we have *you* with us?" Making scary gestures with her hands, she teased Sonya, "Hell, if there're any ghosts, we'll find a cosy place for you to chat with them."

"No!" Sonya argued. "I'm not kidding! Did you pay attention to where *our* abandoned house is? It's next to Bachelor's Grove Cemetery! Don't you remember the stories of the *white lady*? The lady that's been seen in the graveyard holding her dead baby that she's buried next to? That's REAL!"

The legend of the 'White Lady' of Bachelor's Grove Cemetery has been longstanding in the Chicago area. At the risk of sounding cliché, everyone who has lived in the Chicago area knows about the *white lady*.

"I'm not worried. If she's real, she won't bother us. She's mourning her baby. Besides, we won't be in the graveyard," Nina reasoned. "Hey, a toll booth is coming up, get some change out."

During the rest of the drive, Gayle and Sonya studied the clues for locating their hidden items. Gayle needed to find an old red change purse; Sonya, a pair of tiger-striped eyeglasses; and Nina, a pair of antique brass hair combs.

Following the navigation system, Nina turned onto a pitch-black dirt road lined with giant elm trees; its canopy gave the illusion of being in a cave. Sonya pulled forward from the back seat to gain a better view as the house came into view. "There it is. There's the house."

With headlights aimed at the front porch, Nina parked. "Okay, let's do this." The girls turned on their phone lights and started for the house.

On the rickety porch, a ripped screen door hung on one hinge, moaning like an old man whenever a breeze nudged it. Gayle shoved it aside while Nina jiggled the main door's knob. It opened with the sharp, ear-splitting scream of rusted metals scraping against each other. Sounds awakened beyond the door.

"Wait. Did you hear that? Something's inside. This is a bad place, bad energy. I feel it!" Sonya did not want to cross the threshold.

"You wanna stay out here? Fine, but we're not gonna look for your eyeglasses and you'll be out of the sorority." Nina walked into the foyer with Gayle. Muted, creaking footsteps sounded from above. Frightened, Sonya scurried close behind the others.

"It's mice, or bats," Nina scoffed. "Now hurry!"

Gayle found the red change purse in a kitchen drawer and helped Sonya find the eyeglasses in an ash bucket near the fireplace. Nina, upstairs in a bedroom, searched for the hair combs when the others joined her. Sonya saw something shining on the window ledge in a small closet. "I found them!"

In the bedroom, Nina noticed a glimmer behind the woodwork. She pried the wood aside to uncover two engraved brass hair combs. "*I* found them!"

In the hallway, Sonya and Nina compared items. The pair that Nina found appeared older than Sonya's. "I don't know what you found, Sonya, but mine are the *real* ones."

"*Real?* As opposed to what—*unreal?*" Sonya argued.

"Never mind. Let's get outta here. We'll take both of them. One of them has to be the pair they hid."

On the drive back to Omega Kappa Xi, Gayle and Sonya examined the antique hair combs. Trying to decipher the engraving, Sonya snapped a picture on her phone and enlarged it. After much deliberation, the two girls agreed the word on the combs was *Lydia*.

"Lydia who? I'll bet these belonged to the *white lady*, the ghost that carries her dead baby around. Oooo, I don't feel good. I'm dizzy. Something's wrong." Nina pulled off the road so Sonya could barf.

Returning to the car, Sonya handed the combs to Gayle. "I can't hold these; they're making me sick. They're cursed!"

"Give them to me." Nina grabbed the combs and put them in her hair. "Do I look cursed? You're reading too many stupid ghost stories."

At the sorority house, all the girls turned in their scavenged treasures and camped out in the great room. Sonya slept far away from Nina, who still had the combs in her hair. They were not planted by the sorority for the scavenger hunt.

***

The next morning, Nina returned to her dorm room. She ditched classes, spending the day binge-watching her favourite shows. Late that afternoon, Sonya returned from classes. Miffed at Nina for missing the editorial staff meeting, she blasted her, "Hey, I had to meet with Mr Thomas without you. Why didn't you answer my texts?"

"I've been busy."

Sonya leaned over Nina's shoulder to see what kept her so busy. "What the hell? You've been binge-watching this crap all day?" She pulled back, "You smell like you haven't showered." Feeling woozy, she reached for the chair behind to steady herself. "You ditched classes too, didn't you?"

"I'm hungry, go down to Tony's and pick up some pizza." Nina paid no attention to Sonya's chastising.

A wave of sickness gurgled from Sonya's stomach; she grabbed a waste basket and barfed. "Screw you. Get your own damned pizza."

"I can't stay in this room with you and those cursed hair combs." She grabbed a carry-on bag and started packing.

"I'll spend the night at Gayle's." Dropping the carry-on, she hurled again.

"Damn it!" Sonya headed to the door. "I'll be back tomorrow to pick up the rest of my things when you and your cursed hair combs are in class. When you've come to your senses and throw them away, I'll move back. Maybe."

The next evening, Nina skipped the *Future Astrophysicists* conference, attending the Alpha Paedra Psi's *Free for All* instead. Thinking that Nina would be at the astrophysicists' gathering, Gayle accompanied Sonya to retrieve the rest of her belongings. They found the room in utter chaos. Clothes, from both girls' closets, lay strewn about the room. Sonya's jewellery scattered across her dresser and floor. She collapsed to the floor, sifting through the mess, tossing Nina's dirty clothes to the side.

Gayle gasped, "You were robbed!"

"It sure looks like it!" Separating Nina's clothes from her own, she noticed some of hers were missing, "My brand-new suede boots are gone! So is my leather skirt and silk blouse..." Scrambling to her feet, she sifted through the jewellery, "...and my brand-new gold earrings!"

Gayle rang campus security who arrived within half an hour. They took Sonya's statement and photos and filed a robbery report. They also changed the lock, gave Sonya a new key and texted Nina to pick hers up at the security office.

After packing the rest of her belongings, Sonya heaped Nina's things on her bed then left for Gayle's room. They talked most of the night about the strange events since finding the hair combs.

Their phones began ringing at six o'clock in the morning. It was Omega Kappa Xi announcing their invitation to the sorority. The ceremony would begin Sunday at noon. The girls wondered if Nina had received an invitation; both texted her. No response.

Nina partied all weekend at the fraternity. Late Sunday night she returned to her dorm room discovering the lock had been changed. She went to the security office to complain and retrieved her new key. Once inside her room, she shoved the clothes from her bed onto the floor and laid down, still dressed in Sonya's new clothes.

By Wednesday afternoon, Gayle and Sonya, concerned they had not seen Nina for days, paid her a visit. When Nina opened the door, the girls could not believe their eyes. Nina was wearing Sonya's black leather skirt, silk blouse, suede boots, golden earrings and, of course, the hair combs. She hadn't showered since the day of the scavenger hunt seven days ago. The room was in disarray, worse than when Gayle phoned security. Bags of take-out food intermingled on the floor with clothes, books and magazines.

Sashaying to her bed, Nina plopped down and asked, "What's up?"

Sonya looked at Gayle. "I can't do this. She's still wearing them. I'm already feeling sick. I have to go."

Gayle walked into the room and questioned Nina about her negligent behaviour—missing classes, the sorority induction ceremony, Chess club and editorial meetings.

"What are you so worried about? I'm just having a little fun." Nina showed no concern, turned on her laptop and began binge-watching GoT.

***

Sonya convinced Gayle that intervention was needed from someone who could break the curse. They arrived at Sophia Vanga's home in Schiller Park, a Bulgarian suburb known for their old-world cuisine and culture.

Sophia's niece greeted the girls and led them into the parlour, "Aunt Sophia will be here shortly. Please sit." She motioned to a round table.

Shuffling sounds came from the hallway where the old blind woman, born without eyes, manoeuvred perfectly to the table. She sat with the girls and listened to their concerns ever since Nina found the combs.

When the girls finished their story, Sophia began to speak, "I know of the white lady. You are right. She was cursed by the witch who wanted her husband.

"Lydia, who you call the white lady of Bachelor's Grove, loved Jed. He was well to do but a hard worker, not afraid to get his hands dirty. He gathered stones from his farm to build his home. He had many farm animals and owned hundreds of hectares of rich farmland.

"Even though Jed was wealthy, and I've been told, handsome, he was a friend to anyone in need. He helped with barn raisings and re-routed streams running through his lands to share with neighbours.

"He met Lydia at a church picnic. She was a young schoolteacher who lived with her parents, brother and sister. Her father was a farmer too, but he made most of his money selling honey from his bees.

"Jed was smitten with Lydia from their first meeting and after a brief courtship, they married. Lydia quit teaching to run the household, garden and help Jed in any way she could. They were the most loving couple anyone knew."

"Life was pretty normal for everyone in the little town until a gypsy family moved in; most people shunned them for their strange ways. But they kept to themselves—didn't bother anyone.

"One day, Jed decided to drop by their little shack and welcome them. He gave them some hens, a rooster, goat, pig and some baked goods from Lydia.

"Bavol, the old gypsy man, thanked Jed and told him if he ever needed help with sick animals or crops, his daughter, Minka, could heal most anything.

"Minka visited Jed twice a week, bringing special concoctions to keep on hand for ailing animals and a dust which made his crops double in size. He was thankful for Minka's neighbourly help.

"Minka wanted to be more than neighbours. She

wanted to be his wife. She started dabbling in black magic. She devised a plan to do away with Lydia.

"On their first anniversary, Lydia gave birth to a daughter. Jed called her his little angel. Lydia cared and fussed over the baby's every need while still cooking, cleaning and loving Jed.

"I think Gloria was about three months old before Minka showed up with a gift. She bought a pair of brass hair combs and had them engraved with Lydia's name. Lydia graciously accepted the gift and put the combs in her hair right then and there.

"Minka knew it wouldn't be long before Jed would call for her help. She knew Lydia would grow lazy from the curse of Sloth she had cast on the hair combs and Gloria would need care. She thought that between Lydia's laziness and Minka's special brews, it wouldn't be long before Lydia died."

"Lydia's demeanour began to change within days. Jed thought she was merely tired after having the baby. He waited on her hand and foot, refusing Minka's help, thinking Lydia needed peace and quiet.

"Poor Jed. He worked the farm, cooked, cleaned and cared for the baby as best as he could while doting on Lydia. He was sure she would snap out of the darkness when spring came in a few weeks. She didn't.

"Along with spring came lots of baby animals, newly planted fields and a tuberculosis epidemic. Jed stayed away from town to avoid bringing any germs home to Lydia and the baby. But Gloria became sick anyway. Jed stopped his farming chores to care for her. He tried all the old wives' tales—cod liver oil, vinegar massages, steaming hemlock for her to inhale under blankets. Nothing worked. Gloria grew sicker and died a week before her first birthday.

"Even her baby's death couldn't break the evil spell of Sloth inflicted on Lydia. She did grieve and withdrew into a worthless shell of her previous self. She followed her baby to the grave six months later.

"Jed lost his mind with heartache. He neglected the farm, spending days in the graveyard. Friends and family tried to help. He told them to leave him alone; he said he was already dead."

"Eventually, he sold the farm animals and the majority of the farm, keeping only a small area where the stone house stood. He lived the rest of his days alone, with memories in that house. That's the house where you found the hair combs.

"When he laid Lydia out for the wake, he took the combs from her hair, later throwing them against their bedroom wall. He never liked those combs—they contorted her beautiful, long hair into a matronly bun on top of her head. In death, Jed arranged her hair loosely around her face and down her shoulders.

"Lydia's death freed her from Minka's curse, but even though she reunited with her baby, she walks the grounds carrying Gloria and blaming herself. That's the part of the curse that lingers—undeserved guilt. As long as evil still exists in those combs, Lydia cannot rest. Her soul is tortured by an evil that was done to her, not by her. The evil must be broken for her to see the truth and be freed from unfounded guilt.

"Those combs have cursed your friend. They must be destroyed; only then will your friend be saved and Lydia set free to finally rest in peace.

"Go now." She handed the girls a carved wooden box. "You will be safe from the curse if you put them in here. Return them to me. I will remove the curse."

***

Sonya and Gayle found Nina playing video games in her room. Sonya stayed in the doorway as far away from the combs as possible but still within range if Gayle needed help.

Trying to reason with Nina about the truth of the hair

combs, Gayle's efforts were met with laughter and a threat if anyone tried to take the combs.

"That's it. Hold her down, I'll get those damned combs from her." Sonya charged in, struggling as Nina tried to break free from Gayle.

"I've got one." The words barely escaped from Sonya's lips before she upchucked all over Nina and the bed.

Still battling, Nina's legs broke loose and kicked Gayle off the bed. Sonya launched her fist into Nina's face, disorienting her enough for Sonya to rip the other comb and a clump of hair from her head.

Gayle got up from the floor and tried to run for the door when Nina lunged and dropped her again.

"I don't have time for this!" Sonya punched Nina hard, this time incapacitating her long enough for the two girls to escape through the empty corridor and to the parking lot.

***

The girls sat in the parlour again after giving the box to Sophia. She sat in a rocking chair beside the fireplace, opened the box and pulled the combs out. Blue sparks flew from her fingertips as the evil in the combs repelled her touch. Sophia whispered something in her native tongue. The combs reacted, glowing bright orange against the blue sparks still wielding from her fingertips.

One comb in each hand, Sophia made the sign of the cross and threw the combs into the fireplace. The glowing embers screamed out with heinous laughter as the combs melted away.

When it seemed to be done, a quiet peace filled the room and an apparition appeared behind Sophia.

"Holy shit!" Sonya yelled, "It's a ghost!"

The apparition manifested clearly enough to see that she was smiling and holding a baby. Sophia raised her arm to touch the spirit's face. "You are free now."

Sonya couldn't believe her eyes. "That's the white lady of Bachelor's Grove!"

"No, girls," Sophia said, "This is my sister, Lydia. The white lady of Bachelor's Grove is no more."

Cursed

by Stacey Jaine McIntosh

My eyes fluttered, closed briefly. Then snapped open with a start. Sleep would claim me soon, but for now I fought it and yawned.

It was my curse to bear as the daughter of the Grim Reaper. The sins of the father rested on the heads of his children. This I've been told from the time I was old enough to understand.

The last time I succumbed to my curse, I slept for three months. The time before that, I slept for six years.

Time was destined to pass me by, only I could never tell exactly how much time.

Bone Idol

by Stephen McQuiggan

At first, Sam found it funny, even oddly endearing in a way; the fact that anyone could be so shamelessly bone idle tickled him. The stories of Alastair McDonald that did the rounds on the factory floor were told in such an affectionate, playful way; it was hard not to smile. Of course, Sam believed them to be little more than exaggerated lies, just a way for the wage slaves to pass the drudgery of the shift before clocking out and returning to the dull reality of their own lives.

Nobody could really be that lazy, thought Sam, though he was careful to feign shock at every new instalment of the Lazy Ass Al Show. He even began to feel a little sorry for this much maligned man he had never actually met. Then one godawful wet Tuesday night, he punched in for his shift to find that the legendary Al had been transferred onto his squad.

Sam spent that first night in slack-jawed wonder at the study in indolence that was Alastair McDonald—he moved like a man caught in a perpetual strobe light, the whole world wavering as he trundled by in aching slow motion as if he were but a vision from a parallel, stationary dimension.

"I saw him downtown walking his pet tortoise," Big Jeff, the line manager, told Sam in the canteen. "Damn thing nearly pulled his arm out." But Sam couldn't raise the customary chuckle. He had a bad feeling that Al's arrival was going to have a negative impact on his heretofore cushy job and, sure enough, after break, Big Jeff cornered him to tell him that "Lightning Al" would be his new partner on the Thumper.

Sam protested, listing Al's faults in alphabetical order, but Jeff cut him short by simply agreeing with him. "Tell me about it, I've been lumbered too," Jeff shrugged. "There are two lazy bastards on the factory floor and Alastair McDonald's both of them." It was obvious that Jeff had stuck Al with Sam down in the basement just to get him out of everyone else's hair.

The massive compactor that squatted in one corner of the basement was known to everyone as the Thumper due to the sound it made when, having its capacious throat stuffed with all the rags and off-cuts from the machines upstairs, it spat out its heavy square bales. One half of the basement was filled with scrap to be fed into the Thumper, the other with tidy neat bricks of compacted material ready to be taken away by the dayshift forklift crew.

"Come on, buddy," Sam said, putting an arm around Al, determined to befriend him, make a worker out of him and prove everyone (including himself) wrong. After an interminable half hour, he dropped the pretence of mentorship and camaraderie and started contemplating murder instead.

He had let Al feed the Thumper, but the guy was so damn lethargic he didn't even bother separating the bundles. No matter how many times Sam warned him he'd jam the whole system up, he just flung great clumps of rags down the chute. Al was beyond help, beyond talking to. Sam could only gaze at him in wonder. Other lazy people would surely prostrate themselves at his feet and worship him—he was the bone idles' Bone Idol.

"I need to go to the toilet," Al declared with the voice of a badly charged robot; Sam nodded curtly, glad to be shot of him, glad of the break. He watched him go, the basement slugs leaving him trailing in their wake as he trundled over the dank floor toward the flickering light of the exit. Sam marvelled at his undertaker gait if Al was lugging a coffin, his fellow pallbearers would die of old age before they ever reached the cemetery.

Sam busied himself loading the Thumper; he had a full bale done and there was still no sign of Quickdraw McDonald. Surely, he couldn't still be on the toilet? Sam fumed; my wife had a shorter labour. Was Al married? Sam couldn't imagine what kind of woman would put up with that—maybe she was a blur of multi-tasking speed; they did say that opposites attract after all.

He was just about to go in search of his workmate when he saw a shadow crawling across the far wall. "Hey, Usain Bolt," he called, trying to mask his anger with humour, "hurry up and lend me a hand here." Sam still ended up doing the lion's share, almost putting his back out along with his temper.

He bit his tongue for as long as he could but Al's half-assed manner boiled his piss to such a degree, it was all he could do not to fling him down the chute with the rest of the scrap. "You're gonna clog the damn thing," Sam told him for the umpteenth time, feeling the vein on his temple telegraphing. "Pull the bundles apart before you dump them in. Just take your time and…" He trailed off, realising the sheer idiocy of his last statement.

Al merely nodded, his head moving up and down with all the haste of continental drift and carried on unloading huge bundles into the machine regardless. Sure enough, with a demonic rattle, the Thumper let out a groan as it jammed.

"You happy now?" seethed Sam, clambering over the Thumper's lip and reaching down an arm to clear the blockage. There was a metallic scrape as his watch strap snagged on a bent and rusted hook beneath the debris. "Turn the damn thing off." Sam spat over his shoulder as the machine whirred into gear again. "The big red button on your left." But Al didn't move. There was a hiss as the Thumper began its slow, inexorable descent and something in Sam's guts began that sinking journey too.

"For fucksake, Al, hit the fucking button!"

Al stared back, his face frighteningly blank, as he began the painstaking chore of processing this information. The Thumper let out a whoosh as its thick steel plate began to slide down its oiled hydraulic shafts. Sam yanked on his arm, feeling something give in his shoulder, but it was still stuck fast.

"Jesus, Al, turn the machine off NOW!"

Al turned like a kebab on a spit, placing one foot in front of the other in a parody of movement. The Thumper's squashing plate was slow, but Sam feared that Al was even slower. He watched in horror as Al inched toward the stop button as the terrifying thought that Al was doing this on purpose suddenly took root in his mind.

Sam tugged on his arm until it went numb, screamed and cajoled until his throat was raw, and still Al crossed the short yards like a torpid sloth, his hand finally reaching out for the glowing red button just as the plate connected with flesh and bone.

There was a crack that, in Sam's fancy, sounded like his destiny snapping underfoot. Then there was only agonising darkness.

He awoke in a hospital bed; his wife seated on the side closest to his stump as if she wished to take up the slack. He had to come to terms with it, the doctors kept telling him, for there was a lot he had to do—learn to walk again for one thing; he had never realised the weight of a single arm, and how he'd struggle for balance just to remain upright. Dressing, tying up his shoes, opening bottles and a million other little chores he had taken for granted were all fresh skills he had to acquire.

Without a job, he was stuck at home, snipping at his wife and kids until they eventually left; another amputation he had to learn to live with. All the money he had received was no compensation for their loss. The dreams were the worst though; forget phantom limb, the dreams were the real itch he couldn't scratch.

They were always the same, replaying that awful night over and over, as the Thumper descended in deadly increments and Al McDonald moved toward the stop button at a glacial pace—but just at the moment when he was about to shut it off, he turned toward Sam instead...and on his face a knowing grin. The slow burning insistence of his dreams fed his hatred, flattened it down and compacted it into a murderous thing.

He would have his revenge on that lazy bastard, but he would take his sweet time, for revenge was a dish best served frozen. He had learned that much from Al. He would kill him, but he would do it slowly, and he would relish every drawn-out excruciating second of it because he would be there to watch...and to grin knowingly.

Sam spent most of his compensation on an old meat locker on a piece of scrubland on the outskirts of town. He didn't add to his expense by renovating it; it had all he needed: two rooms, a partition window and doors that only opened from the outside. The realtor thought him daft no doubt—a yuppie throwback intent on converting it into a quirky homestead; Sam did intend to live there, for forty or fifty days at least. He prayed it might even be sixty or more.

He camped out on a few random nights to check the traffic flow (non-existent now that the new ring road had been built) and reconnoitre for partying teens, ramblers, dogwalkers and the like. Nothing—he may as well have been the last man on earth. Satisfied, Sam shifted his languid reconnaissance to Al, a process akin to watching a tree grow. During his time in the hospital, Big Jeff had informed him that Al had been discreetly made redundant after the 'accident' and he was still out of work.

Sam would park outside the McDonald burrow, learning his routine and following him to the shops; watching him browse among the aisles while everyone else bustled around him was as transfixing and unsettling as watching time lapse photography. One morning, his phantom fist flexing after one dream of smirking Al too many, Sam decided to put his plan into action.

He stood in the supermarket as Al listlessly made his way toward him, not so much pushing his trolley as leaning on it for support. It took an age for Al to recognise him, his mental faculties as slow as the rest of him; how many one-armed men did he know, for Christ's sake?

"Hi." He nodded; the greeting slowed down to sound like an unoiled hinge. Sam furrowed his brow as if trying to recall the face. "It's me...Al." The human slug eventually offered. "We used to work together."

"Al! Jesus, I hardly knew you; it's been that long. How you been, buddy?" The smile Sam plastered on felt like it would crack his jaw.

"Fine," Al said, his eyes darting up and down Sam's body before resting on the stump; "You working?"

Yeah, Sam felt like screaming into his moronic face, *I got a job as a Fruit Machine, just pop a penny in my ear and give my one remaining elbow a tug*, but managed to retain his good-natured grin. "Not since the accident. How about you?" Al shook his head like a buckled metronome.

If he apologises, thought Sam, then fuck the plan, I'll kill him where he stands. "I got a shitload of cash out of it," he said, his grin stretching to breaking point, "bought some prime real estate and I'm setting up my own business, so it was a blessing in disguise really. Say, I remember the guys telling me you are a bit of a whiz with computers, that right?"

Al nodded again; Sam was convinced he could see hordes of lice fleeing his body in search of warmer climes. "Well, when I get up and running, I'm gonna need someone to look after that side of things. You interested?" He was willing to bet Al had never been interested in anything in his waking life, that his narcoleptic demeanour wouldn't crack if Lucifer himself appeared to claim him.

"That'd be dandy," said Al, each word drawn out torturously.

"Tell you what, if you're not busy, I could drive you out to the site now, show you the set up."

"Okay, I s'pose. What kind of business is it?"

This time Sam couldn't hold back the yucks. "We're going into the dietary game, Al—it's the one trade, save for undertaking, that never has a downturn."

It was as easy as that—dangle a job in the lazy prick's face and before you knew it, he was sitting in the car, speeding along country lanes to his unwitting end. Sam parked up on the rutted grass close to the meat locker with a jaunty whistle on his lips.

"I love my new car." He smiled. "I always hated the driving stick. That's another thing I owe you."

Al stared out at the crumbling squat building amid the trees, blinking every half century or so. Sam lit a smoke as he waited for him to extract himself from the car, no longer irritated by his sluggishness, relishing it, if anything. "It doesn't look much at the moment," he conceded, putting his arm around Al's shoulders, "but use your imagination. Have a look inside, see where you'll be tapping those keyboards—it's gonna be like the Starship fucking Enterprise, my friend."

A fetid stench seeped out of the dank interior. Al stepped inside with all the haste of an eroding coastline and Sam slammed the door shut behind him. Finally, he could release the pent-up hilarity he had been struggling to contain on the drive over. After a badly coordinated jig, he hurried round to the other side of the locker, jamming open the door on that side with a log he had left there for that very purpose.

Sam's stump was itching with excitement as he made

his way to the Plexiglas window in the dividing wall. It was through this little portal that he would watch Al die, and die slowly; no quick exit for Ol' Lightning Al, he would go out in the same lackadaisical manner he dawdled through life.

It took a human being between thirty and sixty days to starve to death and Sam hoped to be still coming here, munching on a chicken leg as he observed, in two months time. He had supplied enough water for that time period and had set out a timetable of three hours a day, and three at night, to document his deterioration and suffering.

Sam pounded on the unbreakable glass and Al ambled over. "Do you know what's going on?" He laughed. "That room is your tomb. Don't worry, you'll love it, because you don't have to do a thing, just take your time and die at your leisure, you dozy fucking…"

There was a crack; a crack that in his fancy sounded like the thin bones of destiny snapping. Sam spun round, but before he could so much as curse, the door on his side slammed to with a vicious, deadening thump. Sam beat on it but knew it was no use. Al peered at him blankly through the partition, his hateful face as vacant as ever.

Sam wasted whole days banging and shouting, scrabbling at the plaster for loose brickwork, tearing his nails as he clawed at the floor, until acceptance finally kicked in. Surely someone was bound to notice his car eventually and investigate, weren't they?

Al hadn't so much as raised his voice or lifted a finger in a bid to escape; he just sat in the corner, a Zen dummy sipping on water. Sam glared at him through the window, glad he would see every second of his demise. He still had a few chocolate bars and a packet of nuts in his pockets left over from his stakeouts.

He waggled the nuts in front of the partition to torment Al, tore them open and popped some into his mouth before the realisation hit that he would have to ration his meagre supply. He still believed that someone would rescue him (preferably after Al had snuffed it)—he couldn't bring himself to believe that Fate would be cruel enough to take his arm, then his life.

The idea that not only could Fate be that cruel but would take every opportunity to prove it only began sinking in after the second interminable week was over and his paltry food cache was spent. The water was starting to taste brackish, exacerbating his cramps, and in the gloom his favourite snacks danced before him in a torturous parade, singing their Siren song: a sickly, sugary dirge that made his shrunken belly howl.

The only solid thing to look upon was Al and even he had begun to resemble a hallucination, a stationary, never changing mirage. Perhaps he was already dead...but no, his eyes occasionally darted up to meet Sam's as a sly smile rippled at the corners of his mouth.

When the cramps kicked off in earnest Sam forgot all about Al, too consumed with vomiting over the stench of his own liquid shit, convulsing as his internal organs shut down, his gut attempting to digest itself for want of anything else to do.

With the last of his strength Sam propped himself against the window, his breath now too feeble to mist the image of Al on the other side; if only he could see the bastard die, he could go to his skinny grave happy. His heart was capable of a few desultory beats, as if it were Al's heart locked in his chest intent on killing him with its laziness. Staring at the inert lump propped against the far wall, Sam felt his life ebbing away.

Al's hand moved slowly—oh, so slowly—into his pocket; was that a knowing grin suddenly animating his face? A rattling breath accordioned Sam's paper-thin lungs as he began sliding downward, his last sight that of Al meticulously unwrapping a chocolate bar. There was no mistaking the smile on his face this time.

As Sam collapsed onto the dank floor, he heard something inside him crack, though he had no time to fancy what it might be.

Couldnt be Bothered

by S.Gepp

I didn't want to go, but it had become a tradition. More to the point, I wondered if Ignatius would really be up for his annual birthday drinks after everything that had happened only eight days earlier. I guessed I would soon find out.

Ignoring the doorbell as I always did, I knocked on the door of the modest house I knew so well. When Simone had kicked me out, I'd ended up spending three months here before getting my own apartment. Then there were the many nights of playing poker, watching bad black and white movies, and just drinking and talking— even after Ignatius had married Katherine—which marked some of the happier times of the past ten years. Of course, the birthday tradition stretched back before then, to when we were still at primary school, back almost thirty years: July 12, every year since 1981.

There was no answer, so I took a step back and gazed at the driveway. The black Toyota sat there as it always did. I sighed and tried again, louder.

"Come in!" The voice seemed distant.

I walked in. To my right was the lounge room and ahead of me the door leading to the kitchen. "Ignatius?" I called.

"In here, Pete." I followed the voice and found him sitting at the kitchen table, his eyes fixed on a piece of paper in his hands. I placed a bottle of Scotch whisky in front of him. "Happy birthday," I greeted, trying to inject cheer into my voice.

Only then did his eyes shift. "Yeah. You know, it *is* a happy birthday." He smiled.

"Even after…after all that shit last week?"

He nodded. "Yeah, Kath left me. My fault apparently. I'll give her what she wants. It's cool."

"Hang on. Eight years of marriage and you're just giving up? Just like that?"

"I can't be bothered fighting. Too much hard work."

I paused briefly. Then, "I spoke to Kath yesterday."

"Thought she'd talk to you." His tone was resigned, not angry.

"She said you didn't get a promotion at work in the last round. Again."

"Didn't get around to applying," he replied quietly. "Couldn't be bothered."

"How long have you been there?"

"Twelve years."

"Have you ever been promoted?"

"Once. My boss did all the paperwork for me. I hated it. There was a lot of extra work to do."

I stared at him. "Remember in high school when you tried out for the squash team?"

"Yeah. So?"

"You looked good, especially for someone who'd never played before." I grimaced. "Why didn't you give it a go?"

"Training and all that hard work? Couldn't be bothered."

"That's what pissed Kath off so much. She said you're getting lazier and lazier. When you're not at work, you're watching TV. It's only when one of the guys comes over that you even show any sign of life. She reckons you've given up."

He did not say anything as he cracked the bottle of Scotch and poured a little into two mismatched glasses that happened to be nearby. "What do you think?" he asked cautiously. I decided that honesty was the best policy here.

"I think you're a lazy sod, and you always have been," I stated.

He smiled and raised a glass in my direction. "Yep," he agreed, "and now I'm rich." He slid the piece of paper across the table and then placed an open newspaper beside it.

'Mystery winner!' blared the page three headline. One winner, twenty-five million dollars. And Ignatius had the numbers. All I could do was stare at him as he downed his drink and poured himself another, the grin across his face as wide as the ocean.

JULY 12, 2009

I was nervous when I knocked on the door, more than I had been a year earlier. It had been three months since I'd last caught up with Ignatius, visiting him the night the divorce had been finalised. The next day, he apparently cashed in his lottery ticket and quit his job. I didn't go to see him. But now I was back. Tradition demanded it.

The door swung open before I knocked, revealing Ignatius.

It took me a few seconds to recognise him.

He'd shaved his hair off and he had dark circles under his eyes, but that wasn't what shocked me.

It was his size.

He was double the man I'd last seen. Three months ago, he'd been certainly bigger, but...this?

"Glad you remembered, Pete." He looked genuinely happy to see me.

"Of course." I forced myself to smile.

He shook my hand and took the offered bottle of Scotch, then led me into the living room. A home cinema dominated everything, the screen covering what had once been the front window and surround sound speakers all focused onto the large couch in the middle of the room, where a pronounced indent showed exactly where he preferred to sit.

I dragged a kitchen chair into the room as he lowered his expanding frame into the couch, filling all three of the spaces. His breath was laboured, even from simply answering the door. Without saying a thing, he swivelled the laptop on its table in front of him and tapped quickly at the keyboard. Finally, he nodded and turned to face me so he could begin the inane chitchat of males everywhere. But I could not concentrate on what we were discussing.

This was Ignatius? He had no ankles that I could detect. His triceps hung from his uncovered arms like wings. He had no shape beyond round. He had chins, jowls and no neck. He was still Ignatius, but...

The doorbell rang and in walked two young men, each carrying three large, flat boxes and two bottles of soft drink as well as a pile of foil-covered garlic bread rolls. They placed them on a table by the lounge room entrance and then left without saying a word. They had clearly

71

done this before. "Isn't the Internet wonderful?" Ignatius gushed. "Order, pay, give instructions, leave a tip, all without moving. Perfect."

I smiled as well as I could as he hefted himself up and waddled to the table. He placed two of the boxes on my lap, one of the bottles and a few garlic breads before carrying the rest over to the couch. Two pizzas for me? I didn't think I'd eaten more than one, ever. But I thanked him, opened the first box and watched as he used his laptop to load a movie onto the screen.

I don't think he even noticed when forty minutes later I placed an uneaten pizza and a half by his side and left as Vincent Price and Agnes Moorehead discussed a bat.

JULY 13, 2010

The front door looked different, but it was only when I knocked that I realised what it was—a television screen was set into it, one that flickered into life at my rapping.

Two eyes regarded me briefly, coldly, and then they widened with apparent joy. "Pete!" came a voice from the speaker grille above the screen. Ignatius' voice sounded too deep, slurred a little, husky.

I heard a series of clicks and the door swung open.

The odour struck me first: stale sweat, old cooking

oil and mustiness, unpleasant and nauseating. It hung in the air like an invisible cloud. My eyes watered a little, only growing worse when I entered the living room.

I could see him in profile, sitting on that couch and watching that huge screen. "'Ey, Pete," Ignatius greeted affably. Then, "Ya shoulda been 'ere yestadee." He was having trouble speaking and I could barely see the mouth move between his floppy, rubbery lips.

"Worked late. Sorry," I lied. How could I tell him that it had taken me forty-eight hours to build up the courage to come? "But I'm here now."

"I'm glad." He smiled and moved his hand expertly across a keyboard attached to the laptop at his side. I had never seen a board with such large keys before; but then again, I had never seen fingers like the sausages Ignatius had at the end of his featureless hands: no knuckles, no joints, nothing, just off-white coloured meat stubs.

That was when I noticed he was naked, but thankfully the folds of skin that fell over him hid anything I didn't want to see. He realised I was staring and glowered. "Clothes?" I asked, and he relaxed.

"Never leave the house," he replied with what I assumed was a shrug of his immense shoulders, the waves of movement running over his entire body. "Don't need 'em. Man comes once a week, cleans the house, cleans me. Couldn't be bothered doing it myself. All cool."

I made myself smile as my eyes automatically took in every detail of his body. He seemed to merge into the couch: the pale colour of his skin fading into the material of the furniture. It was just about impossible to tell where Ignatius ended, and the couch began. Even the way the folds of skin on his back hung over the rear of the chair added to that strange impression.

I grabbed a chair from the kitchen, taking my time, still just watching him. I saw his feet and lower legs, no ankles at all; his thighs lost under a mound of his lower torso. The soles of his feet were smooth and pink, as though he hadn't stood on them in a long time. I could not say anything.

The doorbell rang, breaking the uncomfortable silence. "Hope ya like Chinese," Ignatius said with a wide, hungry smile. Then he stared at the webcam so that his eyes filled it. "Service entrance," he barked.

I heard movement in front of us and then Ignatius tapped again. A panel opened in the wall below the huge screen and a tray slowly slid out on metal casters, laden with more boxes and plastic containers of food than I had ever seen in one place. The tray slid right up to his leg and he grinned at me. "Help yaself," he slurred, drool trickling out of the corners of his mouth. "Wanna watch summat on TV?"

"Got any new films?" I asked, just trying to divert my attention from Ignatius O'Toole.

He tapped yet again and the screen in front of us flashed into life like a movie theatre. "Got the Doc Phibes films with Vincent Price." He grinned. I nodded and the opening of a film I had not seen in twenty years started.

I went to grab a dim sum. My chair slid out from beneath me and I crashed to the carpet. "Ya okay?" Ignatius asked anxiously. He knew he could not help me; I'm sure his concern was self-protection.

"Sure," I muttered, grabbing the couch to help me up, digging my fingers in.

Ignatius yelped.

But all I could think about was how soft and spongy the couch felt.

Our eyes met.

I looked at my hand, then back at him. Almost on instinct, I pinched the edge of the couch.

He winced.

I ran.

JULY 13, 2011

I recognised the house straight away. It had been on my mind all week. Just the thought of going back there, as I knew I should, was making me physically ill. So, when I saw Ignatius' place on television, surrounded by the police, with the words 'Live From The Siege' in a caption box beneath a pseudo-concerned reporter, the glass I was holding dropped onto the carpet, spilling my drink everywhere.

"Everything okay?" My girlfriend of eight months came out of the kitchen looking concerned.

"I've gotta go," I whispered.

"Peter?" She was scared, but I was already out of there.

It only took me five minutes to get my car close enough to be stopped by an angry police officer. "Area's cordoned off," he snarled.

I quickly climbed out, looking at the end of the road where I could see everyone was. "I know. But look, that guy in the house, I know him. What's happened to him?"

"Excuse me?" He tried to tower over me, but I was ignoring him.

"I know him…"

He suddenly pushed me back against my car, his forearm across my throat. "I'll check. And if you're lying, so help me, I'll…"

"Sergeant"—came a warning voice from behind him and he released me immediately. "What's going on?"

"Another so-called friend, sir."

The new arrival looked at me. "So, what's his name?" He jerked his thumb over his shoulder.

"Ignatius O'Toole. Mother died in 2002, father a few years before. He went to St Francis High School, but dropped out at…"

"Enough. Come with me." This new officer led me past the fuming policeman. He would not answer any of my questions as we made our way up the road. But words soon failed me as I took in the scene before me. Official vehicles surrounded the building and blocked the streets off, and several men in dark clothing were pointing weapons at the house. But that was not the oddest thing.

At least five cars were parked around the house: two marked with the logos of pizza places, one of the others advertising ÜberEats and my first thought about the other two was Chinese food delivery.

I could see Ignatius' black Toyota in the driveway, covered in bird droppings and a thick film of brown, the two visible tyres completely flat. The house was dark and quiet, the front door slightly ajar, and yet it did not feel still. There was something about it that had everyone clearly on edge, something about this that was just wrong.

"So…what's happening?" I asked eventually. As far as I was aware, this was just some sort of a siege.

He hesitated before responding. "Six delivery guys have gone in since yesterday; none have come out. Their cars are still here, mobile phones ringing inside, and that's about it."

"Is Ignatius okay?"

"We don't know. He won't answer the phone. We don't know if there's someone in there with him or what. There's some sort of security system keeping us all out."

"So, you don't even know if he's okay." I was panicking. He was rich and so obese he could never hope to defend himself against someone who just wanted what he had.

"Can you try to call him?" the officer suddenly asked.

"What? You said he's not answering…"

"We think there's caller ID. Someone he knows might get him to answer." My stomach lurched. That comment told me they thought Ignatius was behind all of this.

"Okay," I finally replied.

"Do it now."

I took out my mobile, found his number and hit the call key. From somewhere in the house came the sound of an old-fashioned telephone ringing. Then it stopped abruptly. "What?" growled a voice in my ear that sounded like it was spoken by a man with cotton wool in his cheeks.

"It's me, Pete," I said carefully. "I came here for your birthday and I found…"

"I know." There was a pause, and then, "I waited f' y', but y' didn' come…"

"You could've called me."

"Couldn' be bovvered." Another pause. "Come on in."

I looked at the officer and then at the house, and I sprinted faster than I had since leaving high school. None of the police were ready for it and they were only just reacting as I reached the front of the house. The door swung open and I started inside.

"Shoes off," Ignatius' voice said through the speaker grille.

I obeyed quickly and almost dove in. The door slammed behind me as the police drew nearer, then the lights flickered on. I gagged. The whole place smelled of sweat, rotten food and urine. I took a few steps forward and shuddered. It felt like I was walking on a children's bouncing castle filled with molasses. Even the walls were spongy to the touch.

I had to fight the urge to just flee.

"Welcome." Ignatius' voice seemed to come from all

around me, making me jump, my heart pounding in my throat.

"What are you doing?" I managed. I felt like I was pleading.

"As li'l as possible." Was he laughing? I couldn't tell. "Ev'rythin's done fer me. I c'n use th' 'puter t' git whatev' I want." The next noise sounded like a sigh. "Couldn' be bovvered doin' anyfin' else." A pause. "Couldn' be bovvered doin' anyfin' at all."

I peered through the door into the lounge room. The home theatre screen was still on the wall, the flickering black and white images of Lon Chaney's Phantom casting a grey glow across the room. But the place felt smaller than I remembered, as though the walls were closing in. It was claustrophobic and the need to vomit once more hit me. I took a step backwards.

"What wron'?" he asked. The tone of the voice had changed a little.

"I'm sorry I forgot your birthday, Ignatius," I said. "Again."

He laughed heartily.

The floor moved as he did so.

"Had a feast all ready f' us. Lotta food. I ate it." He laughed again.

"But eating sounds like hard work." I tried joking.

Sloth

All movement stopped and I had the distinct impression that I had really upset him. I felt suddenly, incredibly vulnerable. "Only th' chewin'," he finally replied.

I took another step backwards, but as I did so I heard the door click locked behind me. The floor moved beneath my feet, undulating in spasmodic waves. Then the kitchen door in front of me swung open.

Two legs were all that were visible. They looked thin and red, the pants ripped and torn, the skin pock marked. A drop of liquid fell from the roof of the kitchen and landed on the exposed flesh. It smoked and sizzled.

"Oh, come on, Ignatius. Please."

The whole place settled and I was sure I could hear heavy breathing, panting as though out of breath.

"You need help, mate." I tried.

"Couldn' be bovvered." The voice sounded tired. I risked a pace backwards. "Couldn' be bovvered doin' anyfin'. Ev'rythin's…jus' too hard."

"Everything?"

"Yeah…" Another step back. "Good t' see y', Pete." Sounding more distant. I risked yet another, smaller step. "Don' be a…strangerrr…" Two more steps and my hand found the door handle behind me.

"Goodnight, Ignatius," I whispered.

81

"Nighhh…" The door clicked open and I almost fell out, then I just ran backwards until I tripped over my own feet and rolled on the front lawn, unable to take my eyes from the building.

The atmosphere grew tense. The building shuddered, rattling the few windows left in their frames. And then…

Nothing.

With a sudden 'crack!' the roof over the lounge room sank down.

The sound of a sigh came out, followed by the faintest breeze which held the odour of old meat and stale cooking fat.

Then it all fell still. I could *feel* the change. There was nothing left.

The police officer only now made his way across to me. He squatted down; his own eyes fixed on the silent structure. His face told me that he was not sure what he could sense. "What did he say?" he asked, his voice sounding like the growl of a frightened dog.

"He did it," I replied quietly. "He ate…killed them."

"Is he gonna come out?"

"He can't."

"What?"

We looked at each other. "He's dead," I muttered.

"What? How?" He was so confused that I almost

laughed.

But instead I said, "I guess he just couldn't be bothered to breathe anymore."

One Hit Wonder

by A.L. King

James looked around. It was seemingly all he could do. His eyes went to the coffee table, where a nicely packed bowl of One Hit Wonder sat. He thought about leaning forward and grabbing his pipe for another toke, but he couldn't muster the will to move. He was lit, and all it had taken was a single hit.

He watched the plastic cat clock on the living room wall. The black and white thing with its shifting stare appeared to mimic his current state. However, its tail also swayed to and fro in sync with its peepers, revealing quite clearly that it—unlike the man on the couch—could move more than just its eyes.

After thirty minutes, he understood that he was experiencing more than a deficiency in willpower. He tried standing but lacked the necessary flow of energy from brain to legs. It was almost as if the single puff from his recently acquired stash had blown a fuse in him.

He turned his attention to YouTube, which was still playing on his large flatscreen. He'd started a short video when he first sat down: *10 Movies You Should Only*

Watch Stoned. Whenever that list had reached its end, a series of auto-plays continued. Now, for some reason, the service was showing a documentary about Chernobyl.

Looking back at the clock, he discovered it was only fifteen 'til six. His single hit took place shortly after getting home at five. Surely, by the start of the next hour, he would be fine. In the meantime, he studied the cracks running through the walls and ceiling. How was the place still standing? Miracles of modern architecture, he supposed. Such things could truly be appreciated while zoning out on furniture covered in dog hair.

Where was Zoomie anyway? He strained his eyes left and found her sitting at the end of the couch, staring expectantly at him as her stomach gurgled. Either she was a hungry girl or she was late for a business meeting in the backyard.

James figured it was probably food she wanted. He let her outside when he first arrived home and then packed his own bowl rather than filling her dog bowl. He wondered what would happen if she became *too* hungry. He imagined her teeth digging into him, yet still he could not move.

Such morbid thoughts were quickly dismissed. Zoomie loved him. She would rather starve than scarf him down like a can of Pedigree. *Mmmm. Pedigree.* As he recalled the smell of her food, there was something appetising about it. The overwhelming scent that greeted him each time he popped off a lid was reminiscent of Vienna sausages. That was likely because both canned foods—one intended for canines while the other passed just barely for human consumption—were derived from the same meaty slop.

It was only 6:17 pm. The music video for *Zombie* started playing, the original version by The Cranberries.

The stupor of a high was taking longer to wear off than James anticipated, but he told himself that he would be fine. Soon enough, he would get up and make his way to the kitchen. Although he didn't think he would find the Vienna sausages he was craving, he would finish off whatever crumbs were left in the Doritos bag on top of the refrigerator. He often placed food up there so Zoomie couldn't get to it.

Thinking about food caused a deep sort of pain in his stomach. Had he ever experienced such a frustrating case of the munchies? James decided he better relax. He'd eaten a late lunch at 2:30 pm, only about four hours ago. No way could he be starving.

Except, as his eyes settled on the living room window behind crooked, torn-up blinds (thanks Zoomie), he understood that more than four hours had passed since his last meal. Night had come, and now it was going from darkness to light.

There was a fresh loaf of dog shit in the corner. He looked at the other side of the coffee table to see Zoomie sitting there with an apologetic look on her face. He wanted to tell her not to be sorry—that it wasn't her fault, it was his—but he could not speak.

So for a few hours, he glared at his marijuana pipe. Whatever was in there was not pot. At least…it wasn't *simply* pot. There was no doubt in his mind. One Hit Wonder had been laced with something.

He told himself that he would be fine. The brightness outside indicated that it was at least Saturday. If Monday came and he still remained homebound—couch-bound—perhaps his co-workers would notice he was missing.

Or would it seem business as usual? James was typically ten to twenty to thirty minutes late on the regular. At least once a month, he failed to show or even call in his absence. If he thought everyone at Best Buy was going to pile into the dinky Geek Squad car like clowns in a clown car just to come check on him because he missed a single day, he had another thing coming. It would be Tuesday at earliest—maybe Wednesday, Thursday or Friday—assuming anyone bothered checking on him at all.

An advertisement for Life Alert started on YouTube, catching his attention. The product was simple. Elderly people wore a button they could press if they happened to take a nasty fall while alone, and medical assistance would somehow be signalled to send help.

James wanted to laugh as he watched the commercial. Not even one of those magical buttons could save him now. Even if he had one, he would first have to lift a finger.

***

A week passed. He counted days by the very slow lightshow outside. Approximately seven dusks and dawns had come and gone. He wondered how he was even still alive, going without food and water for so long. Thoughts of starving or dehydrating to death were only a part of James' overall panic. What if there were a fire, a flood or far worse?

Although his ability to move seemed as lost as his long-removed appendix, James still possessed his sense of touch. He knew this by the wetness in his crowding pants. Like his ability to breathe through his nose (and inhale the stench surrounding him), his bladder and bowels had continued working involuntarily. The stench of his own bodily evacuations blended with that of Zoomie's politely placed cluster in the corner.

He considered himself lucky that he wasn't yet experiencing the wrath of an unfed dog. Rather than eating him, his good girl had proven to be quite resourceful. From the empty wrappers scattered on the living room floor, it was clear that she had become desperate enough to scale the counter and knock his stockpile of junk food off the top of the fridge. He knew he had no right to be upset, but that was *his* grub, and despite not yet dying from a lack of it, there remained a gnawing sensation in his stomach.

It was more than starvation, James realised. He had the munchies. Because somehow he remained high. So high that he *still* could not move.

Zoomie, meanwhile, continued eating. She must have learned to bite down on the handles of cabinets and drawers to pull them open, because pretty soon, she was dragging every bit of his bachelor chow into the living room.

***

YouTube auto-played nonstop for the first eight days. That incessant flow of videos generated by algorithms was maddening to James, who wondered how the service could go for so long without giving up the ghost. Surely, by then, some message prodding for signs of life should have popped up. He'd seen such inquiries at least a hundred times before: *Video paused. Continue watching?*

Constantly slipping in and out of consciousness, he recalled crossing that slumbering threshold during a rather strange video with puppets. When he came to, the screen of his smart TV informed him that it was having trouble connecting to the WiFi network.

Midway through his eleventh day on the couch, he started missing those stupid list videos over-saturating the format. He was silently praying for just one more overly speculated production—perhaps the five best and five worst Bond villains or something like that—when he heard the bombs, gunshots, and screams outside.

Zoomie ran from the bathroom to the foyer, toilet-water flying off her muzzle as she barked her way through the living room. From the flushing sounds he'd been hearing, she must have learned that pawing the silver handle on the side of the tank would refill the bowl. Smart girl. Good girl.

The front doorknob turned back and forth. Whoever it was began groaning something awful. The moaning and knob rattling echoed all the way into the living room. Zoomie had stopped barking, but she continued growling lowly. She sounded as if she were right by the door, prepared to attack. Prepared to defend.

The door was of course locked, but James mentally braced himself for whoever was trying to break inside. From what he could hear, the whole world might be coming to an end. Was someone hoping to call his place home? And if so, why? Had they taken a good look at it?

There was a thud, followed by familiar voices.

"Good job, Luce," said Garret Kensington. "That's how you kill a zombie. Say…wasn't he one of our local winos before he turned? I guess it wasn't his first time getting hammered, but it *definitely* was his last."

"That's not funny," snapped Lucy Quinn. "Keep it down or you'll draw more of them."

James wondered if maybe too much sitting had caused him to go insane. Perhaps he was only imagining their voices or hearing them incorrectly. Had Garret really said *zombie*? Had Lucy really said *more of them*?

Something shattered, and it wasn't a window. His female co-worker must have tipped the flowerpot off the top step as she reached for the spare key underneath it. His flowers died years ago. Not a big loss.

"Now who's being loud?" asked Garret.

"Shut up," said Lucy.

James heard the key whisper sweet nothings inside the lock, the door ease open and the visitors cry out in apparent surprise. Then there was a gunshot that should have (but didn't) make him jump. Following the loud bang, he thought that Zoomie should be barking her head off.

But she wasn't.

A single tear broke through his paralysis and spilled down his left cheek. She'd been such a good girl. She deserved better. It wasn't fair.

***

"Why did you shoot her?" asked Lucy.

"Was I just supposed to let her attack you?"

"She wasn't going to attack me. She knows me. I let her out for James sometimes. She's probably just a little out of her head because she's been trapped in this house for so long."

"We couldn't risk it."

"She was harmless."

"You don't know that."

Garret and Lucy stopped arguing long enough to close and bolt the door and enter the adjoining living room. They gasped upon seeing James on the couch.

"You're alive!" exclaimed Lucy.

Garret said, "Of course he is."

Lucy's peeved expression revealed all he needed to know. One had come there hoping that he was still alive, while the other secretly wanted to find a corpse.

"What's wrong with you?" she asked, setting a bloody hammer on the table as she kneeled to examine him. "You smell awful. Did you shit yourself? Is that piss all over your pants? Why are you frozen in place like a gargoyle?"

Garret issued a superficial chortle. "Look at the pipe on the coffee table, Luce. He's high as a kite right now. Higher, even. I bet he's as elevated as a hot air balloon. I just shot his dog, and he doesn't give a damn."

James gave more of a damn than he could show.

Lucy wiped the single tear away from his cheek, turned and held up her dewy finger. "Look. He's crying. He does care. Unlike *you*, he has a heart."

She spun back around to again face James. Behind her, Garret said nothing as he stared intently at the gun in his hand. James wished he could warn Lucy, who was crying herself now. She cried easily, often set off by co-workers or customers at Best Buy.

She placed her palms on James' cheeks and peered

into his eyes. "Are you in there? I know you're probably scared right now, with everything that's happening, but you need to come out and face the world."

Garret stroked the handgun as if it were a magic genie bottle. "I get it now. You knew where the spare key was because you were fucking him. You just said that thing about letting his dog out to spare my feelings. But seriously, Luce! *Him?*"

James felt a sudden stinging in his right hand. He looked down and saw that he was making a fist. He usually bit his fingernails, but thanks to his paralysis, they had grown long enough to cut into the flesh of his palm. He tried to scream a warning, but only a baby-like coo would come out. She was still facing him as she responded, rather than looking back a final time to see Garret extending the gun.

"I wish I did fuck him," she said. "Maybe I should have stayed one night after letting Zoomie out. I could have crawled into his bed naked and hoped he came back from the bar alone to find me. Even sitting in his own filth, he's more appealing than you are, Garret. What I did with you was a mistake, and I only did it because I thought I was as good as—"

Lucy's tirade and life ended with an abrupt *POP!* The back of her head exploded at an angle that spared

James of everything but the spatter of brains and blood.

He wanted to leap off the couch and attack the killer. Instead, he faded.

***

When he came to, Garret was sitting on the coffee table and looking at him. The man who had killed Lucy was apparently trying to justify pulling the trigger, but his excuse was just as weak as the one he had offered after shooting Zoomie.

"I just...I couldn't stand the thought of sharing her with someone else," said the former member of the Geek Squad. He then pointed at the pipe beside him on the table. "Say...you mind if I hit that?"

James nodded and Garret took the cue. He partook in One Hit Wonder. A few minutes later, he was completely quiet, completely still. He just stared, as if it were all he could do.

***

James bit into Garret's throat.

At first, he wanted to convince himself it was because of the sudden rush of adrenaline.

As he chewed, he tried desperately to believe he was driven by vengeance.

But after he swallowed and licked his lips and took another bite, he was forced to admit that his former co-worker might soon become the most satisfying cure to the munchies he'd ever tasted.

Zombies moaned outside. He moaned along with them, albeit in ecstasy. He finished every chewable piece of Garret and even licked the bones clean. He then walked to the window and peered through the blinds that Zoomie had long ago demolished.

Outside was a fiery mess. There were hordes of the living dead. There were survivors with weapons. There was a whole lot of hassle to look forward to if he left the house. It was quite possible that someone would take one look at the blood on his face and all over the rest of him and think that he too was a reanimated corpse and end his life.

So, James returned to his couch, where he had been sitting for a week and a half. He picked up his lighter and pipe and thought, *Why the fuck not?*

He toked up. As he again froze in place, he stared at his cat clock. There was a bit of blood on the white part of its left eye. It went back and forth and back and forth and back and forth as the end times passed and the cracks in the house failed to bring it down.

Day 97

by Catherine Kenwell

I scratch the offending spot behind my right ear and let my fingertips dwell for a moment, navigating a scaly patch. Lift long fingernails to my nostrils, to inhale. Musky, gritty, a little sour. I flick the detritus from under my nails and watch it fly a few inches in front of me.

I lay here, wondering. How long can a body go without showering or washing or even changing clothes? I'd stopped showering every day after I lost my job. When the job prospects dried up and I had nowhere to go, I found I stopped washing altogether.

Sometimes, depending on the temperature, I'll change from a sweatshirt into a short-sleeved t-shirt. Being overly warm or becoming sweaty is uncomfortable, and besides, I don't want to stink. I don't *think* I do. I raise my arm, crook my elbow over my head and lean down to inhale my armpit—sweet, a little salty, slight musk. A faint onion-like odour? A human being smells. Nothing cosmetic to mask nature. Not unattractive at all.

I stopped wearing socks and shoes when I noticed my feet were itchy all the time. Couldn't have been an allergy to wool socks—I wore the same pair every day. But my toenails grew thick and yellow; the ancient nail enamel peeled away, and the skin between my toes started to flake and scale. It wasn't pretty. So, I just watch, fascinated, as my feet transform from delicate to disgusting. It's kinda cool, how the body reacts to neglect.

I remain still most of the time these days. I've lost interest in getting up for much. I autopay for my groceries now, and the delivery person leaves boxes outside my apartment every Thursday afternoon. I open the door and quickly pull them inside. Cereal, frozen entrees, milk and protein bars. Instant coffee. Orange juice from concentrate. Sometimes bananas, although they tend to turn black before I get around to eating them.

When I first became housebound, I admit I pigged out. I ate everything in sight, all the time. Chips, chocolate, cookies, entire loaves of fresh bread slathered with peanut butter and jam—I'd eat until I almost burst. I'd gorge until I threw up. And then—then, I lost my appetite. The mere thought of preparing a meal repelled me. I don't know if it was because I overdid it or whether it was just too much work. Often now, the milk will spoil before I finish it. Oh well.

The fabric of the sweatpants I've been wearing has stretched to the point of no return. I'm sure if I washed them, they'd fall apart; but anyway, a hot dryer would never shrink them to their original size. At first, when I wore panties under them, they stayed clean enough. But when the underwear elastic disintegrated, I went without. They've become crusty at the crotch, and a foul bouquet greets me whenever I squat on the toilet. When the crust becomes overwhelming, I take the tangy patch between my fingers and rub until the harder fragments fall to the floor and the fabric softens once more.

I should probably take out the trash sometime soon, but it's a gargantuan effort to traipse to the end of the hallway. I'm intrigued by the stench and the rot, and when the piles of bags began wriggling and holes became visible, I figured the mice and bugs wouldn't bother me as long as I kept providing new bags. So, the piles grow.

Besides, I probably look a mess. Haven't brushed or washed my hair in 97 days. I don't look in the mirror anymore—it's grime-clouded and dusty—but when I started pulling out clumps of hair; I figured bald was easier to maintain, anyway.

After the first few days, my teeth lost the sweaters they'd gained. It felt different, for sure, not having the minty fresh toothpaste taste, but when I ran out, I didn't add it to my shopping list. What was the point? Crunching cereal is probably all the abrasion I need for sufficient oral care. My breath doesn't seem foul; certainly, I can't smell anything.

Since I lost my job, I've become a Law & Order SVU aficionado. Maybe I should enter a trivia contest; I think I can identify the outcome of every episode just by viewing the preliminary segment. I know when each character joined the team. Tutuola is pretty consistent, but I still like Detective John Munch the best. And Ghost Adventures—that's my other favourite. Zak and Aaron, what an awesome team! And the places they investigate—it's like a travelogue for haunting enthusiasts. Between those two shows and their syndication, I'm ok watching TV 24/7.

My work settlement paid me enough to last for a while. I don't spend much, only groceries and rent. I can live here for a few years before the landlord can even think of kicking me out. Funny how the credit company doesn't mind if I only submit the minimum payment, and even that, only sometimes. I can't be bothered to open up the computer to pay the bills. Not even interested in hearing from anyone. Don't care about the news. It's just a bunch of crap anyway. Give me Ghost Adventures anytime.

Now the furry throw I used to keep as a sofa accent is my sleeping blanket. Can't remember the last time I slept in my bed. The throw used to smell like fabric softener, a chemical redolence that never really sat well with me. Now, it emits a more natural fragrance: sweat, sleep and greasy hair. Pungent yet palatable.

The sofa, it's giving way to my body shape: lumpy, sagging, wearing thin. I tossed my pillow—a sofa bolster—on the floor when it started turning mould-black. I still kick it around the floor when it blocks my way to the fridge.

Sloth. It's become a challenge: a bar that continues to lower and rise simultaneously. I discovered something I'm good at, and I try to better myself every day. What used to be disgusting is now delightful. I find I revel in my laziness.

I need nothing.

I do nothing. Besides L&O, it's the only thing I try to do more of.

When a Good Man Does Nothing

by K. B. Elijah

The angel perked an eyebrow over his book as the machine beeped twice, a green light blazing on the console. He glanced around, but other than his own, not a single feathered wing was in sight.

His usual trick of getting slowly to his feet and sighing in feigned disappointment as another angel *happened* to get there before him wasn't going to work this time, at least not very effectively.

Could he pretend he hadn't heard it?

As if it had heard *him*, the machine beeped again, a higher-pitched and longer tone this time that screamed impatience. Zaphkiel growled, pulled out a feather to mark his place in his book and stalked towards the machine, tentatively flicking the switch that would release the soul catcher into his palm.

Zaphkiel eyed the glass ball dubiously, swirls of midnight blue with flickering flashes of gold. Yet a trail of murky red, the type that was almost brown, cut through the other colours in a streak of dominance.

"Kimaris!" he called, unable to pull his gaze away from the soul. "Get your ass over here!"

A disparaging grunt reached his ears, and Zaphkiel frowned. A flash of light, a beat of wings, and he was pulling Kimaris away from his poker game by one of his horns.

"Get off!" Kimaris squawked. "I was winning!"

The other three demons at the table chuckled with derision at his words, not lifting a talon to help their friend. They continued to bet and raise as if nothing had happened.

"We..ll..." Kimaris admitted, stretching out the word into two syllables, "I *was* on a little bit of a...downturn in luck, you might say. But that just means things can only get better." He pulled out of Zaphkiel's grip and rubbed his horn despondently. "What do you want?"

The angel held out the soul catcher, and just like he had been, Kimaris was immediately captivated by its depth and colour.

"Ooh," he said, rubbing his claws together excitedly. "That's pretty. Can I keep it?"

"It's a soul, Kim," Zaphkiel said impatiently, trying to resist the urge to roll his eyes. Then he wondered why the hell he was trying for a demon, and just rolled them anyway. "We have to decide where it belongs."

"Don't we have computers for that?" Kimaris wailed plaintively, his black eyes flashing in disgust. "You know, robots of the future and all that? They've replaced every other job in Hell, including the torture; why shouldn't they make this one redundant too?"

"The computers sort the vast majority of souls," Zaphkiel confirmed, pleased he knew the answer for once, "but for the ones on the edge, like this one—" he gave the sphere a shake "—it requires a good old-fashioned argument between an angel and a demon."

Kimaris looked at him blankly.

"You know," Zaphkiel said, shrugging. "You and me. Battle of the ages. Ancient rivalry, bitter enemies, all that."

"But you're dating my sister and we play D&D every weekend together. Not to mention our fortnightly sundaes at that ice cream parlour you introduced me to. Are we...are we *bitter enemies*, Zaph?"

"I don't think so," said Zaphkiel. "But there are no other angels here, and well. I don't really know your friends." He finished lamely, gesturing with a white wing at the poker table.

Kimaris clicked his forked tongue. "Then shouldn't they be a better fit for your enemies?"

"I don't think so," the angel said again. "It's hard to hate people I don't know. I, errr...*hey*, you never returned those shoes I loaned to you! I'm angry about *that*. Does that count?"

"I suppose," Kimaris said. "You know you're never going to see those again, right? Talons and leather don't go so well together." He gave a nasty grin.

"Seems good enough. The work, I mean. Not the shoes. You're paying me back for those." Zaphkiel shrugged. "So how do we do this?"

"Don't look at *me*," said the demon. "I've only just transferred to this shift, you know that."

Zaphkiel peered at the machine. "Ah, there's background info on the soul." He pressed a button with the edge of a fingernail. "Male, died at forty-two years of age. Gustav Davidson."

"What did he die of? Forty-two is quite young for humans. I think."

Zaphkiel checked. "He was run over by a truck."

"Oh, he was reaped by Death himself!" Kimaris said excitedly, leaning over Zaphkiel's shoulder to read the data. The angel tried not to wince at the smell of dead rats and mould. "I didn't know that guy was back in the game; last I heard, he was stuck in executive management and it was his Reapers doing all of the groundwork. Good on him."

Zaphkiel shuddered, using the movement as an excuse to step away from the demon and his pungent odour. "I don't like that guy."

"What, Death? He's a good bloke."

"He eats all of the angels' kitchen snacks whenever he visits," Zaphkiel pointed out. "Like, literally *all of them*."

Kimaris shrugged. "He has a sweet tooth, I know that. But he's never stolen any of ours."

"That's because none of your snacks could be described as 'sweet'," Zaphkiel said pointedly, trying not to imagine the oozing hearts and slippery entrails that adorned the demons' side of the little kitchenette.

Kimaris stretched his wings, black feathers flickering out behind his skeletal body. "We're getting off track."

"Hmm," the angel said, agreeing with him but not wanting to admit it. "Let's see…Gustav made monthly donations to a children's charity, adopted a rescue dog, never deliberately hurt anyone…"

"All points for you." Kimaris yawned. "Why is he here again?"

"Stop being so impatient. He also let a toddler drown, watched a dog be mauled to death and was part of a major fraud."

The demon's pointed ears perked up. "I'm listening."

"It's almost an entirely even list of good and bad," Zaphkiel complained, one pale finger scrolling down the screen. "It's impossible to decide one way or another. Oh, he does have a Sin listed."

"Which one?" Kimaris asked excitedly, almost clawing at the angel's hands to see. "Wrath? Lust? Ooh, I love lust."

"Sloth," they said together, as the word appeared on the screen. They stared at each other.

"What counts as sloth these days?"

"I don't know anything about that one!"

"If only Belphegor were here..."

"Let's wake the soul up," suggested Zaphkiel. "Ask him about it."

"Can we do that?"

"Sure," the angel said, and before the demon could stop him, he had shoved the soul catcher into a circular slot next to the screen and pressed the big red button on top of the machine.

"Reviving"—came the dispassionate mechanical voice—"Please wait."

They waited, shoulders pressed together, the dripping ichor of the demon leaking onto the starched whiteness of the angel's shirt.

"Soul revived."

"Where am I?" A man's voice sounded from inside the machine, and a face suddenly appeared on the screen. Gustav looked a lot older than his forty-two years: his face gaunt and his eyes pale and watery. They were the colour of old dishwater, lifeless grey with dull flecks of brown.

"Processing Facility Two," Zaphkiel said imperiously. "Also known as the Gates of Saint Peter, although you've probably noticed that there's not a gate in sight. We thought about having some installed, to help with the image, you know, but decided it would look weird to have gates without a fence."

"What my colleague *means*," Kimaris muttered, shooting a glare at his friend, "is that you have arrived at your judgement. We are both here, as representatives of Heaven and Hell, to decide your eternal fate. Although they *say* eternal, but really it's—"

"Time for you to start talking," Zaphkiel cut over the demon, who clamped his claws over his mouth as if realising he'd said too much.

"Well?"

"Well, what?" Gustav asked, his voice quavering a little. "What do I have to do?"

"Tell us about your life! What you've done! The good and the bad: we want to hear it all."

The demon nodded. "We do!"

There was silence for a long time. The angel started fidgeting with a loose feather.

The silence continued.

"I don't know where to start," the soul finally said.

"Clearly," Kimaris growled, "what about the toddler you let drown? Tell us about him."

"Her," Gustav said and then sighed wearily. "I was doing some laps before work one morning, and this woman turned away to chat to her friend. The kid jumped into the deep end of the pool."

"So, you tried to save her?" the angel asked, a note of hope in his expression, but the soul shook its digital face.

"No. I thought someone else would. I wanted to, but at first I thought the kid was just having fun, and how awkward would that be if I got in the way? I would probably offend someone in this day and age, trying to save a life. So I just waited for her to surface and she didn't, but I didn't know whether to go and help or call for the lifeguard because they always say you shouldn't put yourself at risk for another and I'm not a very good swimmer and then someone went over there and I thought he was going to help but he was just messing around with his friends and..." He paused his rambling to take a breath. "It didn't end well. I should have done something but I couldn't think quickly enough and then…it was all over."

"Er," Zaphkiel said, chewing his lip. "Tell us about your charity donations instead. You probably saved a few kids' lives with those, right? Did good in the world?"

Gustav stared at him blankly. "I donated to charity?"

Kimaris let out a little cackle.

"Yes," Zapkhiel said firmly. "A children's hospital. You had a regular monthly payment going for nearly 20 years."

The soul frowned.

"I don't… Oh, yes!" he exclaimed, and Zaphkiel smirked at the demon. "I remember now! I got cornered on my first day at university by these people in red t-shirts and hats. Wouldn't leave me alone until I signed up. I meant to cancel it for years afterwards but never found the time."

"That doesn't count, Zaph," the demon crowed. "Being bullied into charity because he can't stand up to a bunch of clipboard-wielding students and is too lazy to make a single phone call does not a good man make."

Zaphkiel nodded gloomily and waved a pale hand to allow the demon his turn.

"The dog," Kimaris said. "Tell me about the dog."

Gustav shuddered. "You mean the one that was killed in front of me in the alley that time, by the crazy coyote thing? That was horrible. I..."

"Let me guess, you froze that time too? Let it happen instead of stopping it?"

"Was I...supposed to fight the coyote instead? It was protecting its young, and that dog was rabid. It had huge teeth!"

"So do I," Kimaris hissed, snapping them at him. "Unfortunately, that isn't enough to land you in Hell. But the fraud...that, my friend, is a moral and legal crime. Share your depravity with us, your darkness and deceit, your wicked wantonness and—"

"I didn't commit fraud!" Gustav objected, his eyes narrowing until they were barely visible on the tiny screen.

"Why does your file say you did?"

"I..." he faltered. "I knew my manager was siphoning money from the company, and I didn't report it. I didn't want to get anyone into trouble, and I knew he would work out that it was me who dobbed him in."

The demon fell into disappointed silence, and Zaphkiel seized his opportunity to speak. "I see why you're credited as never deliberately hurting anyone," he said kindly. "You're just a tad indecisive, little human.

114

You'd rather do nothing than risk anything at all. But you adopted a dog, hmm? Surely *that* was an act of goodness?"

"My sister left me with him one day and got arrested for possession that night," Gustav sniffed miserably. "I never got around to taking him to a shelter."

"I give up!" Zaphkiel declared dramatically, his wings fluttering with exasperation. "I can't get him into Heaven on that!"

"Nor me Hell," Kimaris mused. "He's not evil enough."

"He's not good enough!"

"So, what do we do now?"

"Give the soul the choice," a voice called out, and both creatures looked around to find one of the demons seated at the poker table waving his forked tail at them. "Procedure 78(a)(IV) is *quite clear* about such situations."

"We'll take your word for it," Kimaris said hurriedly, looking at the angel who nodded enthusiastically in support. The other demon shrugged and turned back to his cards.

They rounded on the soul. "Gustav Davidson," thundered Zaphkiel. "Your scales are balanced. You may choose whether you wish to spend your afterlife in

Heaven or Hell. Take a minute," he added kindly, as the man's face paled.

"Uh…"

"Don't you want to spend eternity with fluffy clouds and cherubs, in nothing but blissful happiness?" the angel asked, but the demon waved a hooked claw.

"Don't listen to him. Heaven is way boring. Come with us. It's orgies and booze as far as the eye can see."

"If you're not being boiled alive," Zaphkiel said distastefully, "or dismembered by demons."

"Ah, it's a bit of fun," Kimaris scoffed. "Better than getting those stupid arrows up the ass from that crazy Cupid fellow who hangs around your place."

"I don't know," Gustav said. "I don't know what to choose! It's like the truck all over again!"

"The truck that killed you?" Kimaris asked, rather insensitively, the angel thought. "What happened with that?"

"I didn't know whether to keep crossing or turn back," the soul wailed. "And it just…"

"Hit you nice and square in your indecisive face, got it. Have you ever actually made a decision in your life?"

That was Sloth, Zaphkiel realised. Not necessarily laziness but failing to act when one should: when a toddler was drowning two feet from you, when an orphaned dog needed a home. The tentacles of lethargy and sluggishness, of choosing not to offend or risk by acting, but failing to do anything at all when action was called upon.

"Well?" the demon demanded. "Have you made your choice?"

"He has not. But I have."

Zaphkiel's mouth fell open and he saw Kimaris' head swivel round on his shoulders.

"Carmel?"

"Hello, darlings," the woman said, her grey wings stretching out to encompass both of them in a gentle embrace. "It's been a while."

"Only a few millennia," Zaphkiel said, dazed, unable to believe she was here. "Everyone thought you were dead."

Carmel gave a light laugh: the sound of bird song and windchimes before they are dropped into a woodchipper. "What a silly idea, cousin. Hello, Gustav."

"Hello," the soul said hopefully. "You said you would help me make my choice? These two gentlemen have been quite unsupportive."

"I take offence to that," the angel began and the demon stuck his middle claw up at the machine.

"I said I made your choice for you," Carmel pointed

out. "You were given a minute to decide and you wasted it. There's no orgies or clouds where you're going."

"What?"

"Yeah, mate, you blew it," Kimaris said, making a loud smacking noise with his mouth to emphasise his point. "You had the chance to choose your eternal afterlife and you couldn't even do that."

"Sorry friend," Zaphkiel offered. "If Carmel is here, it's out of our wings now."

"Indeed," the woman cooed, easing the glass sphere out of the machine despite the soul's desperate protests.

"No! I'll decide, I promise, I—"

Gustav's face blinked and then disappeared.

The angel and demon gave Carmel a wave as she disappeared back to purgatory with a flash of light and an unpleasant waft of lemon-scented cleaning products.

"Poor bloke," Zaphkiel mused. "That's worse than what even any of you lot get up to. At least you get to have fun. I heard *nothing* ever happens in purgatory."

"In that case, he might actually like it down there. There's a first for everything." The demon clicked a tongue and waved a wing.

"Now that work is done for the day, want to play some Texas Hold 'Em, Zaph?"

The angel's face broke into a smile, which then

quickly faded. "Oh. Isn't gambling a Sin? I'm not allowed to Sin." His voice was quiet and sad.

"Gambling is a *vice*," Kimaris corrected. "Vices lead to Sin, so you'll just have to be careful. So you can't win, because then you'll be proud of that win. You can't lose, because then you'll be envious and perhaps wrathful. And...you can't be indecisive at any time in the game, because as we've seen, Sloth can be the worst Sin of all. Got it?"

"Got it," the angel said happily, following his friend over to the poker table. "That sounds simple enough."

Equals

by Jacqueline Moran Meyer

I've been walking miles every day, desperately trying not to die. My leg muscles have tightened, and crows' furious calls make me want to run. I glance up to see the birds circling in a vertigo-inducing pattern below the swirling purple clouds that have been dumping rain on us since yesterday. The bleak calls and pitch-black wings of the crows announce the nearby zombies.

We position ourselves for a possible attack, facing outward, backs touching, weapons drawn. I clutch my butcher knife, the knuckles on my shaking hands turning white from the strain. I scan the horizon for zombies— and a hiding place. Kelly holds her axe above her head, grasping it with both fists. Henry, whose wide range of skills must include ambidexterity, wields a heavy hatchet in one hand and a baseball bat in the other. We look ready. I'm not so sure.

After several minutes, the birds move on, and I relax since there has been no sign of any walking corpses. As the desire to rest overwhelms me, I slide to the ground, ambivalent about the muddy water. I'm exhausted. I'm

121

not moving unless I absolutely must.

"Get up, Bob," Henry barks.

"Lazy bastard," Kelly mutters.

I stay put because I'm used to the name calling and people ordering me around. Pleasing others is impossible. Why try? Clean your room. Take a shower. Stop drinking. Lose weight. Get a girlfriend. School bullies called me fatty. My own parents called me lazy and selfish. It's easier not to try at anything; no one will have any expectations. I have always wanted everyone to just leave me the hell alone.

My boss called me slow and inept. She fired me from my boring but rent-paying job at Shopmart, where I washed the floors and cleaned the bathrooms. But that turned into good luck. Yeah. I lost my job, but had I kept it, I definitely would've been attacked and turned into one of *them*. Once infected, humans turn quickly. Any place a lot of people congregate gets hit hard: malls, stores, schools, stadiums.

"There," Kelly whispers, the word coming out like she's asking a question. In the distance, I hear the echo of a caw. I want to burrow into the earth and disappear.

I turn to see her pointing toward the field opposite the one we just crossed. We're about fifty feet from a tall figure wearing drenched, tattered clothing. He, or it—I never know what to call zombies—stands deadly still.

"Damn it," Kelly says too loudly.

Abruptly, the zombie moves toward her voice. Its missing lips expose broken, blackened teeth in a macabre grin. This one has seen some action. Its neck is broken, head resting on one shoulder. The creature's movements are stiff, unnatural. An arm is missing, and its torso exhibits many cuts from someone who tried to fend off an attack. It also has bites about its face, neck and exposed arm from the zombies who forced him to become one of their own.

Zombies I had seen in movies, like in *28 Days* and *28 Days Later*, were fast, loud and ate people. These creatures are slow moving and just bite the living, aiming only to infect us. In fact, they don't seem to eat or drink *anything*. Zombies will bite a chunk out of a live person, immediately spitting it out. If you're unfortunate enough to be cornered by twenty of them, they'll take turns biting pieces off you. I've seen zombies with so many bites they have no insides, only hollow ribs and an exposed spine. I would rather just die than spend all my life hiding from these creatures that just want to turn me into one of them.

"There's only one," Henry says, breaking through my thoughts.

"A whole mess of crows for *one* zombie? Unlikely,"

Kelly says, biting her lip.

"Murder," I say. Their icy glares cut down at me, but I can't stop myself. "It's called a 'murder' of crows, not a 'mess'."

Henry grabs the back of my jacket, dragging me to my feet. I choke as the zipper digs into the flesh of my throat.

"Who gives a crap, Bob?" Henry growls, his red face an inch from my own.

He spits out each word, adding his saliva to the water dripping down my face. Henry is built like Superman, with the wholesome good looks of a country boy who has taken good care of himself: clear skin, muscles, bright eyes. There's nothing similar between us except our age. My face is scarred from acne. My body, obese two months ago, is thinner but not attractive. Unfortunately, sickening loose skin hangs from my bones.

"You're lucky we don't kill you," Kelly hisses. I know she's alluding to Maya and what I caused.

"Shut up and pay attention," Henry adds with a warning.

My two companions and I continue to travel a country road surrounded by open fields and the too-familiar sight of abandoned cars. The map we took from the last gas station we passed claims a town called Mt

Pleasant lies ahead. We need food and water and rest. Dear God, do we need rest.

Everything is too quiet. The scariest feeling may be not knowing what horrible event will happen next. We don't know where the first zombie came from or why our world changed overnight. We haven't seen a single zombie since the day Maya died, several days ago. We haven't seen another live person or heard a gunshot in two weeks.

It doesn't matter how far we walk; the zombies will either already be there or catch up to us. What's the point of going anywhere? The fear of seeing them is worse than when they actually turn up—unless you wake to see a zombie's mouth attached to your friend's neck, like with Maya.

Maya insisted on taking me along.

She found me hiding in the walk-in refrigerator of the deli I lived above. I was heavier then. I sat against the refrigerator door, blocking everyone, hoarding all the food and wearing plenty of layers. I came prepared to stay for as long as necessary. No one knew where I was—not that my family would've looked for me. I don't know what happened to them.

I heard the deli owner, Mr Jeffrey, banging on the door, puzzled about what was blocking the door from the inside. The next day, I heard him and his family screaming as zombies bit them. Another difference between movie zombies and the real ones is that ours are quiet. We can hear them shuffling around and ripping flesh, but no sounds come from their mouths. The silence adds to the fear. Over the next week, I lived in the refrigerator, figuring I'd stay there until everything blew over. Or until my life was over. I was prepared for either outcome.

I was happy to have food and beer, and the coldness masked the smell of my waste. I slept on the floor wrapped in the blankets I'd brought, feeling no more need to guard the door. No one had tried to open it for days. But the electricity went out, and I sat in the dark for three days. The smell was unbearable, but at least I had food.

Maya found me asleep in the rancid refrigerator and felt sorry for me. No one else saw the value of bringing along an obese, drunken man. Maya convinced them to let me try joining them. One stipulation was that I needed to carry a weapon. The second stipulation was that I be prepared to use it whenever necessary. I'd found a large kitchen knife in the refrigerator and brought it with me. Since the moment I joined them, food has been scarce, and I've been caught hoarding food several times. Maya always convinced Kelly and Henry to let me stay, even though they think I'm untrustworthy and slow. They took me in, but I didn't ask for this.

"If nothing else, they'll get to *him* first; we can run," Maya said to them. We all knew she was right.

"There's plenty for them to bite," Henry agreed. They all laughed. I couldn't blame them, I guess. That didn't mean I was laughing.

Maya and I were on lookout duty last week, at a house we'd been staying in for five glorious days. We slept in shifts while the others paced the ground level. I fell asleep during my watch, which I'd done every night and always gotten away with. I awoke to shattered glass and Maya's terrified screams coming from the next room. I glanced in and saw a zombie biting her neck, another one entering through the broken sliding glass door.

I should have helped, but I knew if I waited long enough Kelly or Henry would take care of everything.

Henry and Kelly ran down the stairs past me to help Maya. They killed five zombies while I stood by, watching at the doorway. My feet were frozen in place. I wanted to help Maya—I also wanted to roll up in a ball in a secure hiding place—but my feet were frozen, rooted to the ground. I had let everyone down, but I'm not built for bravery. I can't apologise for that. I won't.

I walked toward them when the fighting ended.

Henry looked up at me with murderous rage. Maya and Henry had a thing. She was bitten; it was just a matter of time before she turned. He cradled and kissed Maya's head until she died—and then he smashed her head in with a stone. The only way to kill a zombie is to destroy their brains. I lied and said I was pacing to other side of the house when I heard the glass shatter, but they knew I didn't attempt to help Maya. Henry, understandably, hasn't been the same since. Carrying out that type of violence, even if it's necessary for survival, changes you, drains you. They have barely spoken to me since that day, but they let me tag along. As bait.

I'm lucky to have met Kelly and Henry. Kelly was an attorney, with a brain trained for strategy. She's used to suits and well-groomed hair, not the dirty mess she is now. She's nearing forty, about fifteen years older than me. Her time at the gym before this nightmare comes in handy; she's an excellent zombie fighter. Henry is, or was, a twenty-six-year-old gym teacher and a former Boy Scout (Be prepared!). Henry the do-gooder zombie slayer. He mentored as a Big Brother and delivered Meals on Wheels when he wasn't mountain climbing or scuba diving. He wants to save humanity. Still. Kelly and Henry are good people to hitch a wagon to during a zombie apocalypse. They're also dangerous for someone who has always felt 'less-than'.

I'm not going to lie; part of me is relieved society has broken down. I don't have to work or worry about how I'll pay rent. Without social media, I'm not jealous of how everyone else's lives seem so much happier than mine. I just worry about the things I need to simply stay alive: food, water, safe shelter. But mere survival is becoming more challenging as more people turn and the zombies' numbers increase exponentially.

They may not be pretty, but zombies have it made. No worries. No responsibilities. I'm not convinced the zombies are dead; they're just transformed. I think I could live with that. They're slow, but they're in no rush to get anywhere. They're not hiding, like me, trying to get away from all the things creeping up on me. They don't need to worry about how they're perceived, how they constantly fail to measure up. All I want to do is sleep. Zombies don't need to sleep. Maybe I don't need to be afraid.

We reach the deserted town. The zombie, who had been following at a safe distance, is now out of sight. That disconcerts me.

The rain stops.

I follow Kelly and Henry, trekking through the desolate town and down a tree-lined suburban street. Other than grass that is a little too high, oddly placed cars and broken windows, the quiet Victorian-house-lined street seems normal. The world has changed dramatically, but physical signs of decay haven't yet appeared: no peeling paint, no weeds sprouting through the blacktop, no roofs caving in. It's easy to think things are okay.

Kelly and Henry stop in front of a three-storey house with intact windows.

"The less damage, the more food," Henry says, his eyes wild with hunger, his lips dry. We haven't eaten in two days and can't stay hydrated, despite the rain.

We trudge around the house.

"Looks empty," Kelly announces, sweat forming on her upper lip. She skittishly looks over her shoulder.

"Tons of windows. Three doors on the first floor." Henry's always thinking of an exit strategy. We usually need one.

"It's too quiet." Kelly's brow furrows, her eyes darting around.

"We need food. It'll be fine," Henry says, frowning. I'm thinking he's trying to convince himself.

We climb the front steps, and Kelly turns the brass handle of the scarlet-painted front door. An appropriate colour given the world we live in now and what will come. The door clicks open anticlimactically. We hold our weapons overhead while Kelly pushes the door open with one foot, peeking into the empty foyer for signs of movement. The honey-coloured parquet floor leads to a curved, floral-carpeted staircase, lined with white spindles set off by the banister's dark wood. The walls are covered with photos of a family—two attractive parents and three obviously loved children. There are school portraits, vacation photos and holiday pictures. There's a strong smell of rot, but no sign of zombies. We enter.

Kelly nods toward a hallway leading to the back of the home, where we saw the kitchen while casing the house. We follow her, our clothes dripping, creating puddles on the floor. Our boots squish loudly, leaving footprints. In the empty kitchen, we open cabinet doors containing useless rows of drinking glasses, white dishes and decorative vases. The normalcy of what we find is all the creepier because of the desolation that lives here now.

Kelly gasps. I misinterpret this to mean she sees a zombie, so I open a nearby door and dive in, closing it behind me. I find myself in a light-blue-painted bathroom. Light streams through a tiny stained glass window, too small for a child to fit through.

"Food! Awesome!" Henry exclaims.

I peek out. Kelly and Henry are stuffing their backpacks with cans of food. I step out of the bathroom.

"Great," I say.

They look up and aim their weapons at me. My knife shakes in my hands.

"Drop it, Bob," Kelly says, scolding me like a child. The knife clinks on the tile floor.

"We've been thinking..." Henry begins, glaring at me.

What follows is a long-winded diatribe that catalogues my failings. Kelly chimes in occasionally. This is the end of our time together. They're not wrong about any of it. That makes it worse.

Behind them, I see movement. The windows facing the backyard reveal zombies shuffling out of the woods and toward the house. There are so many. Former men, women and children from walks of life. Some wear uniforms: a police officer, a doctor in scrubs and children in school uniforms. With each word Henry speaks, more emerge. They are almost to the windows. I try not to react, but I assume they'll attribute any expression to me being upset about being dumped. They don't turn their unforgiving gazes from me.

I try to stall by pleading, "Please. Give me one more chance."

They laugh.

"I'll do anything."

The shattering of the windows is jarring, even though

I knew it was coming. Kelly and Henry turn and scream when they see the hundreds of zombies crawling over each other to get through the window. A throng of arms and mouths reaches for them. They bravely hack away at the dead flesh, determined to fight off this swarm. But Kelly gets too close. One of the gnarled hands grabs her arm and pulls her through the window. Her terrified, desperate screams are difficult to bear. I quietly reenter the bathroom, locking the door behind me, leaving Henry to fight alone. I find that I simply don't have the strength for this.

Though I try to drown out the noise on the other side of the door, I hear Henry cry out. His voice is breaking, anguished. I try to imagine what befell him to elicit that scream, but I don't really want to.

There is a pounding on the door. The frame rattles with the force behind the knocks.

"Bob! Let me in!" Henry yells, rattling the doorknob.

I unlock the door and Henry pushes through, swiftly shutting and locking the handle behind him.

"Were you bitten?" I ask calmly. I know the answer; part of his hand is missing. I just want to see what Henry will admit to.

The zombies are banging on the door, their nails *scritch scritch scritching* on the weakening wood.

"Kill me," he pleads. His voice is weak. Thick blood stains the white-tiled floor, spreading slowly around us. "I'll make *you* one if you don't."

I smile, shaking my head. "You'll only bite me once. *They'll* make a mess out of me."

Henry's eyes widen when he realises that I don't plan on leaving this bathroom alive.

"Sick bastard," he says.

"We'll get out of this bathroom eventually, even if we have to wait for the house to fall down around us."

He crawls to the toilet, pulls himself up and begins to smash his head against the ceramic rim. Lacking the strength to finish himself off, he slides to the blood-drenched floor.

"We'll be equals soon," I say.

I sit next to him and wait.

Belphegor Dont Surf
by Hari Navarro

Charles Manson sits on a small three-legged stool and stares at the naked vision as I prop splay-legged before him. His thoughts hurt, as they often do, when his mind draws the chemicals and the alcohol up through his veins and into his head. It hurts, but the son of Man enjoys its sting as he milks the scruff beard at his chin.

"Tell me Charlie, do you like what you see?" I say and open my legs just a fraction of an inch wider, shift within the discarded Camel packets and torn, yellowed porn and finger the holes in the bourbon-and-ash and fuck-stained couch.

"Who are you supposed to be?" he says and for an instant I ponder with the idea of not telling him. But instead I shrug: there is so much effort that goes into creating this thing that I am, this sticky entrapment, these sleight-of-hand diversions that I enlist to capture those that are weak of mind and easy of will.

I look down across the slender curves of my form and feel fat. I feel heavy; I puff out my cheeks and wish that I could just lay on a beach and watch the perfection of salt-stained bodies as they ride the rolling whip of the waves.

I will tell him. Fuck it! I'll tell this jumped up little shit just who I am and just what it is I am here for. Might be fun, though he is such a wantonly smug little man.

"Who are you supposed to be?" he repeats and I'm not at all sure if he is repeating himself or, if rather, he's forgotten that he'd already asked.

"You, humans, you always have to label things. You have to give things a name. Even your fucking pets, you could call your cat Syphilis Stevenson for all it'd care and it would still come a running for food. Me? I am nothing. I am but a reflection of you, Charlie."

"A reflection, you say? Well, then, I do so like my titties. My titties look fine," he scoffs and I, too, cannot help but smile at his cheeky retort. He is infectious like so many others that are as diseased as he of the soul.

"If it makes things easier for you, Charlie, then you can call me Belphegor. The lord of the gap. I am the disputer, the grand marshall of licentiousness and orgies, the seamstress of discord, the patron of Moab, chief adversary of the Sixth Sephiroth or Love as I believe that you know her. I am that which draws you from the light and into the tarpit trap of sloth. I am many things and I am one thing."

"You are here to tempt me? Then colour me

136

tempted," he chirps and I move uneasily as the worms and the grubs within him twist and turn in the sticky filth of their mess.

"Actually, Charles, this time I am here for myself. I have grown tired of the luring and the moulding of fools. I want to experience the rush. I want to feel its release for myself."

"The rush, she says." He holds out his hands and spirals the flat of his palms before me. In an instant, he grabs the power of the moment. And like that, it is he that is conducting me. I feel him. I feel that he truly cares who I am. I know that he is gravely concerned for my soul and I, also, know with the utmost of certainty that when it comes to fucks, he does not give the slightest of one. But, still, I love him. This is dangerous. He is dangerous. He is special.

"I wish to experience the thrill rush of the kill. I've never actually done it. Never taken a life, can you believe that? Always the puppeteer and never the puppet. But, now, surely though you have killed, haven't ya Charlie?"

"Well, I did shoot me a black bird once; Bernard Crowe was its name. Left it blowing big ol' red bubbles curling and foetal in its own blood. It tried to cheat me. Threatened to wipe out this here ranch if I didn't pay it its fucking dues. I shot it but, it's kind, they are hard to kill, ya' know? Surprised me though, its blood, it was red just like they say. I should have finished it off right there. One less to worry about on the day of reckoning, I believe. One less to worry about when the panthers skulk out from the shadows and tear the sweet liberty out from the fronts of our throats."

"You are an angry man, Charlie. An angry, angry man. There is nothing more dangerous than a man with charisma who bends only to the rot in his own head." I say and think that I really cannot stand this waste of a thing. I can't stand him, but I love him. So maybe, just maybe, he can be yet of some use.

"You like me don't you, honey pot? I like you. I like your titties and your face and I like this beautiful urge that you have for the kill. I love that the best. It's part of you and don't ever fight it, you hear?" he says and I can actually see the glint that sparks from the coals in his eyes.

"I want to kill the rich. I care not the colour of their skin, I want them to die. You see, in all of humanity, through all of my forevers, it is the rich who most ridicule my existence. Sure, there are those of wealth that do nothing but wallow in the inherited sloth of their privilege, but I'm talking about those who have shunned laziness and have built for themselves the magnificent lives that they lead. The fat famous rich self-made pigs.

Do you know of anyone like that, Charlie? Do you know any pigs?"

"Yeah, I know people just like that, Bells."

"Charlie?"

"Yes."

"Don't call me that, don't ever call me that again! And are you staring at my vagina?"

"Well, ma'am. Yes, I guess so. That is quite almost exactly what I'm doing."

"Remember Charlie, I am but a reflection. Have you ever tried to make love to a mirror?"

"Well no, not the mirror as such…"

"What you perceive of me is but a surface. I'll show you, pass me a beer, would you, Charlie? One of those tasty cold brews you love so much," I say and the little big man diligently jumps and makes for the refrigerator that sits dripping and humming like a stalled truck in the corner of this filthy pine-panelled room. He returns and snaps off the bottlecap with the yellowing tips of his teeth.

"You're such a man, Charlie. Now you watch, you watch and you learn." I pour the amber foam to my lips and it deflects from my open mouth and streams down my chin and courses into a delta of rivulets that finger out between the full curve of my breasts. I feel its smooth caress and his eyes as they watch as it then drips down to the hungry sponge of the couch.

"Now, that right there is fucking wild. Do it again. Do it again. Ok, so don't then. Little bitch tease. Let me get this straight. Let me get you straight. There is to be no fucking today, so instead you want to go out and hunt for yourself some piggies?"

"Well, now Charlie, it's true that was the intention. But, you know, I'm thinking about all the planning that goes into such a thing. Then, I have to find something to wear. I mean, you may not have noticed but you've imagined my legs to be unnaturally long. It's going to be a nightmare finding anything to fit. Then, there's the weapon. I was thinking about guns but, then, I kind of set my heart on knives. But they are so...you know...stabby. Such mess. Not that I have to clean it up but I kind of have this thing for order and cleanliness. I know, I know, so sayeth the prime daemon of sloth. I just don't think I can be bothered any more, you know? But maybe you could. You could do it all for me, Charlie. What do you think? Would you do that for me, Charlie? Would ya?"

"What's gotten into you, Bells? What's gone and done stole your fire?"

"I don't know what it is. I feel...I feel exhausted. You know that some say that I am just a metaphor, the manifestation of depression and anxiety. Sloth. I rob you of your will to achieve and to overcome the walls that we stack in our paths. Maybe, I've been doing this for too damn long. It's a shame, I was also going to hit the beach while I was here. Take in some of those famous Hermosa curls," I say as I instinctively, and without prior thought, reach out and lock my fingers with his.

"Well, let me tell you a little somethin', Bells. I could do as you want me to but I ain't gonna. See, I learnt a long time ago that if I want something done to not hesitate in gettin' someone else to do it first. All care and no responsibility. I have people. I have family and they are like you are now. They will do anything for me. Anything, and I will lead them up to the altar of the lily-white swine kings and queens and I will put the swords in their hands. There is a race war a brewing, ya know? I will sacrifice my family, my children and through their bloodied palms I will rise. We will rise. Survival takes many forms. The world will herald us as daemons both and neither of us will need fire a shot nor run a blade and watch the blooming maw of the fat," he says as he gazes into the empty couch before him and he smiles and he knows that, like the true Christ, he is not a deity.

He is madness.

He is Man.

He is Manson, yes, that's it. He is truly the son of Man.

Goodbye Tomorrow
by M. Sydnor Jr.

"Ms Fiona's Psychic Reading," Ty read the handwritten sign above the booth.

"Oh! My dude—dude. You gotta do it." His friend, Darren, slapped his shoulder and stumbled into him, thanks to drunken legs.

Ty felt a little buzz coming on, too, and giggled at his friend. "Nah man, that's stupid. Let's just get on the Gravitron." He pointed to the ride in the opposite direction. "Empty line."

"Just ask a few questions, man—look, I'll even pay for it."

Ty loved that idea. "You pay? Let's go." He walked ahead to the booth placed strangely in the middle of the dirt path. People walked around it, ignored it, didn't even stop to look at the colourful stall that shined brighter than some of the surrounding rides, but not these two.

Ty approached the booth and looked at the woman sitting behind the table. First thing he noticed was her hat, a long black pointy hat with dark letters stitched along the brim that he couldn't make out. Her gown was black too, all formal-like as if she were headed to a ball. Then he got a look at her face, old and wrinkly with mean, grey hair coming down each side of her face, some of it covering her eyes. She looked more like a witch than a psychic.

"Welcome. Come for a reading, have you?"

She sounded like she looked: old, tired, scary, like a wooden door slowly creaking open. Then she laid her palms out on the desk and nodded toward the empty jar at the corner of the table. She had black gloves on that were see-through and he could've sworn through those gloves were only bones, no skin. He wouldn't dare look back down, once he lifted his view back to her. He cringed and said, "No thank you."

Then his stupid drunken friend came crashing in, almost tackling him in the booth. Ty had to grab the table to keep himself from falling into the lady. "Don't start without me," Darren said then threw a couple bills in the jar.

The old lady looked at the money, then grabbed each of Ty's wrists. "Okay. We start."

As blood rushed from his wrist to his shoulders, his legs felt weak and wobbly. His head started to throb, but he thought it was the few shots he took in the parking lot earlier. Ms Fiona scared him a minute ago, but not anymore. Her hands touching his wrists didn't feel like

144

bones, but skin, soft skin. Suddenly, she didn't seem that old.

"First, your friend must leave," Ms Fiona demanded with a stern grip on Ty's wrists but an even harder look at Darren.

"Fine, fine, fine. I'll grab me a deep-fried Snickers bar. You want one?" He elbowed Ty in the shoulder.

"Nah, I'm good."

Then he was off, leaving Ty and Ms Fiona alone, his wrists caged in her grip. Their eyes locked on one another.

"So how does this work, you read the lines in my hands or something?"

"Not quite. You ask me five questions and I give you five answers. That's all."

"That's it? Hmm." His brain completely turned to mush, and he couldn't think of a single question to ask this lady. "Umm, first question…what is today?"

"Monday."

Shit. "No, not the day day—I meant what is special about today?

"It is opening night for the carnival."

"Ugh. Come on, lady. You know what I meant."

She smiled.

"Do those count?"

"You have three questions left, Tyler."

"Shit—okay, okay." *Three questions left. What can I ask—wait...Tyler?* "You know my name?" She opened her mouth to answer.

"Wait! Don't answer that," he yelled.

She smiled. "Today is your birthday, Tyler. That one's on the house."

He mirrored her smile with a great big one and nodded. *Okay, she's the real deal.* That excited him and he wanted to know more, but he only had three questions left. He dug deep into his brain to think of the most important questions he could ask.

"Will I ever get married?"

"No."

Bachelor for life. He loved that idea. But all twenty-year-olds did. "What are the winning numbers for this week's lottery?"

"Five. Twelve. Twenty-seven. Thirty-seven. Forty-one."

He tried to release his wrists, but she had a hold on him. "Can you—" he tugged, but she was stronger than she looked. "I just want to write those down really quick."

"One more question."

"Can you repeat—no, no, never mind." *Five, twelve, twenty-seven, thirty-seven, forty-two—no, one. Forty-one.* He repeated the numbers over and over and over until she

146

squeezed his wrists.

"One more question," she demanded.

"Okay, um…whatever. Uh, when will I die?"

She wasn't as quick answering this as the others. She looked away from him for a moment and looked around. He followed her gaze to nothing, no one, then looked back at her when she released her hold of him. "Tomorrow," she said. Then she erupted from her seat and gathered her things.

Tyler jumped up and stood there in shock. *Tomorrow?* "You're joking, right?"

She pretended as if he weren't there, folding her table, pulling the sign down from the top.

He approached her. "Hey lady? You tell me—"

"Beware of the yellow monster," she murmured. Then she jerked her head toward him, scowling, conjuring all that creepiness from before.

"Wh-what does that mean?"

She ignored him.

"Ty," his friend yelled from behind him.

He turned to Darren and approached him, unsure of what to do, how to act. *What the fuck?*

"Yo, what's wrong, man?" Darren asked, struggling to hold on to a pile of treats.

"This fucking psychic lady is messing with my head,

man."

"Oh yeah, I almost forgot. How'd it go?"

Ty had lost his buzz. "Fucking ask her." He turned around and pointed to the booth, but it was no longer there. No sign of her, no trace. Just an empty pathway. He took a step forward. "Where did she—what?"

Darren stepped next to him and whispered, "Shall we Gravitron now?"

Ty wasn't in the mood anymore. "Nah man. Just take me home."

"Dude, you sure. I'm as drunk as a…as a…raccoon."

He didn't even have the energy to correct the stupid saying. "It's fine. I'm not dying today."

***

Safe to say, Tyler didn't sleep that night. He hadn't gotten on any rollercoasters but his mind made up for that. The way his emotions climbed and dropped then curved, spun and twisted. He didn't cry, but he cursed himself for even going to that lady, then a minute later he'd laugh at the whole thing. He even called Darren to see if it was some sort of sick birthday joke, giving the lady information about him, but Darren denied it. Then, he tried to remember those lotto numbers, *three, fourteen, twenty-one*—he gave up. He had nothing, and that brought him back down to the angry part of the ride. All this back and forth gave him a massive headache and he took three pain pills to go with his coffee. So, he played video games, watched movies, caught up on his favourite shows until the sun crept in his window.

There was no way he was going to class. Hell, he didn't plan on leaving his dorm room. He'd made that decision last night in between movies. And after coughing on a breakfast sandwich, he'd given up food, too. Only water.

A few of his friends stopped by to check on him later in the afternoon, but he didn't let them in. He acted like he was sick, contagious and didn't want to infect them. They backed off and told him to get well. Indeed, he did feel a fever coming on, so he ran to the shower, turned it on and undressed. It was a cold shower and the sprinkles splashed against his bare skin felt good. But as he dipped a toe in, he had a thought that he might slip—so much for the shower. He put the same clothes back on, grabbed an ice pack, slapped it on his head and watched some more television, trying to think of anything but death.

He couldn't shake this creepy-ass woman from his head. He grabbed his laptop and searched for her. Perhaps, when he found her, he could ask more questions.

He'd pay anything at this point to save himself from whatever it was that would take him. He found the webpage for the fair and scrolled down the contacts, rides and events, but there was no Ms Fiona or psychic readings at all. He googled her name—nothing. He called all the local psychics and they'd never heard of her. But that didn't matter because he made it. All this investigative work carried him the rest of the day, unharmed, undead, and it was five minutes past midnight. He felt the weight of the world roll off his shoulders. He wanted to run to the fridge for a proper meal, but sleep won and he closed his eyes.

***

He's floating in the air. Got his backpack on, his earphones in and he's flying through the halls and down the steps, ready for class. His feet touch the pavement outside the building, and he walks to the rhythm of the beat blasting in his ears. Not a care in the world. Smiling. Every now and then, rapping the lyrics to the song, waving at strangers, loving the air, enjoying the outside, appreciating life until he finds himself in the middle of the street, a loud honking noise overriding his music. He pulls the earphones out of his ear but couldn't turn in time to see. It smacks him.

***

It felt so real that it jolted him out of sleep, off the sofa and onto the floor. Only one thing stood out in the dream, one thing he could remember: Death.

So, the next day he stayed home, again, doing the same shit as the day before. This went on for a month straight and, every now and then, he'd have the same nightmare. His friends stopped coming over; they stopped talking to him. After complaints of a stink coming out of the room and clogging the halls, school authorities paid him a visit and kicked him out. Campus security had to physically remove him, and it took four guys to do it. His parents were waiting outside with a van; they couldn't bear to see the filth their son had lived in. Security tossed him in the van and his parents drove him away.

Tyler had transformed into a different person. He was significantly skinnier than he was when he last visited home, and he felt like he'd aged twenty years. Greys were scattered across the top of his head and wrinkles surrounded his eyes. He even talked slower, deeper and when they pulled up to his childhood home, he walked from the van to the house like a snail.

They'd arranged for him to temporarily stay in the basement while they sought help and he was all good with that. His own personal hell.

Once they found help, he didn't want to go. Couldn't go. He even threatened his parents with physical violence if they tried to force him. After that they left him alone and he was free to repeat in that basement what he did in the dorm room. Light eating, no showers, no nothing. Television was his life. The couch was his world.

He couldn't escape this feeling of death waiting for him outside—upstairs—in the shower—he'd become obsessed with it to the point where it felt natural to him. His way of life. He'd abandoned his education, his friends, his family, his reason to live. All he cared about was making it to the next day. Surviving. But he even did a poor job at that as he sat rotting away in his parent's basement.

Ten years passed, twenty years, thirty...he'd changed into some basement mutant unable to function in society. It was so bad, Ms Fiona could have appeared before him and told him that he'd be safe and fine and would live for a hundred more years, but he wouldn't have believed her.

When his parents died, one after the other, he mourned but in the basement. And he started to think like a rational person, question the meaning of his existence, but the thought didn't stick until ten years later. He'd gotten so sick, he couldn't move. The man was literally glued to the sofa. Couldn't get up to take a piss, he just lay there on his filthy, dingy, pissy, poopy sofa. He'd come to terms that he'd be dead sooner than later and had accepted that.

Eventually, Tyler fought like hell to remember his poor excuse of a life. He'd wanted to be a fireman when he was in elementary school, a doctor when he made to high school, then a movie director because he'd get to blow shit up and get girls, his thinking. But the night before his twentieth birthday, before the county fair opened, he'd decided what he wanted to do with his life. To be a writer. Everyone had always told him he had the imagination for it. That following Monday, the day after his birthday, he'd actually planned on meeting with the academic advisor to change his major. But Ms Fiona's psychic reading flushed that dream away. He couldn't believe he'd forgotten all about that only to have it all come back to him when he was moments away from death. Thirty years wasted on poor tv, horrible food and bad dreams. He cursed himself for ever believing in a psychic. And that was the last thought he had before he closed his eyes.

Tyler sat up in bed with a wicked headache. It was throbbing, pounding, like two big muscle men pushing each side of his face. He reached for the water bottle on his nightstand and gulped it all. Then he got ready for his day.

He brewed some coffee and turned the shower on. A hot shower and he felt the sprinkles splash on his skin as he undressed. Before he took a step in, he thought of yesterday, the fair, the psychic, he couldn't remember her name but it made him laugh. "Yeah right," he muttered, then hopped in the shower and washed up. When he finished, he grabbed two pain pills to go with his coffee and drank up, letting the hot sweet taste warm his body and eradicate his headache.

Tyler put on his clothes, tossed on some music and bounced out the room, feeling better than ever. His favourite song played, appropriate for the special meeting he had with the school advisor that would change his life forever. The thought of being a writer had his mind, the music became his own personal soundtrack and he rapped along to the beat, skipping out of the building, waving at random people and smiling for the hell of it.

This is the first day of the rest of my life. Nothing would bring him down from this high.

Then he heard a loud sound, honking, and he found himself in the middle of the street. He snatched the earphones out of his ear, looked to his side and saw a big yellow bus. In that half-second, he remembered his dream: all thirty years of it, and the psychic's name, *Ms Fiona*. But her last words to him stuck out more than anything else. *Beware the yellow monster.*

Then it smacked him.

I Don't Want To

by Gabriella Balcom

Cami sniffled, the tears in her big brown eyes rolling down her cheeks.

"Don't cry, honey," Lana murmured, gently dabbing Cami's face. "Go ahead and eat your banana. You *love* bananas."

Once the girl began chewing, Lana marched into the living room. "How *could* you?" she whispered fiercely.

Bernice reached for the sandwich lying beside her on the couch, but Lana snatched the plate away. "That isn't yours. You already ate your food."

"It wasn't enough," Bernice retorted.

"You could've made more." Lana carried the ham-and-cheese sandwich into the kitchen, setting it in front of Cami before returning to stare at Bernice.

"You always give the kids extra," she complained. "But you hardly feed me anything."

"How can you say that? You had *two* sandwiches, plus fruit, chips and cookies. I made Max and Cami one sandwich apiece."

Hours later, Bernice sulked. "I don't want to. My

157

show's about to come on."

"You've been watching TV for hours," Lana replied. "All I asked you to do was sweep the kitchen and take out one bag of trash."

"Have the kids do it."

"They did their chores."

"You do it then."

"I worked all day while you relaxed at home. I fixed the food even though my arthritis is acting up. Then I cleaned out the fridge and did laundry. You need to do your share."

Bernice narrowed her eyes. "You've always favoured those brats over me."

Lana studied her daughter with haunted eyes. "Don't start that again. You say it every time I ask you to do anything." She rubbed her back, then her right knee, wincing as she gingerly lowered herself into a recliner. "I love you and I've shown that a million times over regardless of your behaviour. You're a grown woman, for heaven's sake. Twenty-seven years old, healthy and capable. The kids are three and five. And they're *your* children."

"They're a pain in the ass."

"No, they're not."

"Cami's a whiner." Bernice's lip curled.

"She cried earlier because she was hungry and you took her food. How could you do that, anyway? You just walked away like—like…" Bernice began a game on her phone. Realising she was being ignored, Lana frowned. "I'm talking to you."

Her daughter raised her head but only to sneer.

"You were supposed to feed Cami and Max when the babysitter dropped them off," Lana said. "I had to work late. It wasn't fair to keep them waiting till I got here."

"I never wanted them." Bernice's voice was glacier cold.

"Then you should've used birth control," her mother snapped. "Thank goodness they're in bed and not hearing this."

The younger woman shrugged.

"I've been raising them since they were born." Lana's voice cracked. "You wouldn't feed them. Wouldn't change them. I had to push you to do anything. And the last few weeks, I've repeatedly asked you to get a job to help with the expenses."

"I got one."

"You were fired within days."

"I don't want to work."

"I'd love it if I didn't have to, but I'm not rich. I'm fifty-nine and only have a few workable years left, especially if my arthritis worsens. When I do retire, I won't get much social security because I haven't made a lot."

"You can get food stamps for us. And money from the church."

"I don't want welfare or handouts because I'm capable of working. So are you."

Two days later

"Shut up!" Bernice yelled at the kids.

Lana glared at her, then ushered Max and Cami outside to the waiting van. A church friend had invited the children to her son's birthday party, offering to pick them up and bring them home later.

"Those spoiled brats are always blabbing and wanting something," Bernice griped.

"You ask for stuff, too. I stand all day long at work and my feet hurt when I get home. That's why I was soaking them. But you wanted me to make you toast, hand you an apple, paper towels and other things just so you wouldn't have to get up yourself."

"You got the kids more stroganoff when they asked."

"They're *little*. If they'd tried to get it themselves, they could've been burned. You can make sandwiches, open cans, heat stuff…"

"Shh...I can't hear the movie."

Lana sighed. "The laundry is still heaped up in the hallway and the dishes are still in the sink. You were supposed to take care of both."

"I'm not your slave. I shouldn't have to clean up after everyone."

"The laundry and dishes are yours. I do meals every day. You refuse, even if your kids are hungry. All I ask you to do is vacuum three times a week, take the trash out now and then and occasionally clean the tub and toilet. And you're responsible for your own laundry and dishes."

"The kids should do more."

"Max helps with dishes as much as he can, and he and Cami wipe the table. Max sweeps, vacuums and takes trash out, and they help me with laundry. It isn't perfect, but they try. They've learned to put their dirty clothes in the baskets I put out, but yours are strewn around your room and bathroom."

"So?"

"Bending and picking things up hurts me. I shouldn't have to. Putting stuff in baskets isn't hard."

Bernice shrugged.

Lana took a deep breath. "Your attitude really bothers me. No matter how many times I talk to you, nothing changes. When I told you why I was soaking my feet earlier, you didn't care. Asking *me* to do more when I'm hurting isn't right. I'm tired. You'd been home and could've easily..." Lana trailed off when Bernice raised the TV volume. "I've said this so many times; I don't know why I bother. You can't go through life waiting for people to serve you, while you sit around and do nothing."

"You cater to the spoiled brats."

"They're not spoiled brats."

"You blame me for everything."

"No." Lana's head throbbed. "I hold you accountable for yourself. I don't understand why you won't help. You show a total lack of caring."

Turning cold eyes on her mother, Bernice asked, "Why would I care about any of you?"

Lana's stomach churned. "You watch shows, play on your phone and help yourself to food *my* hard work provides. You never clean up, never help anyone. I have to say something a hundred times to get you to do the smallest thing. You leave your dirty dishes everywhere, and you aren't putting a cent toward bills. And don't think I've forgotten how you treated me."

Bernice widened her eyes, but their expression remained hard and uncaring. "I don't know what you're talking about."

"Yes, you do. Last week, I was sick with a high fever,

vomiting and diarrhoea. I could barely stand without doubling over in pain, but the kids were hungry. I forced myself out of bed when you wouldn't help, and I fell in the hallway. You saw me there. I was weak, hurting all over. I asked you for help, but you wouldn't. I finally managed to get up. Then, after I warmed up leftover spaghetti for the kids, you took off with Max's bowl. What kind of mother takes her child's food?"

"I was hungry," Bernice snorted. "Of course he tattled."

"He didn't tattle. I saw you. But that's not the point."

"Point? You never have one. You're a boring old dumbass, nagging all the time."

Lana flinched as if she'd been struck. Turning pale, tears sprung to her eyes. "I have nothing left to say to you. You have till the end of the week to be out of my home."

Two weeks later

"I *hate* her," Bernice growled, voice ringing with resentment.

"Young lady, that's enough," Hildy replied. "That's your mother and my child. She's put up with a lot from you, and you know it."

"Bullshit. She's nothing but a mean bitch."

Hildy gasped. "Don't use that kind of language. And

why would you say such things? She raised and helped you all these years. Asking you to do chores was fair. She has your kids' learning to take responsibility for and help, too. There's nothing wrong with that."

"Stupid kids."

"They're not stupid, and you got pregnant with them, not your mama. She didn't have to help, but she did because she's a good woman. She could've put you out. The kids also, since they're your responsibility."

"I would've dumped them first chance I got."

Hildy's mouth dropped. "You carried them in your belly. Don't you care about them?"

Her granddaughter stared at her, eyes cold. "No."

"You can't mean that." Hildy moved, standing between Bernice and the television.

"Get the hell outta my way!"

"Don't you ever talk to me that way. It's rude and disrespectful. Apologise."

Bernice muttered something under her breath.

"What?"

"So—oo—ry," Bernice said, drawing the word out. She added, "Bitch," after her grandmother walked away.

Four days later

"Today's Thursday," Hildy commented. "Your

dishes from the week are still in the sink. Grab the ones beside you and go wash them."

"I don't want to. You do them."

"I didn't dirty them. You did."

Three days later

"The dishes *still* aren't washed," Hildy stressed. "Your Mama and kids are coming over tonight. I want the house to look nice."

"Why are they coming?"

"To visit. You haven't seen them since moving in. Don't you miss your children?"

Bernice stared blankly at Hildy.

That evening, Max and Cami raced back and forth playing tag. They periodically stopped to play Chutes and Ladders with Hildy and Lana. Although Bernice sat across from the children at the kitchen table during dinner, she hadn't said anything to them since their arrival. They didn't seem to notice.

Cami ran from her brother, giggling, and paused in front of Bernice, blocking her view of the television.

"Get outta my way!" Bernice shoved the child hard.

Cami fell against the coffee table, bumping her forehead before landing on the floor. She wailed, scrunching up her nose and holding her head.

"Bernice!" Hildy snapped, kneeling to gather the child in her arms.

Lana bit her lip, exchanging a glance with Hildy.

Max backed away from his biological mother, eyes shadowed by fear.

***

"May I have a word with you, Bernice?" Lana struggled to keep her voice calm. Her daughter ignored her. "Step into the hallway with me. *Now.*"

"Go with your mother," Hildy added.

In the hall, Lana studied her daughter. "That wasn't right."

"She got in my way."

"It wasn't deliberate. She was playing. And you could've asked her to move."

Lana's words had no effect. Her chastisement didn't either. The offender returned to the living room, dropping onto the couch, and turned up the volume on the TV.

Three weeks later

"I've been talking about missing plates and silverware," Hildy said. "Why didn't you tell me they were in your room?"

Bernice didn't respond.

"You could've put them in the sink instead of leaving them out. I've had roaches before and those nasty things were hard to get rid of. Food attracts them and other critters."

"So pick things up."

"*You* pick them up. And dishes and leftovers aren't the only problems in your room. It stinks to high heaven. There are rotten banana peels and apples everywhere. Towels are piled up. Some must've been damp because mould is growing. The same thing's happening with your clothes."

"I need new stuff."

"No. You need to take care of what you have, wash it and not leave it for weeks." Noticing Bernice's attention on the TV, Hildy turned it off. "It's high time you got a job. We agreed you'd work and help out."

"I don't want to work."

"Well, I'd like to be a fairy princess with a castle and a genie to grant me wishes."

"You've got money."

"I get social security, 947 dollars a month. That's barely enough for my expenses, and you're here now."

"I got a job."

"You didn't go in on your second day and they fired you. The job before that—the manager called me, wondering if you were mentally ill. She said you stood around."

Bernice walked away.

"I don't understand why you act this way," Hildy said, following the younger woman into her room.

Lying on her bed, Bernice began fiddling with her cell.

Hildy frowned. "Did you hear me?"

"Huh?"

Four weeks later

"You ruined them," Hildy said, voice rising. "One was my mother's."

"What are you talking about?" Bernice leaned to her right, trying to see the television around her grandmother.

"My towels. I had to throw all but one away. I asked you to wash them weeks ago. When more and more vanished, you said you didn't know where they were, but I just found them. Stuffing them in a trash bag and hiding it in the shed is *not* doing laundry."

"Buy more."

"I can't afford to. Why did…"

"Shut up, you whiny, old bag."

Hildy gasped, her face turning pale. "Don't talk to me that way."

A week later

Bernice finished the banana, slinging the peel across the room. She ate all her sandwich but the crust, dropping it on the floor. After eating the chips and cookies on her plate, she slid it under her bed.

"Bring me more cookies," she yelled before remembering Hildy had been rushed to the hospital with chest pain.

Once she'd searched the refrigerator and cupboards, Bernice groaned. There was food, but none of it appealed to her, and she had no intentions of cooking.

After ransacking Hildy's room, she found an envelope labelled 'Water Bill', took fourty dollars and ordered pizza.

An hour later, she tossed the half-empty pizza box into a corner.

She bathed, then dropped her wet towel on top of the box. Since she didn't have anything clean, she went through a pile of dirty clothes on the floor.

Relaxing in front of the living room television, she heard a scraping noise and flinched, looking around for the source. She saw nothing. A pair of dirty jeans she didn't remember taking off lay on the floor.

With a shrug, she focused on her movie.

Something grabbed Bernice's foot and she squealed.

Her eyes widened when she saw the sleeve of one of her shirts wrapped around her ankle. Leggings inched across the floor, winding themselves around her other ankle.

The clothing yanked her off the couch, dragging her down the hall. She yelled, flailing around, grabbing for doorways and walls, trying to get free.

In her room, her shoes and bedding rose in the air, swirling around in a frenzied tornado, picking up her other possessions in the whirlwind. A plate sailed toward her, eyes and a twisted mouth appearing on the surface. Maniacal laughter emanated from it.

"Help!" Bernice yelled.

A pair of sweats hovered in front of her before floating to the ground, standing upright. One leg grabbed her right arm.

"Let go!" She struggled to get out of its grip.

"I don't want to," a voice replied, seeming to come from the sweatpants.

"We don't want to either," other voices called out.

Rotten banana peels soared toward Bernice. She tried to dodge them from where she lay, but they struck her right arm before dropping to the floor. The places the peels struck her tingled and shimmered. Bernice screamed as her arm began shrinking, turning a dirty brownish yellow. Within a matter of seconds, a rotten peel hung from her shoulder instead of her arm. But it broke off, dry and shrivelled, and almost totally black.

Apple cores hit her left shoulder, which started to change, shrivelling into a mushy, brown rotten apple.

She blinked in disbelief, crying and bellowing for help. Plates tapped her right leg, which took on a white, porcelain sheen before growing smaller, turning into two saucers.

No longer being pinned down, Bernice hopped frantically toward the doorway, but the clothing that originally dragged her there raced after her. Winding themselves around her remaining limb, they transformed it into dirty jeans.

With nothing left to support her torso, Bernice toppled over, landing with an oomph.

"Why are you doing this?" she wailed, sitting up on her elbows. "Go away and leave me alone."

"We don't want to."

Everything circled her, repeating the phrase again and again.

The discarded pizza box slid toward Bernice on one side, toppling onto her chest, which slowly took on a flat, brown appearance. Soon, several pizza boxes lay where her torso had been.

Discarded underwear dropped onto the helpless

woman's head, morphing it into stained panties as she yelled.

Only Bernice's eyes and mouth remained, and she continued screaming hoarsely—all she could manage now.

A wadded Kleenex she'd blown her nose on weeks before floated over, dropping onto one of her eyes, turning it into a second crumpled tissue.

Old, partially eaten pieces of bread landed on her second eye and mouth—even as a prolonged wail rose from it—and they both elongated into dried bread crusts.

Everything floating through the air returned to their previous positions, immediately becoming immobile once more. Bernice's room looked exactly as it had before, except for a few more discarded items.

Jack of Spades

by Jodi Jensen

Aiden stared at the blank screen; eyes glued to the blinking cursor. He'd been sitting here for hours, maybe longer, without putting so much as a single word on the page.

The computer was brand new, a gift from his wife, but he was starting to think he wanted his old one back. His mojo was attached to the old one, with the successful completion of twenty-two novels, seventeen of which had been bestsellers.

Frustrated, he opened a game of solitaire and flipped mindlessly through the cards. The afternoon wasted away until finally, he closed the game in disgust.

To his utter astonishment, there, on the previously blank page, was a typed paragraph.

***

On the surface, Jack had it all. Wife, family, fame and fortune. He was the envy of society with his classic good looks and charismatic personality. It was said he could charm the panties off a roomful of Sunday-school virgins if he so desired. Problem was, beneath the surface, he didn't desire anything anymore. Not really. Not like he used to. Now he was just bored. Bored with his wife, family, fame, fortune and virgins alike.

***

Aiden's breath caught as he glanced around. Surely someone was playing a trick on him, had control, remotely, of his computer or something. Words couldn't just *appear*, could they?

He scrubbed a hand over his stubbled jaw and read the paragraph again. Whoever had written this didn't have his level of skill, but it wasn't half bad either. His interest was piqued but family obligations called.

Later, after dinner, he returned to his computer. The paragraph was still there and he found he wanted to add to it. His fingers hovered over the keyboard as he squinted at the words. Moments passed but nothing came to mind. He took a sip from his water bottle, cleaned his glasses and leaned back in his chair to think.

Still nothing.

Before long, the inevitable happened. Another round of solitaire.

Card after card flashed on the screen, minutes flew by, turning into hours, until at last his wife called out from the other room.

"I'm going to bed, honey. Don't stay up too late, we have that appointment in the morning."

"Be right there," he hollered back, snapped out of his daze by the reminder. He closed the game and, for the second time that day, sat staring in shock.

Another paragraph had been added somehow.

***

He needed some excitement, something to really make his heart pound and his blood sing again. Skydiving? Nah, too cliché. A flaming love affair? Oh, hell no. Too much effort. Maybe a carjacking? He'd done that once at fifteen. Even now, he recalled the way his adrenaline had spiked, and for a few minutes he'd been invincible. Until the sirens. He shut down that idea. Too risky and he was too old to repeat such a stupid mistake from his misspent youth.

What else was there? Suddenly it came to him.

He'd steal a soul.

***

Aiden poured himself a Scotch, gulped it down, then poured another.

Steal a soul? How?

His mind whirled with possibilities. Instead of itching to write though, he was desperate to find out what, exactly, stealing a soul meant.

He drummed his fingers on the desk, then polished off the Scotch in his glass. Both times a paragraph had appeared, he'd been playing solitaire.

Curious, he opened the game again and flipped back and forth between the document and the cards. When several moments passed with no new words, he moved away from his desk and went to bed.

Aiden tossed and turned half the night, unable to get the mysterious Jack and his soul-stealing ambitions off his mind. Finally, in the wee hours of the morning, he gave up on sleep and ventured back downstairs to his office.

This time, he didn't even pretend to try and do anything else. He double checked the story, nothing new there, then opened solitaire. Normally the game soothed him, allowed his mind to wander until the next bit of the story revealed itself to him. But things were different now. All he could do was wonder how long it would be until something new was added.

His thoughts taunted him.

How does one steal a soul? What does that even mean?

Card after card whizzed by, but it seemed the only ones that even registered to him were the spades. Something about those little black symbols appealed to him and each time one flashed across the screen, his mind registered its presence.

He was so fixated on the cards that he didn't even notice the passing time until sunlight peeked through the slits in the blinds. Heart thundering with excitement, he switched to the document and sure enough...

***

It wouldn't be hard. He just had to find some poor sap who was bored with life, like he was. Someone who had ambition but had lost motivation. Someone he could manipulate into doing nothing while he snuck in and snatched their soul.

Jack rubbed his hands together, anticipating the challenge ahead of him. He already had the perfect fool of a man in mind. One who took his family for granted, whose accolades were so commonplace they meant nothing to him anymore. One who didn't even know what a lazy twit he'd become.

And once he had the soul, that's when the fun would begin in spades.

***

Aiden frowned at the computer. If anyone was the twit here, it was this Jack character. Who made him judge and jury? What gave him the right to do such a thing?

"Honey?"

Startled by the intrusion, he glanced up to find his wife standing in the doorway.

"You're not ready."

"I'm not coming with you." He dismissed her in favour of the drama unfolding on the screen in front of him.

A heavy sigh had him looking up again and a burst of heated anger flushed through his body at the sight of her still standing there, glaring at him.

"Get out!" he roared.

She stormed off, slamming the door behind her.

"Criminy," he muttered. "It's like she's never been to the doctor alone before." He reached for the Scotch bottle, undeterred by the fact that it was merely eight in the morning. His mind was a scattered mess and he needed to relax and lose himself again or the story wouldn't continue.

He downed three shots in a row, then sat back in his chair with his hands clasped behind his head and closed his eyes. Though he really wanted to focus on the story, it was the Jack of Spades that kept flashing through his mind's eye. He was half-tempted to look up the card, see if it had meaning, but the pull of the story was strong. Too strong.

Going back to the beginning, he reread everything on the page so far.

Damn! This guy is both an idiot and a whack job...

What kind of moron had a life like Jack had described and it wasn't enough? If anyone was a *poor sap* here, it was this dude.

As a character, he had no respect for Jack, but the overall story had him hook, line and sinker.

He reopened solitaire and within minutes was lost in the monotony of the game.

***

The first thing was to slip into the man's mind, give him something to obsess over, then capture his thoughts. Make it so he couldn't think about anything else except the seed that was now growing. Soon he'd be lashing out at the very people who loved him, pushing them away in favour of the mindless game he didn't understand.

Then, he'd use the man's indignation and anger to fuel his obsession. Both of their obsessions, really. For now, he himself was as taken by manipulating the man as the man was by their game. The perfect symbiotic relationship.

Next was the tricky part: keeping the man in this state until the death of his ambitions. That could take days, or even weeks, but once he got there, his soul would be ripe for the taking and that's when Jack would swoop in.

***

Aiden didn't even remember switching from cards back to the document, yet here he was, reading and rereading the latest instalment. Somewhere in the recesses of his mind, he heard a car door slam, then the front door. He shoved the intrusions away and went back to his game. He wanted, no *needed* to know what was going to happen next.

Card after card flew across the screen and, eventually, he realised the red ones were getting fewer and fewer. Soon, the only colour to streak by was black.

He forced himself to slow down enough to see the suit.

Spade, spade, spade, spade...

No clubs, only spades. It probably meant something, but he didn't know, didn't care what.

"Aiden? Honey?"

His shoulders stiffened.

"The   doctor   said...he   said...it's—I—I have...cancer." His wife took a wobbly breath. "I have cancer..."

Had he really been listening he'd have heard the heartbreak in her voice. The fear, the pain, the devastation. But all he heard was noise. Meaningless words that were breaking his concentration. He never even turned around, couldn't have said when she finally left.

For two days he sat there, not eating, not sleeping, drinking Scotch and peeing on the ficus tree next to his desk. He faithfully played game after game, yet nothing new had been added to the story.

After a while, he quit trying to guess what Jack's plan was, or what was going to happen next. He simply clicked the mouse as the spades whizzed by in a blur.

By the third day, his desperation had him nearly hyperventilating as his efforts had still yielded no new words. He slammed his fist on the desk, then grabbed his wrist as pain shot up his arm.

"Son-of-a-fucking-hell-bound-whore!" His fingers spasmed, curling in like an arthritic old man's, prompting another round of heartfelt curses. "Goddamn-piece-of-shit-good-for-nothing-jacked-up-hand, that *fucking hurts!*"

He tried to pick up the blue octopus glass paperweight his wife had given him as an anniversary gift, intending to chuck it across the room, but his fingers refused to grasp it.

"Oh, for the love of Satan-in-the-seventh-pit-of-darkness, what in the sacred-bloody-Christ is going on?"

He swept his arm across the desk, sending the paperweight along with a slew of papers flying. The blue octopus landed with a satisfying *thunk* while the papers fluttered to the floor like a whimsical kaleidoscope of butterflies. Laughter bubbled up inside him and burst out in a series of loud guffaws at the sight.

It occurred to him, as he wiped his eyes, that he may be feeling just a little unhinged. No matter, there was only one thing that was important now.

The game.

Time to get back to it.

Despite the pain, he put his hand on the mouse and clicked.

The cards flipping, the black spades flashing by, the monotonous *click, click, click* all worked together to soothe the chaos he'd just experienced and soon he was even deeper in the zone than before.

Minutes went by, or perhaps hours, he couldn't really be sure, and at long last, there were new words.

***

He'd done it! He'd really done it!

Jack bounced on his toes as he embraced his stolen soul. It'd been hard earned, for sure. The lazy dumbass had nearly broken free for a moment. There was a fine line between fuelling the anger enough so he could use it, and too much, which would've helped the man break away, had he so desired. Lucky for Jack, the mindless twit had no desire to rejoin his regularly scheduled life.

Gloating and filled with childish glee, he peeked inside the soul, eager to delve in and explore his newly acquired treasures.

Desire, both lusty and material, was the most prominent. Passion, ambition and drive were not far behind. And oh, the wealth! In that instant he knew about all of the hidden money, the offshore accounts, the investments, the royalties. It'd take him several lifetimes to spend it all.

Best of all though, stuffed into every nook and cranny, overflowing in some places, were the story ideas. A veritable treasure trove of bestsellers certain to grow his fame and fortune.

***

Aiden paused as alarm bells went off in his head.

It was him.

He was the lazy twit, the mindless dumbass, the poor sap and the fool. He searched his mind for the things he cared most about, the story ideas, but they were fading faster than he could grab on to them. His eyes darted back to the page.

***

Mine! Every nugget, every piece of inspiration, every word, mine! Jack sifted through the ideas, tossing the ones he didn't care for over his shoulder and laughing as the lazy twit was helpless to do anything but watch his stories circle the drain until, one by one, they vanished. Once he had the cream of the crop tucked safely away, he moved on to the memories.

He mined everything linked to education, awards, honours, ceremonies and prestige, leaving behind lonely little snippets of childhood traumas and teenage workplace drudgery.

***

A single tear trickled down Aiden's cheek as visions of his wedding day, graduations and all the other milestones in his life were stripped away. By the time Jack was done, he couldn't even remember his wife's name.

***

Finally, Jack had it all, everything he wanted, everything he'd dreamed of, and then some. He sat down at a dusty old typewriter in a secluded cobwebbed corner and typed a few last words.

***

Aiden looked away from the screen. He didn't want to know what it said, did he? He couldn't be sure, but he knew something bad had happened and he knew the words on the screen were making it worse.

Seeing an almost empty bottle of liquor on the corner of the desk, he picked it up and guzzled the last of it. He let the bottle fall to the floor with a sigh.

Now what?

He glanced around, certain he'd been here before, but unable to put his finger on exactly when. The bookshelves were achingly familiar, as was the set of French double doors. Through the glass, he saw the back of a woman's blonde head, sitting in a chair facing a window. He had the distinct impression she was sad, though he couldn't have said why or how he knew.

His eyes flickered to the computer screen in front of him.

***

Beware, the lazy writer. Spades bring death to your mind, your ambition and I, the Jack of Spades, am the happy thief of your creativity.

Beware, the lazy writer. Beware.

Jewelled Sloth

by Cindar Harrell

"Sloth, wake up!" a voice thundered. I didn't need to open my eyes to know that it was my sister Wrath, probably with her fists clenched tightly to the side of her bony hips. "I said, *wake up!*"

I felt the air shift slightly and raised my hand, catching her arm mere centimetres away from my head. Only then did I open my eyes. "I am awake. What do you want, Wrath?"

"You're the only one that hasn't collected a sinner. We're all waiting on you!"

"Fine, I already had one picked out anyway."

I slowly stood and walked away, ignoring Wrath's angry mutters.

Selected   Sinner: Alexandra   Feodorovna Romanova

Russia

1872–1918

It wasn't hard to locate my selected sinner, after all

she was Empress of Imperial Russia.

Unrest had been growing in the country and called Tsar Nicholas away, leaving Alexandra in charge. To say she was an ill fit for the responsibility would be an understatement.

Much to the great concern of the court, and the people alike, Alexandra placed her trust in the mystic Rasputin. She allowed him to control her mind and drive her country further into ruin. When the people, and even Nicholas's mother, insisted she remove Grigori Rasputin from any position of power, she did nothing. Even once her advisor was dead, she still sat in her gilded palace, not even lifting a finger to help her crumbling reign. The Romanov dynasty was being shredded before her eyes, the people crying out for help.

Instead however, she threw a party.

It was the grandest event ever held at the palace with their dresses dripping with priceless jewels.

She sat at the head of the ballroom, regally looking over the swirling colours dancing before her in the opulent hall.

"Your Majesty," I said with a curtsy before walking up to her on her raised dais. "Are you going to dance? I believe your daughters wanted to each have a dance, and probably Alexei too."

"No, not tonight. I am tired and would much rather just watch from here," she replied, rubbing a gloved hand to her temple.

"Of course, Your Majesty, I completely understand." And I did oh so well. I couldn't help but smile.

***

Not long after that, the tensions in the country came to a head in the form of a full revolution. The royal family was captured and placed under house arrest. Months passed and they were left with nothing to do but hope that they would eventually be released. The former Tsar wrote letters to the British royal family—relatives—begging for help that would never come. Alexandra fretted in silence, spending most of her time staring blankly at the walls.

I let them wait for as long as I could, liking the inactivity, but eventually my sisters grew impatient, wanting their final soul. So, I put my plan into effect.

I wrote a letter and slipped it into their quarters where Nicholas would find it. I pretended to be a sympathiser who wished to help them escape to England. I gave them a time to be ready and told them to find a way to carry as much as they could without appearing conspicuous.

Olga and Anastasia came up with the idea to sew

their remaining jewels into the lining of their clothing. Clever daughters who would have made far better rulers than their mother. It was a shame that her inability to act would rip away that possibility from them.

On the designated day, they were lined up with their laced jackets, ready for their false salvation. I disguised myself as one of their captors and led them down to the basement where I told them they would be smuggled out in secret. What they didn't know was that the entire thing was a trap.

While we waited for the other guards to appear, Alexandra began to complain.

"There are no chairs down here for us to sit on! Do you really expect to keep us waiting in these conditions?"

I smiled. Even in the direst of circumstances, her laziness was shining through. I grabbed them three chairs only. I wanted to see if even when there was a shortage if she would offer them up to her children or take one for herself. To her credit, she did at least give one to young Alexei who was sick, but then took the second for herself. Anastasia offered the third to one of her sisters, ever kind-hearted.

The other soldiers entered led by Yakov Yurovsky, each one armed.

"Unfortunately for you, your relatives did try to save

you but were unsuccessful. The time of the Tsars is at an end. Stand up."

"How dare you? We do not take orders from the likes of you!" Alexandra yelled as she was forcibly removed from her chair. However, all protests died when each soldier aimed their guns at the family including me. It was not something I enjoyed, gunning down an entire family, but it was what I had to do. Even then though, I knew that I would only fire a single bullet, my aim directed solely to Alexandra herself.

For the briefest of moments before the gunfire started, she looked me in the eye and recognition flashed across her face. The shots were fired. Screams resounded in the small basement as the bullets found their targets. Confusion reigned as it took far longer than anyone expected for the family to fall, no one knew of the jewels serving as protection. But in the end, it didn't matter.

My bullet pierced the known weak spot in Alexandra's heart, bypassing the ruby sewn close to her chest. I looked over the carnage. Anastasia died trying to protect her brother, a noble but futile sacrifice.

"We need to bury them far out in the woods so no one will find the bodies," one soldier said.

"It might be best to separate some of them in case they are found; that way their numbers don't give us away," Yakov replied.

"Keep the young Grand Duchess together with the boy. Separate them and bury the rest," I said, my eyes never leaving them. Those two deserved so much better than the mother and the untimely death they received.

***

I sat on the same couch that my sister found me on before, my head back, eyes closed.

"Sloth! Are you serious? You are still sitting here doing nothing?" Wrath screamed. "We are so close to our plan coming to fruition and you are going to ruin it!"

I sighed. Without opening my eyes, I pointed to the crystalline container that was designated for me all those centuries ago. Inside was Alexandra, the embodiment of sloth, waiting for whatever destiny my sisters had in store.

"Go ahead and look, Wrath. The job is done, now let me sleep."

Matteez

by G. Allen Wilbanks

"Matt to the front desk. Matt come to the front desk, please. Your one o'clock appointment is here."

Matteez glanced toward the ceiling speaker directly above him in the employee break room. That was Colleen's voice on the intercom, he thought. Not surprising. She spent most of her work time at the front counter. Although she had gone to school to become a personal trainer, the manager of the All the Time Fitness had a good eye for curb appeal and, more often than not, assigned her as close to the front door as possible. Colleen had been a knockout before she decided to go under the knife, and the surgeon she found had a reputation for being a true artist. Now she was nothing short of stunning: the poster child for personal fitness. A tiny nose and perfect tits sold a lot of memberships.

Heaving a sigh and closing the crossword book he had been working on, Matteez stood, stretched and let go with a gut-emptying belch. Time to go to work.

Colleen was indeed at the front desk and, as Matteez approached, she gave him a warm smile and a quick wink.

With a graceful sweep of her hand, she gestured toward a pudding-shaped lump of a human being wrapped in a grey t-shirt and sweatpants.

"Hey, Matt. This is James." Colleen stretched out the name in a flirty lilt, pronouncing it 'Ja-ames'. "He signed up last week for a full year and came in today to start his free week of one-on-one instruction. James, this is Matt. He's one of our best trainers."

"Hi Matt," said the pudding. "I prefer Jim, by the way."

Holy shit, it talks! thought Matteez derisively, though he said nothing to James. He simply extended a hand to greet his new client.

The man's hand felt soft and clammy in his own, pretty much as Matteez had expected. This doughy heap had probably never done anything more strenuous in his lifetime than manipulate a computer game controller. He had most likely been to see a doctor recently and been warned if he didn't start getting some exercise, he would be dead in a year. That, or he had managed to score a girlfriend somewhere and she was getting tired of playing 'where the hell is it?' with his dick.

Matteez was grateful he had neither of those problems. The body he currently inhabited was tall, fit and, from the reaction of most of his female clients, not too hard to look at. A few of the ladies he trained had even paid for private lessons in their homes. Off the books, of course. A couple of the gentlemen as well. Being a demon did have its advantages.

"Thanks, Colleen. I'll take good care of Jim."

Pasting on a friendly expression of earnestness, he clapped Jim on the back and led him into the largest of the three workout spaces in the building: the room with free weights and resistance machines. As they left the front desk, Jim swivelled his head to glance over his shoulder one more time at Colleen.

Matteez noticed the direction of his gaze.

That's it, big boy. You keep dreaming. Matteez grinned but kept this thought to himself as well. A mental image flitted through his head of this mass of human flesh holding a box of chocolates and a handful of flowers as Colleen ran in the opposite direction, leaving a girl-shaped hole in the wall behind her.

Fighting to hide his amusement, he tapped the man on the shoulder to regain his attention.

"So, what are your goals, Jim? Build some muscle? Lose weight? Run a marathon?"

Jim peered at him a moment, perhaps trying to decide if Matteez was making a joke at his expense.

Dial it back, big mouth, Matteez warned himself. It

wouldn't be good business to piss off a customer thirty seconds after being introduced; not even one that had already paid for a year's membership in advance. "Are you looking to bulk up or build your endurance?" he quickly clarified.

"I just need to lose some weight. I'm a bit heavier than I like and I want to get back down to about two hundred. The doctor says my size isn't good for my heart."

Apparently, category 'A' was the winner. The doctor had sent him.

"My girlfriend also would like me to be a bit healthier," Jim continued.

Two for two. Matteez congratulated himself by ringing a mental victory bell.

"Well, you've certainly come to the right place, Jim, and I am the perfect guy to get you back to your old fighting weight. I'm thinking we should start today with some weight training, intersperse some sit-ups and push-ups between sets, then on to a light jog to cool down. How does that sound?"

"Sounds good," said Jim, although the expression on his face was not as confident as his words. "I haven't done this in a while, so we should probably start slow."

"Not a problem," Matteez assured him, resting a

companionable hand on Jim's arm. "I won't work you any harder than you can handle. Trust me."

He squeezed Jim's arm lightly and held it for a long moment, trying to get a sense of the human in front of him. Physical contact helped Matteez look deeper into a person, both physically and mentally.

Jim was indeed in bad shape.

The man's arteries were badly hardened, and his heart had enlarged from struggling to pump blood through so much mass. His liver and kidneys were in the early stages of failure as well, due to a case of untreated diabetes.

"I thought you said you saw a doctor recently?"

"What?" Jim asked, surprised by the question.

"Sorry. Nothing. I was just thinking out loud."

Jim looked sheepish for a moment, his face turning a bright pink. "Well, actually, I saw the doctor a few years ago, but I know he would still be saying the same thing he said back then."

"Um. Yes. Probably."

Physically Jim was a complete mess. His soul was a slightly different matter, however. There was darkness in the man, enough to drag him down, but not so bad that he couldn't turn it around if he found the time and motivation to change his life. Hopefully that never happened; but until a soul was safely in Hell, there was always a risk. Matteez briefly considered making Jim a personal project, but he rejected the idea just as quickly. It was obvious somebody else had already claimed him.

Matteez could smell the subtle handiwork of Ephisties all over this human. From the feel of it, she had been working on him for at least a year, probably longer. Ephisties could be very patient when she wished to be, and her results were undeniable. If Jim dropped dead of a heart attack while working out, she would get the score.

Of course, maybe Matteez could still get credit for an assist.

It was an intriguing prospect.

Matteez led his client to the nearest unoccupied bench press equipment and had the man lie down. "Okay, Jim. You and me are going to have some fun. Don't be afraid to push yourself a bit. That's what we're here for. I'm going to get you ripped in no time at all."

For the next hour and a half, Matteez did everything he could think of to push the pathetic human to his physical limits. He paused to let Jim catch his breath only when he began to fear that the fat man's heart was about to break under the strain. As soon as he stopped panting however, Matteez would move him on to the next exercise.

If Jim died, his soul could be collected immediately, but Matteez didn't actually want to be the trainer working on him when his heart stopped. He could be fired for negligence, and that would impact his ability to meet new prospects. He would have to give up the personal trainer gig and figure out a brand-new scam for befriending potential converts. He could do it if necessary, of course, though it seemed like it would require much more effort than he wanted to expend at the moment. For now, keeping this guy alive was in his best interests.

He pushed Jim right up to his limits, but not beyond them.

By the time they finished the session, Jim's shirt and pants were plastered to his body, dark and heavy with sweat. The man fairly squished as he flopped down onto a bench after dismounting from his 'cooldown' on the treadmill.

"I think I'm going to die," wheezed Jim. "Are all the workouts going to be this hard?"

Matteez tossed him a towel to wipe his face. "Don't worry. It's only this difficult in the beginning. As you go on and your body gets used to the abuse, you're going to find it becomes much easier. I have to warn you, though, tomorrow when you get up, you're going to be pretty sore. The day after, you're going to feel even worse if you don't keep your muscles moving and the blood pumping, so when you come in tomorrow afternoon, we'll hit the machines just as hard as we possibly can to keep everything loose. Even harder than today."

Jim blew out a laboured breath and nodded his head. "Harder than today," he gasped.

"Tonight, I want you to go home and do some carbo loading. Eat as much pasta, bread, potatoes and other starches as you can stomach. You might even want to get yourself some pizza. The bread and cheese are a perfect combo of protein and carbs."

"Pizza?" Jim asked, doubtfully. "That doesn't sound right."

"Hey, buddy. Who's the trainer, you or me? Trust me. You've burned a lot of calories today and you need to replenish them to be ready for tomorrow. If you come see me all weak and tired, we won't be able to do what we need to do to get you in shape."

"Um. Okay," he agreed. Jim did not sound completely convinced, but perhaps it was just the exhaustion in his voice.

"Good job, today, Jim. I'm proud of you. Why don't you go hit the showers and maybe relax in the jacuzzi for a bit? I'll see you tomorrow afternoon at one o'clock and we'll do this all over again."

Jim nodded one more time, not bothering—or not able—to speak. He stood slowly, ponderously, obviously fatigued and unsteady on his feet. Matteez watched him toddle off awkwardly toward the gym's locker room.

***

The next day, Matteez sat at the large circular table in the employee break room, working on a new crossword puzzle in his book. The puzzle was one of the harder ones and remained mostly incomplete, but he enjoyed the mental exercise nonetheless. He lifted his head when the phone beside the room's small kitchenette sink began to ring. It squawked out two quick chirps, indicating the call was coming from an inside line. The plastic, battery-powered clock above the sink indicated the time was twelve minutes before 1 PM.

Matteez wandered over and lifted the receiver.

"Breakroom. This is Matt."

"Hey, Matt. It's Colleen."

"Hi, Colleen. What's the good news?"

"No good news this time, sorry. I just got off the phone with one of your clients. That guy, Jim? I guess something came up and he isn't going to make it in for his appointment. I'll put you next on my list in case we get a walk-in, though."

"Thanks, Colleen. That's sweet. I'll hang out here and you can page me if someone comes in."

"Okay. Sorry, Matt."

Matteez chuckled. "Don't worry about it. I kind of suspected he wouldn't be coming back. Some people just aren't serious about getting in shape."

He hung up the phone and returned to his chair.

"It was a valiant effort, Jimmy boy," he said softly. "But you know what they say: the road you're on is paved with good intentions. You rest up. Finish whatever's left of last night's pizza, and I'll come by and visit you in a year or two when you drop dead in the bathroom, sitting on the toilet. Ephisties and I can argue over who gets the credit."

Matteez returned his attention to his crossword puzzle, humming a nonsense tune to himself.

"Let's see, thirteen down: Five-letter word for 'sinful inactivity'."

Heart's Desire

by Maxine Churchman

Patrick stared out of the window; he could only see a small patch of blue sky from where he was lying on his bed. An occasional bird flew past to break the monotony, but he was disappointed there were no clouds to watch. Hours passed quickly watching clouds.

He could hear movement in the bedsit below: Mrs Brandon tidying up or dusting again, no doubt. His eyes slid around the ceiling of his own bedsit, at the cobwebs, thick with more than a month's worth of dust; that was how long it had been since his sister's last visit, when she had insisted on 'making the place respectable'.

He needed to go to the toilet, but he didn't want to alert Mrs Brandon he was at home. She had asked him—no—told him, three weeks ago, to clear out his stuff from the communal area. With any luck, she had already disposed of it and he wouldn't have to think about it again, but just in case she hadn't, he was keeping a low profile.

He undid his belt and turned onto his side to relieve the pressure on his bladder. He couldn't see the window from this position, so he closed his eyes and thought about

203

his mates.

Bob and Gilbert had invited him on a camping and fishing weekend, but he said he had stuff to do. He didn't but he couldn't be bothered to go with them, not after last time.

He had imagined a weekend of sitting by a river, drinking beer, eating food his mates had cooked, sleeping late into the morning and having nothing else to do but laze around watching his mates fishing. Not so. They had him fetching and carrying, hiking and even digging a latrine. He shuddered at the memory.

The light outside began to fade. His bladder was about to burst, so he sat up slowly and listened. Downstairs all was quiet, but he tiptoed to the toilet and didn't flush. His stomach grumbled loudly, breaking the silence. He had toasted a stale slice of bread for breakfast and hadn't eaten anything since.

He found a pot of instant noodles and put the kettle on to boil while he drank a large glass of water. He stirred the noodles and was just passing the front door when his bell rang. Through the peephole, he saw a confident woman in a tailored suit, holding a small briefcase. She was young, with long wavy brown hair and almond-shaped eyes.

He was unnerved when she smiled at him; he didn't

think he could be seen behind the small glass viewer. He opened the door.

She held out a well-manicured hand. "Good day, Mr Newell. I am Miss Phi. Please call me Tina."

He grasped her cool hand and shook it once before letting go. "Call me Patrick. How can I help you?"

"You have won a special draw. Could I come in?"

She might be alluring but he was no fool. "I haven't entered any draws."

Her laugh was musical and she flicked her hair back over one shoulder. "No, this isn't a draw you enter. You are personally chosen and I am here to grant your heart's desire."

He was even more sceptical. "...And what is my heart's desire exactly?"

"I will help you find out."

He shook his head and started to close the door, but she put her hand against it. "Look, let's have a little wager," she said quickly. She clicked the locks of her case and opened it so he could see the contents. Inside were wads of crisp new notes. "If I can't discover what your heart's desire is, I will give you this money. If I do find out, you will allow me to grant it. For you it's a win-win situation. Do we have a deal?" She looked pointedly at his noodles. "Your supper is getting cold."

How could he lose? "Ok deal." He was already thinking about how he could use the money.

She snapped the case closed and stepped forward, her stiletto heels clicking on the wooden floor. He was keenly aware she was eyeing up his slovenly surroundings, but his sister was right—he had no shame! He pushed some papers off a small table onto the floor and put his noodles down before removing dirty clothing from two wooden chairs and chucking them on his bed.

They sat down and she produced a sheet of paper, covered on both sides with tiny writing.

"Sign this please," she said, handing him the paper and a pen.

He scrawled his signature at the bottom and began slurping his noodles while she ran her eyes over everything in the room.

"Your heart's desire is to be waited on hand and foot for the rest of your life, to have the means and opportunity to do nothing but sleep, eat and loaf around. Am I right?"

He was stunned; she'd nailed it. "Yes, but short of making me a millionaire, I don't see how you can fix it for me."

She clapped her hands gleefully, but her look was feral; a shiver ran down his spine. "It is not a difficult problem Patrick. Come with me." She stood up and walked towards the door.

"What! Right now?" He was looking forward to going to bed.

"No time like the present," she said, opening the door. "Hurry now."

He hastily slipped on some shoes and picked up his keys. He got outside just in time to see her lovingly caress the long bonnet of a bright red sports car.

He ran to catch up. "Wow! What a stunner. I bet she goes like the wind."

"Yes, a wonderful car. Get in." She looked a little sad as she eased into the driver's seat.

"Where are we going?" he asked.

"You will see soon enough. Just enjoy the ride."

The city lights glowed and she manoeuvred the car expertly through the crowded streets. He took great pleasure in the envious looks he got from the people they passed. When they got to the ring road, she took the first road north. The streetlights became fewer and farther in between until they dwindled completely. The rocking of the car and the monotony of the road lulled him to sleep. He didn't notice their increase in speed or the change in engine tone as Tina flattened her foot to the floor. Nor did he see the huge tree looming in front of them.

He woke with a start. Where was he? His eyelids

were stuck together and he couldn't lift his arm to wipe away the crust. He fluttered his eyes until they opened and blinked a few times to clear his vision. He was lying on his back, looking at a white ceiling, unable to move; he must be tied down. He rolled his head to one side and saw a dark, blurry figure rise and approach.

"He's awake," she called. It was his sister's voice. "Patrick. It's Sandy. Can you hear me?"

"Yes," he managed to croak. His mouth felt like sandpaper.

"You've been in a coma. Thank heavens you pulled through."

Her face was blurry, but he could see the tears glistening on her cheeks.

He heard a door open and Sandy turned her head, brushing at her face with the back of her hand. "There's someone to see you," she said, "I'll be outside."

A tall, elegantly dressed man stepped into Patrick's view. He grinned, his teeth looking unnaturally bright against his dark skin.

"Hello Patrick. I'm Maduka," he introduced himself jovially. "You met my colleague, Tina. Perhaps I can bring you up to date on a few things?"

"Where is Tina? What happened?"

He sat in a chair and beamed. "Tina is on another

assignment. She delivers the…umm…prizes; I tie up any lose ends and guarantee customer satisfaction." He took a file from a battered briefcase and thumbed through a few pages, nodding and smiling as he read.

Finally, he looked at Patrick and winked. "Oh, yes. A great solution for you I see. I'm really pleased with how this one turned out, as I am sure you are too. Tina is one of our best operatives; she thinks of everything. The car was wrecked of course, such a shame, but here you are—paralysed from the chest down"—he spread his arms wide indicating Patrick's position—"and a touch of genius to get you to sign an insurance policy first. You will be able to leave the hospital and be cared for in your own home."

He stood up and patted Patrick's shoulder. "Lucky you! Waited on hand and foot for the rest of your life. Just perfect," he said turning to leave.

The Suitcase

by Galina Trefil

She called herself 'Snow' but that wasn't her real name. As 'Joan', she'd moved to the Haight-Ashbury during the Summer of Love, and in those days, plenty of people were exchanging the name they'd been given at birth for something groovier, more cosmic, more in touch with beautiful Mother Nature. She took on Snow as an alias because, much to her irritation, she'd never actually seen any before. The name, she was sure, would push her forward to experience more in this world, and most certainly it did.

She came to depend on the new, fab persona that she created for herself, much like Catwoman had depended upon the concealing support of her leotard. Soon enough, teenage Snow had done all the things which, back in her tranquil suburban rearing, were avoided. She'd railed against the establishment and spit in the direction of 'the fascist pigs that controlled society'. She'd protested in Berkeley against the Vietnam War. She'd opened her mind, and mouth, to more drugs than she could shake a stick at. She'd fallen in so deeply to the free love movement that she lost track of the number of her partners.

Being a truly choice chick, she wound up approached by amateur artists who felt drawn, no pun intended, to the need to paint her in the nude. It was during one of these art sessions that she found herself invited to a party in Mendocino County. Mendocino County, located four hours north, was increasingly a hot spot for communes. Snow had heard many stories of these parties seducing her brethren into permanent settlement there.

"Don't go," one of her roommates had cautioned her, right before she left. "People make the communes seem wonderful and peaceful, like we're supposed to live off the land like that."

"Well, aren't we?"

"Have you ever lived without a toilet before? Because that's what Mendocino County is in a nutshell. And you're going to Albion. That's the worst! There's no running water there. You want a bath? They'll tell you to find yourself a stream in the woods and, believe me, those streams are *cold.* Don't expect more from the communes than broken shacks, sheds or even a row of tents. Heating and electricity? Non-existent. I tell you: dreamers from the Haight go to Albion for one reason only—to strip themselves of illusions, to watch their dreams die."

Snow frowned and jerked her face back somewhat.

The warning was terrible, certainly but terribly more intriguing. Could such an utterly primitive place truly exist, right here in Northern California?

No, she didn't want to live that kind of raw and rugged lifestyle. But to see it being lived by others was another matter, sounding rather like taking a vacation to the island of Robinson Crusoe.

For almost the entire drive, the artist, Pete, proclaimed to Snow the many virtues of the Albion commune. Certainly, it was in its rough stage, he admitted reluctantly, but there was a sense of kinship and deep trust there. This came as a natural result of people being forced to pull their weight together for the good of the group. "Once you live there, you get to be, in a way, like brothers and sisters almost. Everybody depends on everybody else. If you need something, you know who to go to. And other people know what they can come to you for too."

"That sounds nice," she replied politely.

"I think you'll really like it. You're exactly the sort of person that the people there look for."

"Well"—Snow laughed—"don't get too excited. This is just for the weekend."

"I know." He smiled. "But still, just wait until you see it…"

Wait until she saw it? Was he kidding? True enough,

the forest was beautiful, but shantytown was the first word that came to Snow's mind when she saw the houses, some of which were patched together by nothing more than plywood. Doors, windows and even walls all looked as though they'd been salvaged from other older structures. Put together, they looked like an architectural patchwork quilt, whose squares were already plagued with holes.

"Focus on the good," Pete told her. "Remember, we're just getting started."

She tried to do as he asked. It was true that the people all seemed exceptionally friendly and gracious. What little they had, they were quick to share with Snow, and everyone seemed extremely interested in her background and asking her questions about her life back in San Francisco. Regardless of how little they had in terms of material possessions, they all seemed, she noted, particularly happy. It made her question or perhaps they had been the ones to ask: was *she* really happy?

The 'party' was a bit of a disappointment. Besides Snow, no one but commune members had been invited to it. A large bonfire was lit and people played guitar and sang Bob Dylan, Cat Stevens and Joan Baez songs around it.

It wasn't long before drugs were brought out and passed around the circle. After that, things were a blur.

Then there was darkness. Only darkness.

"We're not going to the cops!" Whose angry, panicked voice was that? Pete's? "They'd never believe this was an accident!"

"Then what do we do? Just dump her off somewhere?" a woman demanded.

"Yeah! That's it! We'll drive the car somewhere, wipe it down so there's no fingerprints, and then we'll just leave."

"Oh, that's a genius plan right there!" the woman snorted. "Got a spare car, do you?"

"Well, how do you think that we should get rid of the dead girl?"

Dead girl? Who was dead? And how? And where was the light?

"Look," the woman snapped, "do you even know how old she was? I mean, did you bother to check her ID card before you brought her up here?"

"What difference does that make?"

"You shouldn't have brought a kid up here, man! That was just asking for trouble! We needed new people to join, but we didn't need ones that young."

"That's not why she overdosed. That chick was no choir girl, believe me. So, don't make out that this was my fault... It's just bad luck and we're going to have to deal with it. But we can't go to the cops and we can't let anyone identify the body because, if that happens, she'll be traced back to Albion. The police will inspect the property and we'll all end up in jail."

"What about her family? Don't they deserve to know?"

"We can't think about her family. We have to think about *our* family, about all of these people here in Albion that depend on us. Snow died. Bummer for her. But her death doesn't have to be the end of our lives too."

No! Snow tried to scream. It wasn't true, couldn't be! Dead people couldn't think and feel. She tried to groan. The slightest whimper of a sound escaped her lips, but neither of the hippies outside the suitcase that she'd been shoved into could hear it.

The argument outside continued for some great while. But at last the suitcase, which lay on its side, was hoisted up into a carrying position and, for several minutes, Snow felt herself being jostled about.

Don't flip your wig! Snow thought desperately. This was a terrible practical joke or something. These people couldn't be this irresponsible, this stupid! They either knew that she was still breathing, or they'd check one last time before…

"We'll just bury her."

The suitcase was plopped down to the dirt unceremoniously and, outside, Snow could hear the sound of a shovel undertaking its gruesome trade. Then the suitcase was lifted and tossed down into the hole.

Dear God, no!

One unceremonious clump of dirt plopped down on the synthetic fabric surface. And then another. And another.

"Hey, guys!" a third voice called, "what're you two up to?"

"Nothing much."

"What's with the shovel?"

Snow heard the tool drop, with a metallic clang, to the ground. "I just felt like digging, I guess," Pete responded evasively.

"Man, you *are* stoned," came the laughing reply. "Come on back to the circle."

"Sure," Pete sounded hesitant, but cornered as he was, there was no choice but to return to the commune's merriment.

Then there were no voices. For the rest of the night, only crickets and the distant song of the bullfrogs were heard. If not for a hole in the suitcase, not much bigger than the tip of a pencil, Snow would have suffocated outright. Whatever drugs she'd taken, with the coming of the dawn, eventually wore off. Whimpering, she stared at the precious, miniscule stream of sunlight making its way inside her cage.

She had been small enough to fit into the suitcase, but not by much. Her knees pressed into her chest. Her head had been folded forward, to rest her face against her knees. Her spindly arms were both tight against her sides.

She had to get a finger, just one, to the hole in the suitcase. If she could do that, then maybe she could eventually, a bit at a time, tear it open enough to get her hand outside. Once outside, she could unlock this contraption and break free. For hours, she strained in pursuit of that goal to no avail. Frequently, she screamed. At times, she hyperventilated, which caused her to pass out.

Damn them! Where were these commune people? Had they just forgotten about her? Had they decided to not bury her at all? Were they in one of their shacks now, doing whatever they did to enjoy themselves, displaying all the traits that hardcases like Snow's parents claimed were innate to hippies? Where was their follow-through? She snarled. All it took was one person, just one, to pass by…and Snow would scream so loudly that even the deaf would be startled.

As time passed by and Snow's limbs were

increasingly on fire from their stressed position; fear gripped her more and more that, indeed, the commune members had abandoned her entirely. Being buried alive had been a grim concept, but it paled in comparison to dying from dehydration.

That was the longest day of her life. Come night, something finally managed to shift: her finger... Oh, thank God, she finally made it to the hole. But after twenty-four hours without sustenance and being cramped beyond words, Snow found that she had little strength left to push at the fabric. It was so devilishly thick, so horribly durable besides. Maybe she never had the chance that she thought she did... But she had to try.

Albion, particularly the shadowy redwoods, was a cold, mildew-ridden place. The day before had been particularly foggy, which had been the only reason that being enclosed in the suitcase hadn't left Snow essentially cooked to death. But would that weather hold up tomorrow? Who could say? She had to tear this open tonight! No matter what, she just had to!

She pushed and pushed: pushed until her nails broke. Every once in a while, there would be the slightest degree of give, the tiniest sound of just a few threads pulling apart...but it was never enough. Never enough.

Then Snow felt something, something strange.

Something weighty was moving across the suitcase. Was it an arm? Was someone actually touching her makeshift coffin? They seemed to be caressing it, almost reverently.

"Help!" she suddenly screamed, thrusting two of her fingers out through the hole now and waving them back and forth. Her words slurred, given the swelling of her tongue and lips from the lack of water, but her elation was so intense that it didn't matter. "I'm alive! Please, let me out!"

Then she felt a sharp, ripping pain. The fingers which she had exposed in seeking for help were inside something's mouth! It hadn't been an arm that she'd felt at all but a snake. Screaming now for an entirely different reason, she jerked them back inside the suitcase, tearing both her flesh and one of the creature's teeth out. The injured animal hastily retreated and, quickly, Snow's bleeding digits began to swell.

That's it. She couldn't take it anymore! It was time to just give up!

But no. That was a choice that she could make tonight, which she would regret sorely tomorrow, probably for the rest of her life, however short that was.

Gritting her teeth, she prodded at the wound until, at last, the embedded tooth came free. It would be her tool—her pathetic saw, as it were, at least until it broke…which it did, but not until it had helped pry enough space for two more of Snow's fingers to push through the hole. By morning, she could get most of her hand outside. Her strength was fast fading at this point; otherwise, she would have simply yanked the remainder open with a desperate, savage tug. But it took more time. And then more.

By night, the barely conscious girl finally arched a limp limb out of the suitcase and, fingers trembling, undid the lock.

She could barely move. How did the top come off of her? Had she pushed it? She must have but she was so dazed that she could barely remember. Thankfully, the grave that had been dug for her was only four or so feet deep. Marvelling at the stars, she crawled on her stomach, inch by inch, not knowing which direction to turn in.

At last, she could go no farther. She collapsed and slipped unconscious.

"What are we going to do with her?"

Lying on the badly constructed floor in one of the shacks, Snow's eyelids fluttered open. Several commune members, not just the two that had tried to bury her, were staring down at her dazed, dry face. "I thought she was dead," Pete was protesting. "I really did!"

"No one doubts that," another assured him. "It's just

how hard you bothered to check which we're concerned with."

"And apparently," a woman, the one who had tried to help in the burial, snarled, "that wasn't hard enough!"

"I jumped to conclusions."

"You were lazy! Like you're always lazy! If you weren't so damn lazy, you'd have gone back to bury the body and realised she wasn't flipping dead."

"Accidents happen, Jennet!"

"Kiss my a—"

"Knock it off, both of you," a third commune member ordered strictly. He knelt down, tucking several matted strands of Snow's blond hair softly behind one of her ears. "We're going to all have to make the best of things," he told her gently. "This wasn't supposed to happen, but it did. But that doesn't have to be a bad thing. You know, we need more girls here. That's why Pete here brought you down from the Haight in the first place. We need strong, beautiful girls who can work, who can give us children, who can make this place become all that it needs to be. We wanted you to make that decision of your own free will, Snow. I suppose that Pete's mistakes have thrown rather a wrench in that plan though."

"See, kid, we can't risk you finking on us about this whole thing. We can't risk a government raid. The stakes are just too high... So, you're going to have to stay here."

"For how long?" Snow gasped through cracked lips.

"Forever."

Good God, these nutjobs were worse than the snake that had bitten her! "Or else...?"

"Well," the cult leader sighed, "you need to understand, we don't *want* to kill you."

"We'd rather keep you." Jennet smiled.

"Don't make us do something that we don't want to, Snow," the leader entreated smoothly.

Snow didn't answer, simply fainted.

The group employed all the usual tactics. Sleep deprivation and violence were followed by manipulation and love bombing. When she was thought to be displaying signs of independence, terror tactics were brought out once again.

Time passed. Snow wasn't sure how much, because the leader permitted neither clocks nor calendars on the property. Seasons came and went and, with them, years.

After producing several of the required babies, Snow no longer bothered to think of escaping. But, from time to time, she would wonder why she was there. If she hadn't dropped out of high school and moved to the Haight, so eager to experience everything that life had to offer as soon as possible, would she have wound up here? If she hadn't taken drugs from strangers, would she be here?

While Snow judged herself harshly, taking the cult's advice and blaming herself for her own victimisation, Pete had an entirely different take on the whole situation. Jennet had been right, all those years ago, he knew. Sadly, he had always been inclined towards indolence and panic. That alone was the true reason that Snow had wound up nearly suffocating in a ditch over twenty years ago; why she would remain trapped here until she died, forced to live in a tent with the same tattered suitcase from which she'd only barely escaped.

Sloth. Yes. It *was* Pete's sin. But, as he stared at the smooth-talking, murderous cult leader, who held Snow and so many others here prisoner, Pete was certain that there were worse ones.

Would Snow have agreed with him? It was impossible to say, because the day when she could speak, or even think, thoughts which criticised any of the cult's higher ups had disappeared a long, long time ago.

The Fate of the Simulator Pilot

by Rhiannon Bird

Peta snuck out of the cramped room that they had been squished in. Not that she was allowed to complain, but the fact that they had allowed her and her mother to board the ship was a miracle. Still Peta couldn't help but feel miserable. At least back on Earth, she could go about normal life ignoring the fact that she had been rejected for the pilot academy. But here on a real spaceship, there was no way to ignore it. As she crept through the darkened ship, the anger and hurt from the rejection was replaced with awe and wonderment.

The smooth metal and cool of the spaceship washed over her. It was perfect, a dream. She wandered the corridors; the layout was classic of a space jumper 780. Peta knew it like the back of her hand. With wide eyes she crept towards the cockpit. The thick grey door was ajar, giving her a glimpse of the room; she craned her neck to try and see more.

Peta gasped. Lights blinked out from a real control

panel. The pilot's chair sat empty in the middle of the room. She nudged the door open and slipped inside. Even more amazing than the spread of the control panel was the wide window that looked out into space; stars twinkled out at her. They seemed somehow larger and brighter than on Earth, almost like they were breathing. Peta held her breath walking closer; none of her simulations could come close to the astonishing beauty in front of her.

"Who are you?" a male voice said from behind her.

She jumped and spun. The man had cropped brown hair, a sneer and a distinctive pilot's uniform. "Oh, I just got um lost and I was looking for..." she trailed off, "something else."

He gave her a bored look. "Just don't touch anything." Then he wandered to the chair and sat with his feet propped up on the desk. He sunk down comfortably, focusing his attention on the magazine in his hands.

For a few moments Peta remained frozen. The pilot hadn't looked at her since he sat down. Her gaze moved back to the control panel; she longed to reach out a hand and try it. Fly a real ship.

Peta cleared her throat. "How long have you been a pilot?"

"Two years." His eyes didn't move from the magazine.

"So, you still know people in the academy?"

He sighed and dropped the magazine. "Look kid, I'm not here to chat or get you into the academy or any of that crap. Have your awe-inspired look and then leave."

"But I'm the best simulator pilot back on Earth and I am sure—" He held up a hand.

"I'll let you in on a secret: simulator pilots will never be real pilots." She opened her mouth to reply; he continued before she could get a word in. "That's just the way of the world, you have to be space born to be a pilot."

"That doesn't make any sense, if I'm good then I should be admitted into the academy."

The pilot shrugged and returned to his magazine. Peta crossed her arms and turned her gaze back to the controls. The autopilot blinked up at her across; it flashed the word direct, and the button next to it that said avoid was dull. "You have the direct autopilot on," she said, snapping up to look out the big window.

"Avoidance was broken when I started it up."

"Shit." She breathed. The asteroid belt that surrounded the new planet sat right in front of them and the ship was heading straight for it. "You have to do something."

The pilot dropped the magazine down an inch and gazed at the belt. He shrugged, "It'll be fine."

"We're going to have a head on collision with an asteroid and die."

"Then turn on Avoidance protocol," he shrugged again.

"You just said that it was broken!" she screeched, pulling at her hair.

A large asteroid loomed above them and, on instinct, Peta turned off the autopilot and grappled the steering. She managed to move the ship down, so it scraped under the rock then swerved to the left to avoid a second asteroid. "Are you going to help?" She glanced back at the pilot.

"You seem to be doing just fine without me," he said loftily.

"Damn it." She spun the ship on a diagonal to squeeze between two asteroids. The pilot fell out of his chair and slid across the floor. Peta kept her feet planted and stayed upright at the controls.

"What the hell?" he yelled at her.

She righted the ship and pointed a finger at him. "I'm saving your ass."

He grumbled and stood. This time however he didn't sit in his chair with his magazine. He stood behind her and watched her. "Huh, you are pretty good," he mused.

Peta rolled her eyes. "I already told you that."

A football-sized rock hurtled towards them. She turned the ship fast enough that it didn't crash through the massive window but instead it ploughed through the wing and one of the engines.

"You broke my ship," the pilot said.

"At least"—she gritted her teeth as she grappled with the steering—"I got us through the belt. Now we just have to land on the planet."

He waved a hand. "Turn on the autopilot."

"You are the worst pilot I have ever seen. The auto is calibrated for four engines; with three it will go haywire. Plus," she added, "it's not that far."

There was a moment of silence as he examined her. "You look like you're doing fine with this." He sat back in his chair, propped up his feet and opened his magazine.

"You can't be serious," Peta said. He ignored her. "The academy won't accept me yet they graduated him," she mumbled as she carefully balanced the ship with the unstable engines to land. It took a lot of effort and was very delicate. Once they finally touched down, she let out a whoop of laughter; the academy had to accept her now. She had flown through an asteroid field and had landed a space jumper with a missing engine.

The pilot stood and tossed his magazine across the room. "Now," he said, "follow my lead."

"Follow you…what, hey let go of me." She pulled against the hand grasping her, but his grip was strong. "What are you doing?"

He pulled them to the doors as they began to open. "You should have left it alone. I had an easy job; click autopilot was all I had to do and you had to wreck everything," he hissed at her.

"We could have died."

"You'll regret interfering," he said and pulled her down the ramp. There were people waiting for them.

"Quite impressive Captain March." A plump man nodded his head in approval.

"What?" Peta said in fake astonishment, "you're a captain."

March glared at her mocking, and the official's gaze moved to her. "And this is?"

"A prisoner."

"Hey"—she pulled at him again—"I saved our lives." She raised her voice to get over his as he spoke at the same time.

"She tried to take over the ship."

Peta stomped her foot. "The camera footage in the cockpit, it will show you everything." A big burly man stepped forward and placed handcuffs on her. "Get these things the hell off me. You can't just arrest me with no evidence."

"Shut her up," the official said, and the man covered her mouth with his hand. "You're not on Earth anymore girl," he spat, "Don't try to steal the great accomplishments of Captain March."

March sent her a crooked smile and winked. She tried to struggle free, if they would only look at the camera footage. "Sir," March said, "as you know the camera in my cockpit has been broken for some time." He glanced at her as he said it. "But you can see her on the other camera footage sneaking into the cockpit. She tried to take the ship and forced us into the belt rather than the usual route around it."

Peta tried desperately to get away from the man holding her. If they would only listen to her, then there had to be a way to prove that she was innocent. Or at least prove that she'd saved them from being obliterated.

"We'll lock her up right away," the official said. "But before you rest, we have another ship ready to go with a repair team on board."

"Oh?" March said cautiously.

"Losing your engine then adjusting and balancing your flight path, that takes quite a bit of skill. So, we need you to fly back into the belt and get the repair crew to a ship that misguidedly tried to get through it."

March went pale. "Me, fly up there?"

"Yes." The official nodded eagerly. "Everyone thought you got your licence just because of your Dad. After the performance today, we realised that you are more skilled then we ever imagined." Peta hummed in annoyance. The official turned to her in surprise. "Why hasn't she been locked in the cells yet?" he said to the man holding her then he turned back to March. "You leave immediately."

Peta bit down on the hand holding her and he pulled it away from her mouth. She yelled. The man dragged her away as she screamed at March. He paid her little attention as the officials ushered him towards a lighter spacecraft, looking a little sick as if he were about to faint. She yelled anyway. She yelled once they were off the landing deck. She yelled when they left her in a cell. She yelled as there was a second crash at the asteroid belt that day.

.

The Hoarder

by Dawn DeBraal

Bernadette Grahams was a hoarder. She didn't know this about herself. She couldn't bear to throw anything out. When she did, the very next week, she would berate herself for throwing out the one screw that held up the shelving unit or the piece that made the blender work. She loved going to auctions, bidding on boxes people ignored. The auctioneer would say, "Add another box!" The spotter would pile another box filled with junk on top of the table. The auctioneer's hypnotising chant urged her to bid. Bernadette loved going through that junk. There was always a find, something of value. People tended to look away when they saw boxes in disarray, but those were the kind that excited her. She bought three large boxes for two dollars and fifty cents. Piling them in the trunk of her Ford Focus, she opened the driver's side door. An empty soda can and two napkins fell onto the ground. She picked them up and threw them on the passenger side floor. Well, there wasn't a floor you could see, but it was under there somewhere.

The faint odour of old burgers and dried ketchup

assailed her nose when she started the car up. Upon arriving home, she opened her garage door. A tall stack of auction boxes she hadn't looked through yet tipped over onto the driveway. She cussed as she got out of the car, restacked the boxes, took a boat oar (she didn't even own a boat but it was a damn nice oar) and pushed the last box to the top of the tall stack. Bernadette didn't know what was in all those boxes that towered over her head. She would never be able to get them down.

The glassware that broke from the fall was kicked back through the garage door as it closed. There was no room for her car in the garage, so it sat outside, much to the chagrin of the neighbourhood homeowners association. Screw them! Her former best friend and neighbour Aletha was the worst of them. She called pretty much every week telling Bernadette that she needed to get her car in the garage. Bernadette would tell her to go screw herself, punching off the phone.

Aletha wasn't shocked anymore at her friend's belligerence. She called Bernadette under the guise of complaining, to make sure her former friend was still alive. Aletha knew Bernadette had lost a few marbles after Chet died. She could no longer enter the house and see what Bernadette was doing to herself. Her friend and neighbour often wondered what happened to Skippy,

Bernadette's little chihuahua; she hadn't seen him in months.

Bernadette thought about the new things she had gotten today at the auction. These purchases were things that would be needed someday when the world as we know it ended. She'd be sitting pretty with all kinds of things she would barter for food. The rotary eggbeater was an excellent find today, nothing electric. There would be no electricity in the end, so she steered clear of things with plugs.

The neighbours had stopped coming over after Chet died. Bernadette didn't seem to care about things anymore. She was an excellent caregiver to Chet. Everything was sanitised. Chet was so weak and susceptible to germs. Despite her care, he still succumbed to pneumonia and died. Emergency services were able to turn the ambulance gurney around in the middle of the living room to collect Chet.

He died on the way to the hospital. Bernadette knew if she hadn't kept such a clean house, Chet would have survived the germs in the ambulance. Something shut off in her head, and she started to let things go while she prayed for the end of the world so that she could be with her loving husband. Bernadette would never hurt herself on purpose, knowing that taking her life would prevent her from going through the Pearly Gates where Chet was waiting for her. So, she existed, planning for the end.

She was snaking her way through the kitchen, picking up a pile of unopened mail and tossing the collection into a box on the unseen kitchen table. It wasn't safe to have all that paper on the stove. The pots and pans were all dirty, crusted over with months of congealed food. So, she cut off the label on the can and placed it directly on the burner. She twisted her body to face the other direction and, finding the only chair that was not covered in garbage, she turned on the tv to wait for her canned dinner to heat. The news had to be turned off. It was too infuriating to her. How dare they? What was becoming of the world nowadays? Chet was so smart to check out before the world went to hell.

The sound of the can boiling over alerted her that the spaghetti dinner was ready. She turned off the stove and, taking the filthy potholder, carried the can back to the table. Not finding a place to put it down, she brought it back to the stove to cool. She missed Chet. She also missed Skippy. He ran away and never came back. She thought of how ungrateful that dog was. She'd had him for over ten years. It hurt her to think that he would run away like that, and she hoped the little bastard found a happy home. That is how much she loved him.

The can cooled down enough that Bernadette was able eat from it. Rinsing out the can when she finished, she opened the door between the garage and the house and heaved the can on top of the pile she had behind the boxes. She was aware enough to clean the cans out; rats seeking food could wipe out her entire treasure room.

The phone rang. Bernadette searched for the phone near the recliner. She knew it was there; she could hear it. She scrambled through the papers and garbage. There it was wedged under the recliner.

"Hello?" she asked, hoping it was her son Chet Jr. Occasionally he called. It was the only reason she kept the phone.

"Bernadette? It's Aletha. You left your car out again."

"Go to hell, Aletha!" Bernadette wished she had a phone like the old days that you could slam down onto the receiver; she pushed the off button as hard as she could. The phone beeped; the battery was low. Cussing, she looked to find the charger by following the wall socket back. Moving another pile, she put the handset into the found charger.

Bernadette prepared for bedtime. The shower was of no use anymore. The precious boxes had been stacked up to the ceiling, so she splashed some water on her face.

There were no clean towels. Bernadette used her shirt to wipe off the water.

Making her way down the cramped hallway, she squeezed through her bedroom door. The king-sized bed had been reduced to a twin size with all the boxes stacked up against the wall on Chet's side. Bernadette needed to go through those boxes and organise them. She planned on having an 'end of the world' shop where people would be able to buy things from her garage. It was all too much to think about today. Bernadette lay on the only exposed part of the bed, pulling the cover over her, at least what wasn't under the weight of the boxes, and fell asleep.

When she woke up the next morning, she planned to go through some of the boxes on her bed and put her wares in piles. Maybe even price them. She stepped out of bed in a hurry to the bathroom, tripping over a box in the middle of the room. Bernadette fell hard. The pain was incredible. She winced and moaned; it definitely was her hip. She should have made wider paths was her last thought as she passed out from the pain.

Startled from her sleep, Bernadette's head went up when she heard a noise, wincing when she realised she was still on the bedroom floor. Bernadette had slept the better part of the day. She couldn't get to a phone and she needed help. She knew that if she didn't drink water, she would become dehydrated.

"Hello?" she called out. "Help me! Please." She heard scurrying down the hallway. She sent up praises to the Lord, convinced someone had found her. The rat turned the corner into the bedroom. Bernadette screamed, scaring the rat who quickly scampered off.

"Oh, my God!" Bernadette shouted. She remembered her dolly, the one she left under the pine tree overnight as a young girl. A squirrel or a rat chewed off the dolly's nose. Was that going to happen to her? She cried herself to sleep again.

Sunlight peeked through the window around the ill-fitting blinds. Stiff from a night on the floor, Bernadette tried to pull herself to the hallway. She heaved forward screaming in pain but was a foot closer to the bathroom, where there was water. Bernadette knew without water there was no chance of making it to the phone for help. She could barely talk. Her throat was raw from calling for help. Looking around the filth that had become her life, Bernadette wondered how it had come to this point. When did she stop caring?

She heaved herself another foot screaming in agony. Her hand slid, losing its grip when it slipped on the garbage surrounding her on the floor. She fell on her side. She only had a few feet to go to reach the bathroom.

Bernadette was determined and pulled herself along on her good side. The pain made her see stars. Whenever she came to, she heaved forward, finally making it into the hallway and to the toilet. She dipped her hand into the water, putting it to her face to drink. It was disgusting, but she couldn't stand to reach the sink. The phone rang.

"Chet! Honey, Mama's coming, don't hang up!" she called out as she heaved forward towards the phone, gasping in anguish. After ten rings, they hung up. Bernadette tried not to cry, needing to conserve her water. By the end of the day, she was in the living room but had the width of the house to cross to get to the phone sitting on the charger. At least the phone was on the floor and she had been clever enough to recharge the battery. Slowly she made her way towards the phone.

The rat came out from under the couch. Bernadette could see him in the streetlight shining in her front room. He stood up on his hind legs, observing her, appearing unafraid. The thought worried Bernadette. If the rat decided he wanted to bite her nose off, there was nothing she could do about it. So, she yelled, "Scat!" The rat ran back under the davenport.

When she woke again, she could see that the time on the digital clock was three in the morning. She saw a man standing near her. Chet was looking down at her. He still had the oxygen mask on his face breathing heavily.

"This is a fine predicament you've gotten yourself into." Chet walked around her with the heavy oxygen tank dragging from his left arm. He always had trouble with the weight of the tank.

"Chet, help me," she pleaded. Chet laughed, taking off the mask. His eyes were red. It wasn't Chet. It was someone pretending to be him. "Who are you?" she asked. The way the demon laughed at her left Bernadette cold.

"I'm your inner demon, at least one of them. All your inner demons are trying to find new homes before you have the big one, and you are very close Bernadette. Very close. It's quite alarming. We need to get you some help soon so we can jump into someone else. Once you die, you take us with you."

"Us?" Bernadette blinked her eyes. Now there were two of them. She moaned, putting her head back down.

"Bernadette, you need to get to the phone, don't give up now!" the Chet thing urged her. She heaved her body and went into a painful spasm. The rat came out from under the couch to see what was happening and was promptly eaten by the second demon. Bernadette hid her eyes. She needed to make it to the phone soon or she was a goner. Bernadette pushed forward again, the phone just out of her reach. She cried out in frustration. She gathered the last ounce of her strength and, bouncing forward, grabbed the phone dialling 9-1-1.

"9-1-1, what is your emergency?" said the operator.

"Help, I broke my hip. I've been laying on the floor for two days. Please help!" Bernadette pleaded. The operator paused, asking her address. "124 Oak Haven," she whispered on the phone with her last ounce of strength.

"I'm sorry ma'am, did you say 124 Oak Haven?" Bernadette passed out. She did not answer the operator, but within a few minutes, sirens wailed in the distance. The EMTs knocked on the door, then when there was no response, they broke down the door, finding Bernadette. The demons instantly entered the two technicians.

"My God, the smell," said one of the medics; the other couldn't believe her eyes. There was no room in the house. Everywhere boxes had been stacked to the ceiling. She found the phone near Bernadette's hand. She responded to the 9-1-1 operator.

"This is Emergency Service Unit one ten, responding to the call. We're going to need a coroner at 124 Oak Haven. Female approximately in her late seventies, deceased. We have a hoarding situation. Please make sure everyone wears a mask."

Bethany put the phone in the charger. Pulling a mask

from her pocket, she placed it over her nose. She pushed the garbage away from Bernadette's body. She remembered being at this house ten years earlier when it was immaculate. She had helped carry a man out to the ambulance transporting him to the hospital. She recalled he didn't make it. She was feeling paranoid. She'd never felt that way before with a dead body. Strange.

Bethany picked up a box that had fallen over from the stack against the wall in the living room. Placing the box back onto the pile to give more room for the coroner, Bethany shrieked and jumped back when she found the body of an old chihuahua partially decomposed, melding into the carpet. The poor thing had been dead for months.

Bethany was unnerved; she decided to wait outside until the coroner came. What had come over her? She wondered. Bethany was breathing hard, feeling afraid. She saw her partner felt the same way, but she couldn't help him. She was experiencing her own inner demons.

Murder at Dean Manor

by Matthew A. Clarke

Most people daydream about winning the lottery. It's only natural—waste a few minutes here and there at your mundane job, imagining what you'd be doing instead, if you were rich. Henry Dean knew exactly what he would do if he hit the jackpot: big house, big pool, hundreds of animals (for Jacky and the nieces) and servants. No responsibilities, no one to answer to, just complete and total relaxation.

It is said that you're forty-five times more likely to die from flesh-eating bacteria than you are of winning the lottery. Henry Dean did not die from flesh-eating bacteria, but perhaps that would have been kinder.

Three years after Henry had quit his job after scooping the big win, he had a team of servants (although they preferred the term assistants) on hand to cater to his every need. He owned a six-bed, four-bath mansion on his own private estate, fifteen high-end cars and a private zoo, right on his back doorstep. To top it all off, he still had a tidy ten million left in the bank.

"More coffee, sir?" Samuel Barnes, Henry's favourite assistant, stood a little over five foot, and with his hunched posture, wouldn't have looked out of place reanimating corpses in the basement of a dingy castle.

"No, thank you, Samuel. Could you change the channel before you leave, though?" Henry asked.

Henry had installed a full-scale cinema shortly after he purchased Dean Manor, although the big screen was hooked up to a cable TV box rather than the more traditional projector.

"Of course, sir. Anything in particular?" Samuel slid the remote from the pocket on the side of Henry's mobility scooter. Henry had started using the mobility vehicle to get around the sprawling manor after Jacky had left him. He didn't need it, but why walk when you don't have to?

Samuel flicked through a few channels; Henry decided on a nature documentary. On the gigantic screen at the other end of the cavernous room was a thirty-foot sloth, slowly making its way along a low-hanging tree branch. Henry nodded in approval, "Now *he's* got the right idea."

"Certainly, sir. Was there anything else?"

"No, that will do. I'll buzz you when I need the

toilet," Henry said.

"Very well, sir." Samuel excused himself through the sliding double doors at the back of the room. Henry picked up the coffee mug from the small table attached to the arm of his mobility scooter and gulped it down at once: black and bitter, just the way he liked it.

Henry stretched. He supposed he should probably start getting ready for his guests soon; his nieces would be visiting this afternoon. He made a mental note to arrange for Samuel and Kiai to greet them at the front gates. A muted pattering cried for attention over the nature documentary, like drowned static. Henry craned his head to the ceiling while brushing cake crumbs from his rounded gut. It sounded like rain. Heavy rain. He figured he'd check on the animals before his nieces arrived— perhaps he could have some of them brought indoors for petting if the weather was going to be unfavourable.

Henry steered the motorised chair through a hallway, past towering statues carved of marble and several expensive oil paintings. The more you paid for them, the less they looked like anything. He reached the end of the hall and rolled into the kitchen.

Servants flittered this way and that, trying their best to look busy as the chubby man with the expensive haircut silently floated past. Henry couldn't remember the last time he'd stood from the chair unassisted, but sometimes he would stretch his legs out to relieve the inevitable cramping that came with sitting for such a prolonged time. He was comfortable with the fact that they were just for show now.

He rolled toward a young female with short pink hair that screamed daddy issues and an older male with a busy grey beard and a big gut. They were stood over an eight-ring gas hob, pretending they hadn't seen him. The older man was teaching the young woman how to prepare fresh lobster, a dish that Henry would request several times a week. He interrupted and requested the young woman to accompany him outside, to which she politely excused herself from her culinary lesson and went to retrieve a large black umbrella from a wooden stand by the back door. Moments later, Henry and the servant were nearing the end of the concrete path that ran from the patio outside the kitchen doors, all the way to the entrance of Henry's private zoo. His servant had been holding the umbrella over him, keeping him dry in the downpour, while she herself, became sodden.

"Kelly, is it? Tell me, how long have you worked for me?"

"Uh, Kirsten, sir. And about three months now. My Uncle Gilly, the man I was with in the kitchen? He recommended me for the job," she said, squinting against the rain. The thick rubber wheels of Henry's scooter crunched over fine gravel as they passed under a concrete arch that marked the entrance to the zoo, where a musty smell thickened the air, like dozens of wet animals buried in old straw—which was probably about right.

"And do you enjoy your work, Kristal?" Henry asked, rolling up to the edge of the Emperor Tamarin enclosure. Kirsten followed close behind, ignoring the fact he still couldn't get her name right and keeping the umbrella trained over him as best she could. Two monkeys were chasing each other around the swing ropes, taking turns to fling faeces at one another, while the rest took shelter from the rain out of sight in the indoor section.

"I love it, sir." *Too enthusiastic, reel it in.* "I mean, the pay and the hours are great, and who wouldn't feel lucky to have all these incredible animals nearby?"

"Indeed, indeed. I try to be a fair boss. Would you like to see the alligators next?"

Kirsten had heard Mr Dean even had assistants to clean him up after he'd been to the toilet. She was pretty sure she'd have killed him right there on the spot if she'd been asked to. Instead of speaking her mind, she said, "I'd love to."

The rain tapered off as the pair reached the reptile section. The smell of ozone remained. Kirsten folded the umbrella away and hooked it across the crook of her arm as they watched the alligators wade between thick reeds in their marsh, from the safety of a raised viewing platform. Several large turtles bobbed lazily in the dark waters surrounding them.

Henry turned to Kirsten once more. "In the wild, these guys would normally go at one another, so I make sure to keep them well fed," he paused, as if mesmerised by the creatures, "Did you know that in India, snapping turtles are trained to eat dead bodies? It's true, look it up. Due to the high volume of corpses dumped in the Ganges, thousands are released every year to deal with their disposal."

"I did not know that," Kirsten said, tugging at the sleeve of her blouse.

"Yes. Fascinating…fascinating. Of course, a few good-sized pigs could achieve the same result much more efficiently, but these little bastards are much more adaptable to any environment!" Henry slapped a thigh and began laughing, then stopped, when he sensed the young woman's apprehension. "Of course, you know I'm talking hypothetically."

"Of course, sir," Kirsten was beginning to feel sick;

she couldn't help but wonder if this was how the psychopath had disposed of her sister. She had to get him moving.

"Shall we proceed?" Henry asked, spinning the scooter around to face her.

"Yes, please." Kirsten breathed a silent sigh of relief.

The pair continued around the enclosure, stopping at a large cage to watch a Komodo dragon pick apart a leg of meat. Kirsten shuddered involuntarily. She imagined throwing the idle idiot from his chair and into the Komodo enclosure. How long would he survive? She wondered. If everything had gone to plan, Uncle Gilly would be waiting up ahead.

Henry continued ahead, oblivious to her dark thoughts.

"Sir?" she said. *Time to start applying a little pressure.*

Henry could have turned his head to meet her gaze, but instead spun the little red scooter to face her once more. Conserve energy. "Yes?"

"Do you remember a woman called Jacky? Jacky Tiller? Similar sort of height and features to me?" For just a split second, she thought she saw a glimpse of panic glaze across his ashen eyes, but he quickly recovered his composure.

"Jacky…" He appeared to be deep in thought. "I had a woman named Julie working for me a few months ago. Lovely lady. Gone now, though."

"Jacky, sir. Jacky Tiller is my sister, and I haven't seen her since she came to work for you."

They passed under a giant wood-carved snake that linked two stone pillars on either side of the path. At one end of the carving, two large, sharp fangs protruded from the great head of a snake in mid-strike. Ahead was a large area, the walls of which were formed of dozens of large cages, stacked in a rough semi-circle, six feet high. Each cage had a bronze placard screwed beneath that gave a brief description of the creature that lurked within. Kirsten paused to read one:

Agkistrodon Piscivores aka Cottonmouth Snake. Endemic to the south-eastern United States. Adults are highly venomous—painful and potentially fatal.

A small black skull and crossbones was embossed to the right of the plaque. Henry had the skull and crossbones warning added to each of the venomous snake enclosures after one of the servants had been bitten during routine cleaning. He died shortly after.

"Well, I can't help you with that I'm afraid. She is a good woman, but you should have been told the secrecy of this place when you started here." Henry continued rolling, making it clear that the conversation was over.

Kirsten was struggling to control her anger, that the fat prick could be so blasé about her sister's disappearance.

They passed by row after row of cages, many of which were still and silent. Of course, Kirsten knew Henry would never stand up from his scooter to look at any of those above eye level, so she'd only arranged those to be emptied. She continued following, two paces behind, eyes burning a hole in the back of his head until they reached the small pathway at the other side of the area that would take them down to the first aviary.

Suddenly, Gilly appeared from the path ahead of them, his heavy, worn boots grinding stones into the wet dirt under his stocky frame. He crossed his arms as he came to a stop, blocking the exit. George Bates and Thomby Piller appeared either side of him. Behind, Jerrica Hughes, Graham Isted, and Pratik and Kitty Fairbank—who had left the manor after and followed patiently—appeared and blocked the other exit they had come in.

Henry looked at the three imposing men ahead, then hearing the movement behind, pushed the little stick on the arm of his chair to turn him around to see the others.

"What is the meaning of this?" he asked, sounding angry but also confused. "Why aren't you working? I'm not paying you all to walk around. I have guests coming soon!"

A muffled hiss came from somewhere nearby.

"Oh. Did you want some alone time with Kirsten? Is she your new preferred assistant?" Big Thomby spat. This brought laughter from the others.

"Either you lot get back to work right now or you're all fired."

Kirsten slapped him across the face. Hard.

Henry's glasses hung loose off one side of his head as a pink flower bloomed on his cheek. He looked like he was about to cry.

"Why, Kirsten? What's going on?"

Good, the piece of crap is starting to get that we're not playing around.

"We know what you've been doing with your 'preferred assistants', Henry. Did you seriously think that just because you've got a bit of money behind you, you could make people disappear and no one would ask any questions?"

Henry raised both hands in front of him, a feeble attempt at defence. A second blow, this time from behind, connected with his temple. Kitty had closed the distance while he was distracted, forcing him to steer his chair toward the middle of the area, away from the immediate danger but toward Big Thomby and the others.

"N-No. You don't understand. You think I *hurt them*?" His words came garbled, barely distinguishable as his vision swam in front of him, as if caught in a light breeze. He didn't notice the discoloured patch of earth that lay ahead of him, covered in bent sticks and sun-bleached leaves.

"Only once you're done having your fun with them."

"No, I would never!"

His attackers slowly closed in on him. He panicked. Henry spun the chair violently, looking for an opening. There was none.

The ground beneath him gave way as the heavy rubber wheels spun over the edge of the trap. A loud cracking noise punctuated the chaos as the layer of leaves and twigs fell inward, swallowed by the earth, crashing eight feet down.

Kirsten watched as Henry's mobility scooter disappeared into the hole and clattered to the ground below to a chorus of hissing. Henry clung to the edge of the pit with his legs dangling uselessly below, void of muscle from years of using his electric scooter to get around. He screamed as he realised the hole was *filled* with the world's most venomous snakes, all hungry for a piece of the big man.

"Please, help me." He looked her dead in the eye.

Kirsten scanned the faces of the others, they looked as shocked as she felt. All eyes fixed on the doomed man. Was this going too far? Sure, Henry Dean was a piece of shit and deserved to die, but were they really killers? Kirsten ran forward and fell to her knees; she wrapped a clammy hand around each of his wrists... But it was too late. Henry slipped further, tightening his grip on Kirsten, dragging her down into the sea of slithering death with him.

Their screams became strangled as they were repeatedly bitten and constricted. Jerrica, who had rushed over, clasped her hands to her mouth and vomited through her fingers as she watched a rattling tail disappear into Kirsten's mouth. Graham reached the edge of the hole and immediately fainted. Thomby pulled him away from the edge before he fell in and joined the party. Blood was sprayed about as the flailing in the pit continued.

Twenty minutes later, those that remained walked back toward Dean Manor in collective silence. Unsure how to feel, or what to say.

"Thomby? Pratik... What are you guys all doing out here?" A familiar voice called out to them from the kitchen doorway. Jacky crossed the cedar decking, shielding her eyes against the sun with one hand. "And why do you all look like you've seen a ghost?"

"J-Jacky? You're alive?" Jerrica stopped in her tracks.

"Last time I checked," she said with a smirk.

Thomby stepped forward. "Where have you been? We've all been worried sick!"

Graham muttered something under his breath and blacked out again. Kitty knelt to help him back up.

"I've been promoted. Living off-site with some of the others, handling Henry's finances and appointments. He called this morning and asked me to come over—he knows I love his nieces." Her smile turned to a frown as she noticed the look of concern on their faces. "Guys...what's going on? Is that blood?"

The group looked to each other and silently agreed on what had to be done. At least the serpents would be well fed before they were buried alive.

No Tomorrow

by Nerisha Kemraj

At first it started with little things.

Tiny trinkets and toys for her tiny shelf, little key rings for her display cabinets… all the things she liked.

Tom was ever willing to give in to Judy's little hobbies because he knew it was something to keep her mind off the fact that they had no children. Also, her little fascinations never lasted long. Like that one time she began collecting stamps that now lie forgotten in a drawer somewhere. Then there was that time she started knitting and crocheting, but never really learned how, so the little hat she started over Christmas, never got past the first row. But she could never part with those needles, and now they too, lie unused in some forgotten place. Then came the stationery phase…which never left…collecting things that collected dust, pens that dried up, begging to be used. And books.

Her love for books increased when Tom was gone, and along with those, for over two years she collected his favourite newspapers and magazines. Stacks of them lined the lounge floors, reaching the ceiling.

259

Friends and family tried to break her from the habit, before it became an addiction, but Judy couldn't stop herself. And so, when miscellaneous items began to occupy every surface of the house, they too stopped coming by, refusing to associate themselves with the person she was becoming. "What a lazy sloth," they whispered behind her back. But she heard them anyway, and it didn't surprise her that she didn't care. Nothing seemed to faze her since Tom left. They didn't know how it felt to be stuck in the same nightmare forever, trying to hold on to things so that the shadows don't take you.

So, Judy decided that she didn't need them in her life; she had Salem, after all—the mysterious black cat that turned up the day after Tom passed on.

***

Judy made her way into the kitchen, as Salem growled at something in the dark corner of the lounge. But his paws couldn't reach it and she heard the thing scurry away.

"C'mon Salem, you can catch him tomorrow."

She dropped his cat food into one of the many dirty bowls lying on the floor, then for herself, she grabbed a microwave meal from the freezer.

Her groceries were only a call away whenever she did need them, thankfully.

She looked towards the kitchen sink where a mound of unwashed dishes lay waiting, leftover food crusted into them. Perhaps she'd wash them tomorrow, she bluffed herself knowing otherwise. Because it didn't matter, eating right out of the container suited Judy just fine. There would be no use wasting energy she didn't have to wash dishes she didn't need.

Life was liveable…as miserable as it was. At least she still had her television whenever her head wasn't stuck inside a book. And for everything else, there was always tomorrow.

And so, the days passed with Judy comfortable in her own chaotic mess. And Salem, her cat, creating more as he tried to catch the thing that scratched through the house, especially at night.

The noises scared Judy so much that she now slept and woke in the same place where she spent most of her time—Tom's old recliner. And the shadows…the shadows scared her the most. Creeping up upon her even in daylight, she swore she was losing her mind. It had to be rats, but the traps she laid out proved to be futile, and deep down, Judy knew it was something else. She felt its eyes watching her, draining every ounce of strength she had, and on some days, she barely made it out of her chair. Even a trip to the loo was too much. But it always watched her from afar.

***

A loud crash startled Judy awake from a much-needed nap.

It was Salem. He stood atop the largest tower of boxes, mewling at the dark figure standing behind the boxes. Judy realised he was stuck. She shuddered in horror at the sight of the ominous, dark shadow—he had a hold of Salem's tail. Her beloved cat was trapped.

As she climbed onto a column of books to rescue her frantic feline, the slight shift in weight as she grabbed him sent her tumbling onto the floor, while the large pile of boxes lining the kitchen wall fell on top of them both. Judy screamed as her small frame hit the floor. She watched as Salem cowered, freeing himself to move closer to her, hissing at the dark shadow that rose from the trash on the floor, slowly approaching them.

Judy knew it was time, and she laughed through her pain at the irony of her situation. How fitting? She couldn't save herself from the mess that she created. She couldn't leave the memories of Tom, even when her hoarding overwhelmed her…and now she was dying as a result of the sloth that she had become.

A loud croaking voice boomed through the room.

"I am Acedia, one of the seven deadly sins. By now, you have gathered that I have been watching you as you tried to evade me with all your materialism. But an idle mind belongs to me. And now it's time to claim you as my own."

The creature transformed into a hideous, tangible being and reached its talons towards her, glowing as it absorbed all that she was.

Judy gasped a final breath. There would be no tomorrow.

A distraught Salem brushed himself against a lifeless Judy, blood from his loving owner soaking into his paws.

Not Today

by Eddie D. Moore

Allen buried his face in his pillow. The couple in the adjacent apartment was fighting again. Even with a pillow over his ears, he could still make out every word of their muffled shouts.

"Damn it, Megan. I know you're texting other men. Why else would you spend so much time in the bathroom?"

"Maybe it's just to get a little time away from you."

"If that's how you feel, why don't you take your worthless ass back to your mother's?"

"You know that she's refused to talk to me since I moved in with you."

"I guess that's my fault too."

"If you had at least tried to be nice, maybe things would've been different."

"I can't believe I let you change the subject again. It's your loyalty we're arguing about, not my relationship with your crazy mother." Someone hit the wall hard enough to shake the pictures on Allen's wall. "Give me the phone!"

265

Someone pounded on the wall several times, and Megan shouted, "Call the police! Help!"

Allen opened an eye and saw his cellphone was a couple of inches from the outstretched arm he was lying on. He heard a sharp smack that was followed by silence, and he said softly to himself, "I've never called them in the past. I don't know what makes you think that I'd get involved. You'd probably just take the douchebag back anyway." A moment later, he drifted back off to sleep.

The sun was bright in the sky when Allen rolled out of bed. The frost on his bedroom window crushed his hopes of a warm day, and he put on several layers of clothing before stepping outside. The wind sent a shiver down his back, and he stuffed his hands deep into his pockets as he walked, ice and snow crunching under every step.

Allen cut across the park every morning to his favourite family diner for breakfast. His neighbours considered the walk by the lake relaxing, but he was only interested in the shortest possible path to the restaurant. He could smell the pancakes when he took a deep breath, and his stomach rumbled softly.

The mostly frozen lake was about ten feet down a steep incline just off the walking path. The water was deep on this side of the lake, and during the summer, the neighbourhood kids often took turns jumping off the walking path into the water. Allen always felt uncomfortable in this section of the walkway since there was no barrier to prevent someone from falling, and every morning he considered writing a letter of complaint to the mayor, but he never got around to actually putting pen to paper.

Allen noticed that someone was wrapped in a blanket and sitting on the park bench just ahead of him. A small public water fountain by the bench had a slow leak, which had covered the walking path with a thin layer of ice. He sighed and thought to himself: *that's two more complaints I need to write. The water leak is costing me tax dollars, and the homeless shouldn't be allowed to sleep in the park.*

Just before Allen stepped onto the ice, the person sitting on the bench turned suddenly in Allen's direction with a gasp. Allen instantly recognised his neighbour Megan. The left side of her face was nearly covered in a dark purple bruise, and her left eye was swollen shut.

Startled, Allen forgot about the ice and slipped. An instant later, he was sliding down the bank toward the icy water. The ice on the lake didn't break, and Allen sighed with relief when he finally stopped about ten feet from the bank.

When Allen rolled over, he heard the ice crack and pop. Heart pounding, he shouted, "Help! The ice isn't going to hold me!"

Allen lifted his head enough to see Megan standing on the path and looking at him while holding her cellphone. "I can't swim! I need…" The ice shattered and Allen dropped into the frigid lake. His boots and all the layers of clothing he wore to stay warm instantly filled with water and tried to pull him under. He fought desperately to keep his head above the surface, but the ice broke and wouldn't support any of his weight.

Megan looked left and right before slowly putting her phone back into her pocket and walking away.

Allen tried to shout, but his jaw only shivered. Teeth clicking, the water slowly won the fight for Allen's life.

Of Swords and Shackles

by Sandy Butchers

"Wake up, Pike!" A fist banged on the door. "Come on! Today is the last day we can sell our things. Hurry up, Pike, you're going to miss it!"

From behind the door sounded a reluctant sigh. Slow, dragging footsteps shuffled closer, but the door remained shut. "What do you want, George?"

"Today is the last day before the tournament. We must open the workshop, perhaps we can still sell some shields or swords to the knights and noblemen." George had stopped banging his sore fist. His raven black hair clung to his face—soaked by rain and sweat from the run he had made to the blacksmith's workshop.

"I'll be there in a moment," Pike answered from behind the door, "you go and set things ready."

George sighed. "Sure…" he muttered. With a final, agitated blow against the door, he turned around and took a moment to observe the crowded street. He could have sold dozens of weapons during the past few days, swords he had worked on with passion—swords that he knew would outshine the simple, lazily forged pieces of metal that Pike would sell. The streets were crammed with knights and warriors from distant cities to take part in the upcoming tournament.

He had seen horses ripe for the butcher being sold as jousting mares and curtains being sold as fabric for fashionable doublets. *Surely I could sell some of those swords. I'm a decent blacksmith, so is Pike...if only he would pick up that wretched hammer,* he thought.

His gaze moved along the market stalls that had been set up in front of the stores. Each of them had become an extension of the interior—laden with goods and crafted items. He noticed that most of the crowd lingered around the stalls, rather than going into the shops. A faint smile curled the corners of his lips. "That's it," he whispered.

The church bell rang nine.

"Perfect." George often talked to himself whenever he had an idea. "Mass is about to start. It'll leave me with an hour to set up a shop outside."

Quickly, he ran to the back of the smithy and opened its double doors, from where he made an inventory of the things he could sell. He dragged a cart from under a linen sheet and swept the dust from its bottom. Indeed, he found some decent swords around his anvil, and some half-finished pieces around Pike's, lying around like scrap. From underneath another sheet he uncovered some modest shields, and from another pile of junk he fished some proper war hammers, axes and knives.

"For the love of God, Pike...clean up your mess!" George grumbled as he skimmed through the workshop to see what was worthy to display outside. For a moment, his eyes fell on the small but heavily hinged door to the living quarters. He knew Pike was in there; it was the room on the other side of the building from where he had called for him. He nearly stumbled over some lost tools and broken anvils when he made his way through. When he finally reached it, he decided to knock once more.

"Pike?" he said—hoping that maybe this time he would actually come out.

"What do you want, George?" The answer was the same.

George sighed and bit his lip, to prevent himself from swearing. He lowered his head to look through the keyhole and chuckled at what he saw.

Pike sat in nothing more than a piece of cloth that covered his hips. His blonde hair was unkempt and his beard looked scruffy, while he ground a whetstone lazily along the side of a crooked sword.

"Fine...I'll play it your way," George snickered. He

rolled up his sleeves and started to load the cart with everything he thought would make a decent sale. In a matter of minutes, he had collected a fair amount and decided to push it to the front of the house from where he would call on the public.

The church bell rang ten. George's eyes moved to the entrance of the church down the street and smiled, satisfied when he saw the crowd of nobility and decorated warriors flush back into the streets.

"Come one! Come all!" he roared, beating a sword against a shield to draw the attention, "what a bargain! Swords and shields for your games, good sirs! Prepare yourself for the tournament tomorrow, swords and shields for sale!"

It worked. The laden cart became the centre of attention shortly after the church had closed its doors. One sword after the other was paid for in gold, and shield after shield, the cart slowly emptied itself.

George smiled when he heard a click in the bolted door behind him.

"What is going on here?" Pike asked, as he peered through the opening.

"Well, what does it look like?" George answered with a smug grin. "I'm selling my work. You should try it sometimes."

Pike's eyes moved along the crowd that had gathered in front of his door. Several noblemen, dressed in red and golden garments, shook their purses at George. Several knights, wearing the cross of the holy Lord around their neck, compared their old and damaged swords to those George had on display. Completely stunned by what was happening, he leaned against the door. It swayed open and clumsily, he fell out onto the street in nothing but his underwear.

The crowd laughed when they looked at him.

"Never mind him," George said, "it's only the laziest blacksmith in town. Please, you'll find my weapons interesting enough."

Pike scrambled to his feet. "Lazy? What do you mean, lazy? Come and see, my good sirs, you'll find my work at half his price!" He put a metal hook on the door to keep it open and gestured to the gentlemen to come in. The house was a complete and utter mess. In every corner, junk had been piled up against the wall. But amidst the half bent and broken swords, amidst the crooked shields, the noblemen and knights soon found what they were looking for.

George watched the mob move away from his cart and into Pike's quarters with a frown. The frenzy only took minutes. Before the church bell rang eleven, Pike's store had been picked clean of everything that seemed useful for the upcoming tournament.

Pike walked out—still dressed in nothing but his underwear—with a smug grin on his face. As if wiping the dust from his shoulders, he tossed a stuffed coin purse up and down in his hand. "See that, my dear friend?" he said proudly, "sold out in a matter of minutes. And did I have to strain myself? Did I break sweat in the process? Not. At. All."

George muttered some inaudible words and pushed the nearly empty cart back to the smithy at the back of the house. He wiped his brow as, indeed, sweat did pearl on his forehead.

"Think of it this way," Pike called after him, "all we have to do now is enjoy the show!"

The town square had been turned into a small arena by the end of the day. On the church's terrace, a tent had been pitched to facilitate the Duke and his wife. Two golden chairs faced the gathering crowd around the torchlit tournament field. The people cheered and applauded when the royal couple ascended.

George looked at Pike who hadtaken some effort to get dressed. "Tonight is melee night," he said, "let's make a bet."

Pike shook his coin purse in front of George and smiled when he heard the coins clink. "Money aplenty. What is it you wish to wager?"

"Ten gold coins if my sword reaches the finale." George moved his gaze to the knights who had assembled on the battleground. He could already see three swords made by himself and considered his odds. A confident smile wrinkled his face when he spotted some of the ugly chunks of metal Pike had called swords. He truly considered him the laziest blacksmith he had ever known, since none of the blades were polished, none of them ground to a superb blade. He nodded his head, satisfied at his decision.

"Alright, ten coins it is." Pike smirked.

The tournament started, and the crowd went wild. Knight after knight left the battleground—battered and bruised, after swords and axes, halberds and clubs smashed their armours to pieces. The game crept closer to the finale.

George fiddled his fingers around a coin. "Come on…" he whispered, when he saw there was only one sword of his left in the game. He cheered and screamed, as though his voice would empower his work to win the battle. He clapped his hands and whistled, as though the knight would gain magical powers to succeed. The clanking of swords spread across the field, echoing like the church bell, ringing in victory.

From the corner of his eyes he saw Pike—arms folded across his chest and silent. Jumping and cheering was simply too much effort. He watched him lean on the ropes that separated the crowd from the field, fondling his purse between his fingers.

George's eyes moved back to the battlefield. Two knights were left standing. "I'll be buggered," he muttered when he felt an elbow jut into his side. One of his swords had made it to the finale...but so had one of Pike's.

The audience was called to silence when the Duke rose from his chair and raised his hand. George immediately pressed his hand to Pike's mouth to silence him.

"My dear citizens of Anglobus," the Duke bellowed, "we have found our finalists!"

A wave of cheering and applause rushed through the city like a flood of sound, but the Duke quickly raised his hand again. "The final melee contest will be between Sir Archibald Brickbane, Lion of the Western Wilderness, and Sir Barnabas Brimstone, Lord of the Vaulted Valley. Ladies and gentlemen, please cheer for your champions!"

George cheered as loudly as he could, whistling between his fingers, laughing and howling in joy.

"But!" The Duke continued, once more gesturing to the crowd to be silent, "where would our champions be without the craftsmen who made their weapons?"

George fell silent, his mouth opened in stupefaction. Never had the Duke—or any member of nobility for that matter—acknowledged the necessary skills behind the knights on the battlefield. He looked at Pike who stood at his side: not showing a single move more than necessary to breathe.

"Will these craftsmen please step forward?" George heard the request from the Duke up front. He swallowed hard and scratched his fingers through his beard. He cursed quietly when he realised his hands were still covered in soot but stepped forward nonetheless. So did Pike.

When the Duke gestured to them to come closer, the two blacksmiths walked to the pavilion, where two servants placed two simple wooden chairs at the side of the terrace.

"Before you sit," said the Duke, "please tell me which sword belongs to you."

"Duke." George bowed his head. "It is my honour to have forged the weapon of Sir Archibald Brickbane."

Pike just pointed his finger at Sir Brimstone.

The Duke nodded his head and granted the men a smile, after which he directed them towards the extra chairs.

George bowed—and a second time when he passed the Duke's wife. He cringed at the sight of Pike, who walked straight to the chair and made himself comfortable, rolling the coin purse between his fingers.

"Then let the finale begin!" the Duke roared and raised his hands.

George's eyes moved from the knights to Pike and back—one moment watching anxiously as the swords crashed into each other, and the next rolling at Pike who didn't so much as flinch at the sight of the duelling men. He strained his eyes to focus on the state of the metal. "Perfect," he whispered, "the blade is holding up brilliantly." But when his eyes focused on the blade of Sir Brimstone, the smile on his face disappeared. He could see the blade was damaged beyond repair—the metal bending and tearing whenever the weapons met. Quickly, he turned to Pike and tugged his arm. "Did you harden the blade?" he hissed quietly.

Pike turned to face his colleague and shrugged. "Why? It's pretty as it is, isn't it?"

"You fool!" George cried out, nearly shoving the lazy blacksmith from his chair, "you didn't harden the blade!" It struck him like a bolt of lightning: Sir Brimstone was not only fighting to win the tournament but also for his life. Any moment now, the sword could shatter, leaving him defenceless if Sir Brickbane would smash his weapon straight into his.

George rose from his chair nervously and stepped forward to meet the Duke. "My Lord!" he shrieked, "you must stop the contest!"

The Duke turned to look at him but the sound of another clash between the knights quickly drew his attention away again.

George reached out but was immediately pulled back by the guards. "Please," he urged, "Sir Brimstone is in danger."

His words had barely been uttered when the cheering of the crowd suddenly turned to screams. When even Pike stood up and moved forward to see what had happened, George knew that it was already too late. He turned to face the arena and gasped at the sight that had manifested itself in front of him.

Sir Brimstone lay on the ground with a pool of blood shimmering around his head. His face had been split with the blade George had so carefully crafted. Two pieces of bent and broken metal lay shattered on the field… Pike's sword had broken.

"What happened?" the Duke roared as he faced the two blacksmiths.

"I think Sir Brimstone doesn't have what it takes to win the tournament," Pike chuckled, shrugging his shoulders once again.

"You fool!" George cried, "you lazy son of a heathen! You didn't harden the blade! It shattered because you were too lazy to do your job!"

The crowd fell silent at those words.

"Is this true?" the Duke asked—seething.

"I assure you, I did my job as a blacksmith. It's George's fault; he was supposed to—" Pike stammered when he saw the armed guards reach for their swords and shackles.

"Don't you dare put this on me!" George cut in, "I told you to finish your work, time after time, but you never listened. Now look what you have done. Your sloth has killed Sir Brimstone."

The Duke stepped forward and scrutinised Pike from top to toe. "May the Devil cast you into his snake pits," he rumbled, "and feast on your anguish." He gestured to his guards to clasp Pike in irons. "And until that day, you will know the true meaning of work… Take him away!"

George watched Pike struggle to escape the metal shackles. He knew there wasn't a single chance he would be spared from the fate that awaited him. "This is it," he whispered, "the finale...and the winner is..." A faint smile curled the corners of his lips.

Only One Reason
by J.W. Garrett

She read the email reminder and clicked off her phone, glancing at the catastrophe that was her bedroom. Sammie needed to make an appearance at this networking event…reconnect with some of her former co-workers to increase her freelancing income. The money from her settlement was almost gone. Some days she wished she'd died when that eighteen-wheeler had slammed into her tiny Toyota.

In many ways she had.

For the past six years, she'd left her modest apartment only when necessary. Surprisingly, that had been very infrequently. Anything could be delivered nowadays. Services were only an email, text or phone call away…except for something like this, where her physical presence was required.

Prying herself from her latest read, she closed her laptop. The little bit of income she did earn came from book reviews that she sold to *The New York Times*. Manoeuvring her full-time position into this one had been painless. The job required little to no research and no specific timeline for completion. She could literally do it whenever and wherever. Commitment level of zero.

Come to think of it, it had been a while since she'd sent one in. Had it been two months or three? Time just seemed to slip away from her.

At least in the case of her injuries, time had done its job, physically anyway, and her meds kept her OCD on a tight leash, when she remembered to take them. At first it hadn't been so difficult. Friends would come around, encouraging her to get out, to participate in the world…in life happening all around her.

But as she continued to decline their invitations, the visits lessened. Only her mother stopped by now, once a month. However, uncomfortable with her daughter's surroundings, Mom never stayed long.

Four months had gone by since the last time Sammie had been outside. Only the threat of no more refills on her meds had gotten her ass in gear back then. With meds, money and a little food, she was good. Existing was so much easier and uncomplicated this way, and life required nothing from her. But if that delicate balance shifted, then her world spiralled.

Now though, she needed to leave, and it felt like a bulldozer would be necessary to heave her out the door. Had it been four or five days since she'd showered?

Details... With the prospect of more money on the line, she slowly trekked to the bathroom and, forty-five minutes later, tugged on a top and a skirt, smoothed the wrinkles with her hand, then stepped into some pumps.

Wow, that was a lot of work, and it had only taken her...*two hours*? Shit, the event had already started. Pulling her hair into a knot at the base of her neck, she headed for the door, grabbing her bag on the way out. Inside were some basic cosmetics, business cards from her reporting days, keys, credit cards and phone.

After hailing a cab and sliding inside, she gave the driver the address, then applied makeup on the way. Twenty minutes later, she navigated through the hallways of her old place of employment. Feelings of melancholy echoed through her as she made her way to the conference room. Sucking in a deep breath, her hand hovered for a five count before she pushed her way inside.

Three members of a cleaning crew lifted their gazes to hers. Perched midway inside the room, Sammie paused. She glanced at her phone, then at the three staff members again.

"The gathering ended over thirty minutes ago," one of them offered.

"Thanks," Sammie said, ducking her head and backing out to the hallway. *Of course! It did. This is what*

I get for making an effort. Huffing out a breath, she made a beeline for the elevator, wanting to escape as quickly as possible back to her solitary life.

"Sammie? Is that you?"

She turned. "Jeff, right?" she asked, taking in his calm demeanour.

His lips lifted in an easy smile. "Could you really forget me? After dating for three months?"

She shook her head and crossed her arms, wondering how long was polite enough to stand here in pointless idle chitchat. Names eluded her these days. Sammie just wanted to get home.

"I thought I might see you earlier." His gaze dragged down her body. "Guess you missed it."

She shrugged. "Yeah, well, it's been a busy day."

"I can identify. Hey, what would you say to drinks later? For old times' sake? We can catch up. Say…6:30 at Stella's? Gives you enough time to change…into something more comfortable. You remember the place, right?"

"Uh, sure I do." Her conversational skills were in sad need of repair. But maybe she could still make a human connection today.

Jeff's eyebrows disappeared under his hairline. "Well, whada you say?"

"Sure, I guess."

"All right then. See you soon. Looking forward to it." With a chin lift for a nod, followed by a graceful turn, he sauntered away.

Before the accident she had been completely hung up on him. He'd been the one reason she'd stayed connected to humanity for as long as she did. Now even he wasn't worth the energy.

Twenty-five minutes later, she sighed deep and slow. Done debating, she didn't give her decision any more thought. She wouldn't meet him.

At 6:45, he texted her. Jeff still had her number. *Well, that's a surprise.* A picture flashed before her on her cell phone screen…two martinis, hers with blueberries, his with olives… *He remembered.* Her mouth watered as she stared at the picture. Could she really have that life again?

Ignoring his attempts at communication for the next hour, she surfed the Internet and reheated leftover takeout, then prepared for bed. Rest. She needed rest. Today, the first in so long that she'd ventured out or extended any effort to reconnect with her human existence had brought failure again.

Her eyes drifted shut as snippets of scenes passed through her thoughts: today's missed meeting, her mother's attempts to connect with her, friends who'd long since given up hope of connecting again and last, the martinis—a small thing but an invitation back into a living, breathing community.

People were exhausting. Sammie gave in to a short restless sleep.

Snapping open her eyes at the chime from her phone, she clicked on the latest of even more texts from Jeff and read through them all again. Maybe she still had time to meet him... Lifting her gaze, she blinked slowly, as if she were only now seeing her surroundings for the first time, sparking an awareness she hadn't felt in ages.

The apartment wasn't just cramped and filthy. Layers of grime covered all the surfaces, with stuff piled precariously high. The stench of rotting food crinkled her nose, the decay of something long dead giving evidence to the passage of time.

Street equipment buzzed loudly in her ears. Roadwork at this hour? She threw open the window. A horde had gathered, watching... But watching what? Once the crowd saw her, they yelled and pointed animatedly above.

Pinning her gaze upward, matching the masses below, she caught sight of a fire igniting. Her apartment darkened. The only illumination came from above. Her eyes wide, Sammie felt the icy fingers of fear sliding up her spine. Over a loudspeaker, a policeman called out, "Get out now! The building's coming down."

She lost her footing as she ran toward the door. Mounds of mail littered the whole space, shoved in for who-knew-how-long. She hadn't picked it up in forever because what did it matter? Now sprawled in the middle of it, she snatched up a newspaper and straightened as she read the date, *August 12, 2018.*

Accompanying the mail were eviction notices, lots of them. Her building was being torn down! Flinging open her front door, she saw several more stapled to the door. An eerie darkness filled the hall. The deserted passageway flashed a deep crimson red from the emergency exit sign. Seconds ticked by. She stood frozen with the light boring into her eyes. How had she missed all this, this morning when she'd gone out? Clearly *no one* lived here anymore. She only barely did.

Pulling open her phone, her eyes darted to today's date, glowing there, *November 2, 2019.*

A blast rocked the floor. *Here it comes.* She'd rejected her own existence, and, for once in a very long time, Sammie and this thing called life were in agreement. The martini picture flashed on her phone again. *Thought we had a chance again, Sammie.*

She raced to the staircase. Twenty flights. She could

do this. But her muscles were out of shape from disuse. She floundered, awkward and clumsy. Shaky feet plodded one step to the next. The walls vibrated, while plaster, metal and wood rained down on her head, clogging her throat.

Air…if only she could breathe.

Bricks fell in on her next. Above, she saw tongues of fire lick toward where she lay, trapped. Her finger outlined the picture she held, still gleaming dimly on her phone. The date below it read *November 2, 2013.*

Wait. No… This doesn't make sense. How could that be? Only six months after her accident? But wasn't it just this morning she had seen Jeff? Where had the time gone?

An explosion blew the floor out from under her.

Time slowed as her body floated. A rush of air slapped her face. Fire chased her skin, exhilarating her—and, for a few precious seconds, she soared. For a moment she had it. Life… She was free at last. People below waited; arms outstretched in welcome. Just for her.

Clouds of debris and ash covered her broken, lifeless body. Amid the rubble of the building, Sammie's bloodied fingers still clung to an old flip phone. Pieces of its innerworkings had fused with her hand, creating a gruesome mixture of flesh and plastic. Cracked and crushed, her most meaningful lifeline, the old phone, was finally dead.

    With her.

Reflection

by Stephen Herczeg

"You really need to lose weight, or you'll be dead by Christmas," Doctor Brown said staring down at Morris's test results.

Morris shifted; the chair groaned under his bulk and let out a sharp crack. He froze. In his mind he remembered the last humiliating time a chair had broken and dumped his ass on the ground. It had been in a mall food court. The stupid place had put in cheap wooden chairs. Flimsy knockoffs from China, not made for people of a proper size and shape. The patrons around him had laughed and choked on their food as he was deposited on the floor and writhed around to right himself once more. He'd stood and eyed them all off with a withering look before storming out.

"Come on Doc, I'm trying," Morris said, holding up his wrist to show off 1his new exercise watch, "I bought one of these." He tapped the face; it highlighted the number of steps he had taken. "I've done ten thousand steps."

Surprised, the doctor grabbed Morris's wrist and

looked at the watch face. He swiped the screen and his face fell into a look of disapproval.

"That's for the last month. You're meant to do ten thousand each day," he said.

Morris grabbed his hand away and stared at the watch.

"Every day?" he blubbered, "Fuck that."

"No," said the doctor, "it will fuck you if you don't."

***

Morris put his shopping bags down before his front door. He reached down towards the front of his pants, forcing his overhanging belly out of the way and plunging his thick hand into the pocket hiding beneath one of the voluminous folds of flesh before finally retrieving his house keys.

He was bathed in sweat from his journey of two hundred metres from the corner store. He'd kept up the mantra that every step was good, every step got him closer to the ten thousand, every step would keep him alive longer. Facing his front door, all his mind could think of now was the comfort of his couch and binge watching the latest Netflix series.

He pushed the door open, grabbed the bags and

stepped forward. His shoulders pressed against each side of the door frame and refused him entry to his own house.

"Oh, come on," he said out loud, before taking a step back, turning side on and crab walking into the house. "Stupid house. They should make doors the proper size."

Morris waddled down the hallway and dumped his shopping onto the kitchen bench. He quickly pulled the items from the bags and tallied them up.

Four 2-litre bottles of cola and six bags of chips.

He smiled to himself.

"That should be enough," he said.

Morris's plan was coming together. He reckoned the walk to the shop and back was enough exercise for the day; now it was time to relax and wind down. He'd read on Facebook that mindfulness was just as important as exercise. He planned to achieve a level of mindfulness by binge watching the latest fantasy series.

It had only come out the week before, but already *Keys to the Kingdom* was setting records. The critics were hailing it as the new *Game of Thrones*. Morris had read that there was more of everything, if that was even possible. More sex, more nudity, more blood and guts. Everything a young boy like Morris could want in a television series.

He put two of the cola bottles into the fridge, then

picked up the other two and three bags of chips. He rounded the counter and headed to the couch. He put the bottles down on the side table and dropped the chip packets onto the couch. Grabbing the remote, he turned and let his bulk fall backwards into the specially cultivated groove that fit him like a glove. He snuggled back into the cocoon-like depression and pointed the remote at the TV.

He pushed the *on* button and the TV fired up.

It was then he noticed the reflection of the kitchen behind him. With the TV showing nothing but a black screen, the kitchen was perfectly framed by the TV surrounds. The light still blazed and showed every detail of the room as an opposite picture on the television.

Morris struggled and shifted, eliciting groans from the vinyl of the couch as it grabbed at his sweaty legs, and looked behind him. His shoulders shrank in despondency when he saw the kitchen light ablaze as he'd left it.

He sneered, "Fuck it"—and scrambled back to face the TV again. If it got too bad, he'd consider getting up again, but couldn't be bothered at the moment.

He hit the *Netflix* button and brought up the main menu.

There it was, front and centre, the promotional picture for *Keys to the Kingdom*. With a flutter of excitement in his chest, he pressed the *purchase* button and went through the process of providing himself with an evening of blood, sex and debauchery.

Finally, the opening titles rolled for the first episode. Morris raised the volume and dropped the remote next to him. He grabbed for the nearest bag of chips and tore it open, spilling chips across his wide torso and onto the couch. He grinned and greedily shovelled them into his mouth.

When half the first packet remained, Morris plopped it down and grabbed a bottle of cola. He downed half a litre and let out a long, loud belch that echoed around his flat. He grinned at his effort and gave it an eight out of ten. Not his best ever, but at least there was no follow through.

He plonked the bottle down, ignorant of the splash onto the table, and grabbed the chip packet.

On screen, a blonde-haired knight faced off against an enormous dragon. The dragon outsmarted the knight and bit off his sword hand. Blood spurted from the wound. Morris grinned.

At last, some gore. Now where's the sex?

The dragon closed in for the kill, only to have the knight roll sideways and bring a small dagger up into the dragon's vulnerable throat. Black blood spewed out over the knight, bathing him in the dragon's gore.

Morris chuckled to himself and stuffed more chips in his mouth. One got caught in his throat and he started to cough. He dropped the chips and grabbed the bottle of cola, dragging another half a litre down into his gullet and relieving his tickling throat.

By the time his concentration fell back to the TV, the injured knight was being consoled by a wench in a small-town pub. The knight seemed very happy with her attention.

Now that's more like it.

Morris's hand dropped down towards his groin, but he gave up when he realised it had been a long time since he'd been able to feel or even reach anything down there.

Instead he simply watched the act play out on screen and stuffed the rest of the chips into his mouth. He tossed the empty bag aside and grabbed the cola, tipping it up and draining the last drops. He placed the empty bottle next to him; it would come in useful later.

Back on the screen, the disabled knight, now wearing a golden hand was in deep conversation with the king. There was a disagreement about something stupid, and the king ended up with a dagger sticking out of his chest. As he collapsed and died, the end credits rolled.

Morris smiled and chuckled. For a pilot episode it

had been pretty damn good.

He hit the *stop* button and the screen went full black for a moment. The vision of the kitchen blazed across the screen.

Morris's eyes dropped down to the remote for a moment as he searched for the correct button. He put his finger on it and raised his eyes.

As his sight adjusted to the TV again, something moved behind him in the kitchen.

"What the fuck?"

He turned as quickly as he could and peered at kitchen. There was nothing there. He blinked. Stared again. There was just the kitchen. Nothing more.

By the time he turned back, the next episode had started. He shook his head and grabbed another bag of chips.

Within moments, Morris was lost in the doings of the newly crowned king and his process for choosing a queen. By the time the episode had finished, blood had flown, maidens had been deflowered and another litre of cola and pack of chips had bitten the dust.

Morris's bladder was fit to bursting. He grabbed the empty soda bottle and managed to fit it to his plumbing, much to his own surprise. When he'd finished, the bottle held almost a litre of bright golden fluid. Morris smiled and screwed the cap on to contain the warm liquid. He carefully placed the bottle on the side table, well out of reach, just in case he grabbed it by mistake.

He aimed the remote at the TV in readiness to select the next episode. The black screen reflected the kitchen once more.

Morris's face dropped open as he saw a black figure float across the kitchen and stop. In the reflection, it seemed to be staring directly at him. He struggled to turn around, the vinyl grabbing at his hairy legs like Velcro, and failed to see the figure duck out of sight. By the time he faced the kitchen, it was empty. He turned back, a sheen of sweat bathing his forehead.

I imagined it. Surely.

He grabbed the soda bottle and drank half of the black liquid, before nestling back and starting the TV show to avoid facing any further phantoms of his imagination.

The third episode was a little long and dull. Mostly people talking and plotting. Not enough blood and sex, at least not in Morris's mind. He considered that it may be his own mind wandering and wondering about the figure he'd seen.

He stuffed more chips into his mouth and munched them down. Surprisingly, his stomach seemed to be getting full. A heaviness was growing down there and rising into his chest. After another mouthful, a tightness grabbed at his upper chest, as if the chips were stuck and wouldn't budge. He dropped the bag and reached for the soda. He needed to wash the blockage down.

Suddenly, pain lanced through his chest; it felt like someone had placed a weight on his rib cage and was pushing down. His breathing became heavy. He struggled to drag air into his lungs as the fingers of pain dug into the flesh across his torso. His outstretched left hand shivered as several bolts of agony raced from his chest, down his left arm and out to the tips of his fingers. His hand closed into a claw and shook.

He grabbed at his chest with his free right hand. Thumping it to try to relieve the pain. Nothing. Nothing seemed to work. He pictured Doc Brown shaking his head after another sermon. Morris's eyes started to close. Spots appeared before his vision.

Suddenly, a hand clamped down on his shoulder. A bony hand. Devoid of flesh. A black sleeve sitting just above the wrist.

As Morris stared at the hand, his mind reeled. He shifted his gaze and slowly peered up the sleeve towards the hand's owner. A hooded face turned towards him. As the light from the television shone on its stark white features, Morris made out the skeletal visage that stared back. The eyes were black pits that bored into his soul. Its mouth set in a rictus.

Morris screamed.

"Oh stop! You knew this was coming. You've had enough warnings," said the spectre.

"But, but…" said Morris, suddenly feeling much better.

He stood up, with more ease than he had in years. His eyes darted down and he realised why. His corpse still sat on the couch, quiet, unmoving, the dead eyes staring off into the distance.

"You must come with me now," said Death.

Morris dropped his head in sadness and nodded. He spied the remote and turned back towards the television.

"But I haven't finished watching this season," he said, his mind reeling at the fact he may never see the end of the series.

"Don't worry about that. Where you are going, they even have the next season."

Morris smiled. Maybe death wasn't as bad as everybody made out.

Slowly Coming to Life

by A.R. Johnston

He wasn't sure what was worse, being here in the bar or not having anything else to do. Both things were bothersome and annoying but at the same time, he couldn't bring himself to care. That had been his sin, sloth, not caring about anything and sitting back and watching the world revolve around him. It had been his sin before, and after he fell, he reflected. He shrugged it off though; he really could not bring himself to care.

"Are you going to sit there and watch everyone all night? Or will you finally do something productive tonight?" Issac asked as he slid into the booth on his opposite side.

Adagio tilted his head at Issac, his black locks falling and hiding half of his face. He really needed a haircut but as always, he forgot to do it and then couldn't be bothered. He shrugged at Issac, giving him a careless smile as he reached for his glass to finish off his beer.

"What would you have me do Issac?" He wiped his mouth with the back of his hand, as he placed the empty glass back on the table with the other hand. He tossed his head to get the hair out of his face, too lazy to use a hand to push it back.

Issac sneered in disgust at his fellow brother and fallen angel. Adagio didn't cause trouble necessarily, but because he was so darn lazy it drove Issac up the wall. He couldn't even begin to count the number of times he had been tempted to toss the lazy sot out on his laurels. But Issac had never been able to do it. Adagio with his stunningly good looks and brains always managed to save him. Adagio might be slow as his Italian name implied but he was absolutely brilliant. It's why he was in charge of doing the books for the club and all the other business ventures he had.

"Do your job. The books need to get done and people need to get paid," Issac growled at him, snatching the pitcher of ale on the table and not only filling the spare glass but also refilling Adagio's.

Adagio smirked and picked up his glass, toasting Issac with it and downing it in one long, slow swallow.

"I'll get to it tonight then." Adagio waved him off with the empty glass.

"This the one you were telling me about Issac?" A stunning beauty with long hair made up of so many different shades of brown, it totally fascinated Adagio.

She was something that was actually making him

sit up and pay attention. Not much had ever caught and changed his indolent behaviour before. Issac noticed the change in posture and frowned at him before turning back to the woman who had walked up to the table and was standing right beside him.

"Mmm...yes, this is Adagio. Adagio, this is Lyric," Issac introduced.

Lyric studied Adagio for a moment before reaching out a hand to him.

"A pleasure," she said politely, meeting his hazel eyes with her own cognac-coloured ones.

He gave her a stunning smile as he reached to take her hand, making her stumble slightly to the table, almost landing her right in Issac's lap. She had to brace herself with her other hand on the table, quickly letting go of his hand and shoving Issac over in the booth. Issac moved over reluctantly, looking as though he would have been happier to have her sit in his lap. Then again, as an incubus, he probably would have been happier with that option, rather than have her beside him. Though having her lean into Issac to look over at him and ignoring Issac made Adagio feel rather smug.

"The pleasure is certainly mine, fair Lyric," he spoke with a touch of heat in his voice. Something had finally piqued his interest, and it was a someone.

"Are all fallen angels charismatic, suave and insincere?" Lyric looked at both fallen angels but had directed the question to Issac.

Adagio started to chuckle and Issac looked like he swallowed a bug, which only amused Adagio even more that this female could fluster the incubus.

"I'll ignore that insult, Lyric. But as I was saying, this is who you need to talk to about looking into finance. Adagio does all the books for all the clubs. I hate to admit it, but he's absolutely brilliant with numbers," Issac said grudgingly.

Adagio raised a surprised eyebrow at him, but smirked all the same at the backhanded compliment.

"And I assure you, Lyric, I am completely *sin*cere." He gave her a smile that would have made any female or male for that matter melt into a puddle in front of him.

Not Lyric, she just chuckled and shook her head at him.

She's a null, in a world of magic and fallen angels, he mused, looking at Issac to confirm, which he got in a slight nod.

"Yes, I'm a null to most things. It doesn't mean that I can't do magic. It just means it doesn't work on me." She shrugged it off as if having heard his inner thoughts. Being a null, who was to say what would get past her and what wouldn't.

He leaned over the table, grabbing the glasses sitting there and the pitcher that was quickly becoming an issue since it was almost empty. He signalled for another pitcher as he filled the glasses and slid one over to Lyric.

"Join me in a drink and tell me exactly what it is that Issac thinks I can do for you," he said as he leaned back in the booth, throwing one arm up over the top of the booth and bringing his glass to his lips before drinking. Looking at her with such interest from over the rim of his glass.

She twirled the glass on the table, looking at it before picking it up and taking a long pull from it and placing it back on the table.

"I have a money trail to trace for a case I'm working on and Issac says you're the best. Who am I to say otherwise? Unless you prove him wrong, of course." She winked at him.

He started to laugh. "Oh, I like this one Issac. Wherever did you find her?"

Issac sighed, shaking his head at him. He glanced at Lyric, knowing that comments like that would get her riled up.

"Where did he find me?" She gripped the glass tighter as if restraining herself from tossing it all in his face.

"Aria is her sister," Issac spoke as though this would end the questioning altogether.

Adagio choked on the sip he had just taken, leaning forward coughing, eyes watering as he tried to breathe properly.

"Well, I'll be damned," he whispered, taking a longer inspection of the woman in front of him.

"Ha!" Lyric laughed. "I believe you already are."

Both fallen angels paused to look at her in astonishment. She shrugged as she grinned at them and took another drink.

"What? It's true. You are damned," she chuckled.

"Touché," Adagio answered. "I'm sorry about your sister. She was an amazing guardian."

Lyric nodded. "Thank you. She was. One of the best. Best of both worlds, right?"

Both former angels nodded, thinking about how they never wanted to cross Lyric's father. They may both be amazingly strong and powerful in their own rights as angels, even as fallen ones, but her father was not one to be trifled with. Lyric's father was a fallen angel himself, and his sin had been wrath.

"I'm hoping now knowing who my father is won't stop you from helping me," she queried, sounding slightly aggrieved that Issac having said anything. "Then again, your sin is sloth, right? You may not feel the need to do anything at all."

Suddenly, Adagio did not feel the power of his sin of sloth. He felt like he should get his act together and do all he needed to help the woman in front of him, lest he catch the attention of her father. He didn't feel like dying his final death any time soon, least of all at the hands of wrath.

"What can I do for you in this financial hunt?" He smiled and slammed the rest of his drink.

Are You Done?

by Marcus Bines

"Are you done?" says a rasping voice in my ear.

"I'm sorry, what?" I reply, looking around and seeing nothing. Literally nothing. I can't even see who's speaking to me.

The voice sighs. "Come on, are you done?"

"With what? I mean…where am I? Who are you?" Just a small selection of the questions I have for this voice.

I could swear I was lying in bed a few minutes ago. Now, I'm…nowhere. There's black all around me, and I can smell something nasty, but I can't place what it is. I try to look down, then up, but even that doesn't seem to be possible. I don't have a body, but that doesn't make sense. How can I speak, or smell or look at the infinite nothingness without a mouth, a nose or eyes?

"You are speaking to The Administrator, and it says here that you're a category three, subsection forty-two."

"It says where? What's category three? Where are you, more to the point?"

"Does that matter really? When you're here on a three-forty-two?"

"What the hell does that mean?!" I shout.

"Hey," says the other voice. "There's no need to get testy with me, I'm just doing my job."

"Well, how about you explain your job to me, because I have no idea what's going on. Where's my bedroom gone? My wife and all my stuff? And what about my kids, where are they?"

"Okay, Mister...Carter, is it?" It sounds like a clipboard is being consulted, or something similar. "You have recently died. Now, please try to stay calm."

I can't speak from the panic and existential crisis exploding in my head (do I have a head?), but if I could, I would wonder out loud how this job was assigned to this person...being...whatever. It's like having a nurse with no concept of pain.

"How exactly am I supposed to stay calm when you drop a bombshell like that?!"

"It's not my place to smooth the journey from the physical world to the next. Personally, I couldn't care less how you respond to news of your own demise."

Wow. Talk about heartless. As far as I know this voice is completely bodyless, so I guess that fits.

I try to take stock of the information I have. I'm feeling emotions—especially towards this Administrator character—and smelling something like cheesy feet, and hearing voices, and speaking. But I have no body. I am nowhere, but someone is here with me, trying to get information out of me. Do I hold that information in my head, as I used to? If not, where is it?

I need him or her to say more.

"Okay, so I'm dead," I manage. "Why am I speaking to you? Why aren't I in heaven or something?"

The Administrator laughs. It's not a pleasant giggle, but a low, throaty chortle.

"Oh, they got you good, didn't they? What place and time were you...? Here it is... 1977, London. Yes, that makes sense."

"What makes sense? None of this makes sense to me!"

"Oh, calm down, Mr Carter. No amount of excitement will get you anywhere. Okay, here we go. Now that you've died, we have to work out your next steps together. I asked a few moments ago whether you were done or not, by which I meant have you completely finished in the real world or do you need more time?"

"How would I know? Hang on—you do this with other people all the time, right?"

"Correct, sir."

"Does anyone know? Whether they are done or not?"

"Oh, yes, some people do. Tends to be the ones

who…well, the ones who aren't here on a three-forty-two, that's for sure."

"Okay, now tell me, what does that mean? How many categories are there?"

"Seven, obviously."

"Why obviously?"

"It's just a nice, perfect number, isn't it?"

"Well…sure, but…so's three."

"Too short."

"Okay, then, ten. That's a nice round number."

"But there aren't ten categories. That's too many."

"Categories of what?!" I shout.

"Calm, calm," he or she says again. I still can't work out what gender this creature is, but I decide it's not important. "Let's call them 'problems'. Or maybe 'challenges'."

"*Problems?*"

"Okay, look, some people in your world go for 'sins', but that carries a bunch of associations with it that we just…might not want to get into."

"Are we talking the Seven Deadly Sins here? You should have just said it!"

"Well, okay then, yes."

I pause, and a silence sets itself up between us. It lingers while the information sinks into my…consciousness. I don't think I own a brain anymore.

"So I'm in hell," I say.

"Depends," says the Administrator. "That's just a concept."

"So you're not Hell's admin then? Because that's a hilarious idea!"

He/she snorts. It sounds like I've offended him/her. "Hell's admin." I hear, mumbled under the breath, if he/she has breath.

I need more information. "So what's the third sin? I never can—could—remember the order."

"Sloth, Mr Carter. You, it seems, were a lazy so-and-so in life." The Administrator sounds put out now, like he/she was enjoying our conversation before but isn't anymore.

"Sloth?" Of all the things I could be here for, I've died with *Sloth* on my soul? Not Pride or Wrath or…

"You may have committed a variety of 'sins', if you're happy with that terminology, but Sloth was the one that did it for you it seems."

"And subcategory forty-two?"

I hear the sound of paper being flicked—at least I assume that's what it is. I still can't see anything at all.

"Forgetting to turn the oven off after making yourself a late-night snack."

"You've got to be kidding me." How many subcategories are there? That's ridiculously specific!

"Well, Mr Carter, that's what it says here. And why not? If you get yourself so drunk that the aftermath of your snack making ends the lives of not just you, but your family members as well, why shouldn't that be your category?"

His/her words echo in the empty space.

My family members?

"I...killed them?"

"Yes, sir, you did." His/her voice is emotionless, colder than cold.

"Annie? Georgie? Both of them?"

"Yes, Mr Carter, both of them. And Mrs Carter. All gone because of your half-full pan of..." He/she checks his/her information again. "...Instant noodles."

"But I...they..."

I can't cry. There's no way to without eyes or tear ducts. But I am desperate to.

"It was just a mistake, it wasn't..."

This isn't fair.

"Indeed, Mr Carter. It wasn't deliberate. But it was your fault."

"So Julie and the kids, are they having this conversation with someone else right now too?"

"Oh no, they get a free pass. They can't be done if their lives were cut short by someone else, so they'll have another go around."

"Another go around?"

"Oh, I forgot… London, 1977," he/she says, sounding exasperated. "Heard of reincarnation?"

"I think so," I say.

"Well, your wife and children will resettle in some new bodies, have their memories wiped and get a second chance. Might be third, actually. Or fourth. Or seventeenth, who knows?"

That silence returns as I ponder all that the Administrator has told me. Then that question comes again. "So back to you, Mr Carter. Are you done?"

"What are my options? Why do I get a choice?"

"That's just the system. Okay, on a three-forty-two, it looks like you have three options. Option A—you're done for good; I speed you through and your category decides your punishment. Option B—you have another go around, but you don't get to be human again like your wife and children. You'll be something medium to low, like a…" More consulting of paper. "A small bird or a trout or something."

"A trout? Someone will catch and eat me!"

"There is Option C, of course."

"What's that?"

"An inter-life. You might call it something like a...*ghost*, perhaps?"

"For how long?"

"Until you learn everything you need to learn, of course. That's what this is all about."

"But how do you know when you've learned it all? Is there a curriculum of some kind?"

The Administrator sighs. "When you know, you know. Why do I have to have the same conversation again and again with you people?"

"So just to get this straight, for accidentally killing myself and my whole family, I have to choose between full-on punishment in hell—"

"For want of a better word."

"Sure. Or reincarnation as an animal—for however long it survives—or living as a ghost, for who knows how long."

"Yes, although at least with an inter-life you get to go back to the place and time where you died. It's nice and familiar."

"But no one I know or love will be there."

"No."

"And I won't be able to feel or touch anything."

"No."

"But I could scare the next people who move into my house if I want?"

"Not for a while. Your house is gone I'm afraid, went up in smoke. You'd have to hang around until they rebuild and then haunt the new place. Still, by that time if they glimpse your clothes you will look suitably 'period' to the new folks."

I stay quiet for a moment.

"There isn't a good option, is there?"

"Do you really think there should be?" says the Administrator, with what sounds like a smile. I wish I could punch him/her right in the face.

I keep thinking. I don't know what I'm thinking with, but it's happening. What happened to the bright light you're supposed to see, your life flashing before your eyes? Where was all that?

I wish I could go back and warn people, tell them that no matter what you do, your actions catch up to you— even the stupid ones.

But they've got all their warnings, haven't they? I mean, I had no idea I'd get to choose what happens to me. I kind of thought that would be up to someone else, but I knew there'd be a reckoning. Everyone does. It's obvious, isn't it? We can't just live how we want consequence free, right?

"So eternal punishment, reincarnation or ghost? That's it?"

"Option A might not be so bad on a three-forty-two. But they do know about the murders down there, by the way."

"Now hold on, I didn't commit those. They never proved it in court!"

"There's no court down there, Mr Carter. You gave the order, someone else did the job." The voice falls into a damn good impression of me: "*I didn't commit those. Semantics.*"

I ignore him/her. "Okay, I've made my decision."

"Finally," sighs the Administrator again.

"I'm going for Option—"

Suddenly I hear a horrific noise, like the clanging of a bell, the scream of a child and the scrape of nails on a blackboard all rolled into one. It repeats and repeats, forcing me to shout to the Administrator. I wish I had hands to put over my ears.

"What's that?"

"Oh my word, I'm so sorry! I forgot to tell you at the start—there's a time limit! If you don't choose before the bell tolls, the universe chooses for you! Please forgive me Mr Carter!"

Forgive him/her? Useless administrator! I hope

he/she gets fired!

But before I can say anything, the black around me turns to white, then to black again, then to a murky pinkish colour. I can feel again, and I'm very cold and wet. I can't see much, but I know I'm tiny. I feel like I'm squashed into a ball, in fact.

Nearby I sense many more like me, bumping up against me. I can feel a sensation of being pushed and pulled around by a sort of wave, a bit like it used to feel when I stood in the sea and the water would drag by my legs as the tide went out. I don't have legs anymore though. I'm just a tiny ball.

I think I'm an egg, in fact. In water—that's weird.

Suddenly everything goes dark around me and I'm scooped up with a few of the other eggs, into some huge black cave, and I feel like I'm travelling. Then the ball around me breaks and squashes, and I'm in horrible, agonising pain. Thankfully it doesn't last long.

All around me is black again, for several minutes.

I hear nothing. I see nothing.

Eventually a voice speaks, cold and rasping.

"Are you done?"

I can't believe it.

"Come on, are you—" There's a pause. "Mr Carter?"

"Um, I think so. Administrator?"

"Yes," he/she says, stretching out the syllable in doubt. "But I only just got rid of you! Hang on… Oh."

"Oh what?"

"The universe chose for you. Option B. Salmon."

"Well, I didn't get much time as one. I think I got eaten," I say, huffing slightly.

"Yes, you did, didn't you… Oh, that's funny!" he/she says, starting to laugh. It's a happier giggle than before.

"What?"

The laughter dies down slightly. "Well, there you were worrying about being a trout and you got eaten by one!"

"Brilliant," I say. "What now?" I don't have much patience for this anymore.

"So," the Administrator says, finally bringing his/her laughter under control. "Are you done now?"

"How can I be done now after moments as a salmon egg? What the hell am I supposed to have learned from that?"

"Beings learn in mysterious ways, Mr Carter," he/she says with an enigmatic tone. At least I think that's the intention.

"I don't know, I—"

I pause, which seems to disconcert him/her. I hear

clipboard paper flapping again. "What is it?"

"I need to speak to your boss. You're useless. You've forgotten again, haven't you?"

"Oh, Mr Carter, you're right. I'm so sorry. Please forgive me again."

If I had eyes, I'd roll them. Is there a category on the list for doing a fundamental job really badly? Admin— variable in life, even worse in death.

He/she takes a deep breath. "I'll go through it again. You've died, and…"

"Forget it, just tell me, nice and clearly: what are my options here and how much time have I got?"

I Want My Blanket

by Ann Wycoff

"We gather to welcome in the Age of Aquarius," the grand devil announced to a host gathered upon the Plains of Paradox.

"Six exemplars have been chosen. Those worthies have harvested the greatest number of mortals for our pleasure. They will compete. The winner will be promoted into my service as a full devil while the losers shall writhe forever in the Consuming Pit. It is justice that the soul worms we have reaped during the Piscean Age be fed. Step forward first contestant and proclaim your deeds!"

The imp known as Grim flapped up to the damned soul tortured into the form of a voicecaster.

"I have captured many souls by causing mortals to eschew compromise. Cruel determination has been their touchstone," Grim said.

Each contestant took its turn in due course.

Ominous said, "I have shown them that the roads of all possibilities lead to this place. Auguries were inauspicious. Omens prophesied evil. I am greater than

325

Grim, for all of its works depended upon me!"

Tabulations were made. A billion abaci clicked. Finally, Ominous was cast down screaming into the Consuming Pit.

Envy, Phantasmal, and Nightmarish made their announcements. Each was found wanting. Only Sloth stood between Grim and victory.

An honour guard dragged Sloth forward upon a soporific palanquin.

"All of this is too much trouble. I'm tired," Sloth whimpered. "Can't we just let the humans sort it out for themselves? What could possibly go wrong?"

The mathmancers tabulated for some time. Sloth was soon fast asleep. Meanwhile, several minor wars broke out, but finally order was restored, and the grand devil pronounced its verdict.

"I proclaim Sloth our winner. Let it be written! Let it be done!"

Sloth sobbed and pulled a protective blanket of human skin about itself. The imp began sucking its thumb.

The grand devil chuckled. Four mighty praetorians with beards of wire and brass whips dragged the newly elevated Sloth to its deserved reward.

The Last Stand
by Jo Mularczyk

She stared at the page, mesmerised. The images made no sense and yet they had crowded her dreams. There were pictures of people standing, walking and even more impossibly—running. The words of an old nursery rhyme came to her from across the years, sung to her by her grandma. *Stretch up tall upon your toes, bend your arms and touch your nose, bend your knees and jump up high, let your fingers touch the sky.* She had thought it was just a bit of childhood fun then, but these pictures added a moment of doubt, of hope. She shoved the unhelpful emotions down where she could pull them out and rifle through them in the middle of the night. For now, she studied the factual information in the images, their physicality, the dynamism of the movements, the dimensions of these people standing upright.

"Sarah?"

She shoved the picture inside her pillowcase, clambered on to her roller and hit the comms button. "In my pod Mum!"

"Have you input the week's meals young lady? It's

327

your turn to cook." Sarah looked at the intercom screen. Her mother's face stared back at her sternly. Well, the set of her jaw and eyebrows were stern; but no matter how hard she tried, her mother could never quite capture any harsh emotion with her eyes. They always looked to harbour a subdued joy. Perhaps though, Sarah was seeing her own reflection there—"subdued joy" was really the closest she ever felt to any kind of happiness.

"Sure Mum, sorry, I'll get onto it now. Bye." She waited a polite second before closing the comms channel and flicking over to the food prep app. She scrolled through the hydroponic column and sighed dismally as she perused the exhaustive list of ingredients. A beep alerted her to an incoming call. She saw that it was her mother again.

"Sorry, I didn't mean to cut you off I was just..."

"No, I'm not calling to chastise you Sarah. I just wanted to remind you to include an extra allocation at each meal because Gran is staying with us this week. It's grey mobility week so she's catching a ride over. Actually, she'll be here soon."

"Ok Mum. Thanks." Sarah switched the comms channel off again with a feeling of disgust. The 'greys'...she hated the derisive term for the older generation. Like so many things in her life, it just left a sour taste. Sarah hit the comms screen and called up her sister.

"Ha, I've been waiting for your call! So, what's it gonna be this time?" Jamie said with a smug look on her face.

"What assignments do you have coming up?" Sarah asked resignedly.

"Ancient history."

"Topic?" Sarah asked, continuing with the masquerade. They both knew she would do anything to get out of preparing dinner.

"Twenty-first century—the era of transformation."

"Hmm…sounds a little dull." Sarah tried to keep the anticipation out of her voice. Jamie would need to provide her with her senior student access to allow her to read the relevant texts. At this point she would even agree to take on Jamie's dinner allocation to be able to do this paper.

"Take it or leave it Sarah. If you want me to do your dinner prep this week then you'll write my paper."

"Ok, ok. You drive a hard bargain Jamie. Just send me your access code and I'll get started."

"You're such a sucker Sar-bear. It's a deal. Byeeeee!" Jamie clicked off with a manic celebratory laugh that rang in Sarah's ears, providing an incongruent soundtrack to the inner glee she felt.

Sarah pushed herself over to the window of her pod. It ran from ceiling to floor like all the windows in Polis 2500. It was the only way to allow the inhabitants to see out from their vantage point atop their rollers. She looked down at her legs which were presently thrust out in front of her like the useless protrusions that they were. She prodded them in despair. It made no anatomic sense. Every part of the human body had a purpose. Internal and external components worked together in total harmony. Except for the legs.

She stared outside at the transport tubes joining each polis to another, pods hanging off them like great insect sacs. Hundreds of metres below, she could see a few mobility pods jetting along the ground. "Probably taking the wealthy few to important places to do important things with other important people," she thought. Sarah's thoughts often held this acerbic edge these days. She wished she could be happy with her life: accepting like Jamie. But she longed for more. Something inside her had always suspected there should be more. She rolled back over to the pillow and reached her hand in to touch the piece of paper and assure herself that it was real. It had been a freak find. One day three months ago, she'd been in the lift on her way back from her outside session. She'd been watching the doors slowly close, cutting off her final glimpse of the outside for a week when a pale hand reached inside the lift. The doors careened back open revealing a small wizened old man lying on his roller, arms pulling him along, legs inert behind him. He'd seemed shocked to see her.

"Sorry my dear I thought this lift was empty. I'll wait for the next one," he had muttered, eyes downcast.

"No, it's ok, come on in. There's plenty of room." Sarah had never understood the insistence on keeping the older generation separated from the younger.

The man just shook his head sadly and backed out of the lift, leaving the doors to shut Sarah in by herself. As she was about to protest further, something had caught her eye on the floor—a piece of paper. It must have been caught under the man's wheels. Sarah grabbed it and just as she was wondering how to get it back to the man, she noticed the images. People using their legs. They were tall, athletic and…happy. Without thinking, she'd shoved the page inside her jacket and had spent every day since poring over it.

Her screen beeped again. Jamie had sent the access code. Sarah input it immediately into the research module. She knew they could both be in trouble for this, but it was such a low-level offence it was hardly well policed. Her thoughts lazily tripped across the risks, but she knew that they would not stop her from looking further.

She typed in 'twenty-first century' and scrolled excitedly down the list of topics that were now at her fingertips:

Transport in the twenty-first century

Climatology—a burgeoning movement

Technology as the new frontier

The architecture of the modern polis

She'd read versions of most of these topics before. She scrolled more quickly, feeling a little underwhelmed until one title caught her eye.

Human anatomy—ecological adaptation or sociological intervention?

She felt a tingling as she clicked on the title. It opened straight into the text—no preamble or table of contents as though the author had been in a hurry to share their thoughts.

It was during the twenty-first century that we saw technological developments on such a significant scale that societies were irreversibly transformed. No area of human life escaped the impact. The economic gains were undeniable, as were the achievement in fields such as science and medicine. However, the detriment to social and physical development was (and continues to be) immeasurable. As communication, commerce, education and all facets of life were conducted almost solely via remote access, the need for human interaction, social engagement and physical contact was slowly eroded. This led to the disintegration of huge swaths of the human lexicon, the transformation of the transportation system and urban design, the re-engineering of the entire agricultural and horticultural spheres and the physiological changes in the human condition such as pigmentation, metabolism and eyesight. These many factors are all acknowledged as part of our global history and human evolution. What are not widely discussed though are the physical changes in terms of musculoskeletal development. It is scientifically clear that humans historically walked on two legs. It was their biological imperative, driven by their anatomical design and their survival instincts. They ran, skipped, hopped, jumped and danced. Many of these terms have been largely lost to the current population. There is a reason the older generations are systematically segregated from the younger, for fear that the collective knowledge will be tainted with these distant memories. I have attempted to infiltrate the research module with this text, but I am sure it will be weeded out soon enough. For those of you who may read it before then, I entreat you to carefully look at the next baby you see. There is a biological desire to move *that we have removed through swaddling, tethering and...*

The screen went black. Sarah recoiled in horror, although whether at the sudden disappearance of the text or what she had read, she wasn't sure. She realised now that she had suspected some of this horrible truth but to read it in such stark words brought it into sinister reality. She felt a sudden wave of nausea and wheeled herself into the washroom where she tapped the hydration button and gratefully let the spray of water hit her face. A single thought burst into her consciousness. *Gran!* She needed to speak to her grandma now. She wondered if the grey mobility set had arrived yet. She rolled out of her pod and down the corridor to the lift. There was nobody else about but that was not unusual. Outside of mealtimes and allocated outdoor sessions, there was little reason to leave their pods.

Sarah rolled into the lift and headed down to the transport floor, determined to wait there for as long as necessary. Her wristband started beeping and she saw a message from Jamie.

What did you do? My student access code has been blocked!

She didn't respond. A message appeared from her mother asking where she was but she ignored that too. As she rolled toward the mobility docking station, she saw a lone figure rolling towards her—Gran!

Her grandma smiled as she saw her approach, but the smile froze in place as her eyes traced a path across Sarah's face. She could only guess what emotions were etched there.

"Gran, I need to talk to you."

"So, I see. I always knew it would be you Sar-bear. Your sister is happy to be told but you've always been the one who wanted to ask," Gran answered sadly with a hint of pride in her voice. "Come on then, let's head to your pod."

"Uh, actually I think I might be better off out of there for a little while," Sarah answered cryptically. Gran didn't flinch and didn't ask why. She just gave a little nod and started rolling down the corridor and past the lift bay. Sarah followed until they came to a small alcove behind one of the artificial plants that lined the corridors. They rolled in behind there.

"Huh, I've never noticed this little spot," Sarah said wonderingly.

"Ok, we may not have much time, so I'll just tell you what I know." Gran started in a business-like tone Sarah had never heard her use before. The words came quickly and succinctly, as though they'd been lying formed for a very long time. "My grandpa told this to me and I'm guessing he heard it from his grandparents before that. Humans aren't meant to be lying around in these contraptions all day. We're not supposed to be lying on the floor. The humans who came before us used these useless things." She hit at her legs in disgust just as Sarah herself had done earlier.

"But how, why?" she stammered.

"Well I'm guessing some of it just happened naturally as people started spending more and more time in front of machines and screens, more time inside, less time needing to get anywhere. But then once the cities started being designed around a less mobile population, they didn't want people moving you see. So, they get us while we're young. Right from birth, the parents are told they need to strap their babies down and that's just how it is and how it's always been. But I'm telling you darling it isn't how it's always been and it isn't how it should be."

Sarah felt a cocktail of emotions swirling within her. There was vindication, fear and a desperate sorrow, but beneath it all was a glimmer of hope.

"How can I stop it?"

"Well now, it all starts with one. You'll need to exercise those legs of yours. It will take patience and determination, but I reckon you've got your Gran's grit. Do it in private, get them strong, get them moving and when you feel like they could bear it, you stand right on up and you show them all."

Gran hugged Sarah awkwardly from her roller and mumbled something about being careful and not being seen talking together, but Sarah laid there mute, silenced by the fear and the hope and the burning questions. As Gran wheeled away, she whispered, "Wait a few minutes and then come on out."

Sarah wiped her face and was surprised to find it wet. A few minutes later she wheeled her way back to her pod. It looked smaller than when she had left it, stifling. The enormity of what she had learned lay all around, pressing down on her. She knew what she had to do. Sarah closed the door behind her and wrenched herself onto her bed. She reached one hand inside her pillowcase, took a deep breath and started to stretch her toes.

Beulah

by Bronwyn Todd

Beulah Cracknell raised her head just high enough to spit. A thick gob of phlegm struck the plate beside the bed, pooling amidst the crumpled butts and remnants of last month's butter chicken. She watched the mucous spread and settle, then rolled, stomach heaving, on the sweat-stained mattress. Her belly hung low, like a warm sloppy apron. Its rolls were a comfort: familiar and soft.

She stretched; eyes fixed on the mantle clock. It was noon. Too early. She dozed, mouth ajar.

The mobile buzzed. "Christ's sake…" she muttered, searching among the tangled sheets. She could leave it, send the call to voicemail. But business was business. She needed the cash.

"Yeah," she sighed, expecting a gentleman's voice. It was female. The voice dripped with undisguised judgement.

"Beulah Cracknell?"

"Who's asking?"

"It's Jan from Child Protective Services. You were scheduled for a visit with your children this morning…"

Beulah sighed. When would Welfare take the hint? Those kids were better off right where they were. Truth be told, she didn't have the energy for them. The incessant demands, all that whining, the tears...

"Ms Cracknell...are you there?"

Beulah hung up the phone and switched the ringer to silent. She rolled, one hand beneath the pillow, determined to salvage remnants of sleep. It was useless. She was wide awake. The Welfare bitch had seen to that.

Nature called. She hauled herself up from the bedding and shuffled to a bucket in the

corner of the room. She grunted, squatting above the rim, piss falling like a torrent of pale ochre rain. Better here, in the bucket, than to trek downstairs. She wiped herself dry with a torn piece of cloth.

Beulah stood and watched her reflection. Her breasts, pale, purple-veined and

slack, hung almost to her navel. Her hair was slick with days of grease and a fresh crop of acne peppered her chin. She chuckled and reached for a packet of smokes. No need to fuss with a shower or clothes. None of the blokes had appointments today.

A knock at the door sent her scrambling for a robe. Maybe a client was here for a

drop-in. She smirked. She knew what the menfolk

liked. Her skills had kept them coming back.

"Hang on," she called, snatching her robe from the floor. An earwig slipped from its

crumpled folds and clicked on the tiles. It scurried away.

Beulah opened the door, a seductive smile ready. The smile died swiftly on her lips.

The haggard old woman from the house next door was out there, blocking Beulah's light.

"Ms Cracknell, I've come about your rubbish. There are rats in my garden because of

your mess." The woman had deep brown, sunken eyes. She was hag faced and always dressed in black.

"Yeah, yeah," said Beulah. She pulled the door closed. It was blocked by the hag-

faced woman's shoe.

"It's the last time I'll warn you," the old woman said. "Clean up your mess or I'll

notify the Council."

"Eat shit!" Beulah bellowed and stamped on her foot.

The old woman howled and pulled her foot from the door, cussing in angry, foreign

words. "You'll get what's coming. Mark my words..."

"That's it, speak in fucken English!" Beulah

slammed the front door and thumped

upstairs. The bed was slick with body grease and fragrant with the musk of sweat. She settled like a creature cocooned in its burrow and dozed as the afternoon ticked by.

A tap at the window roused her from sleep. A butcherbird, pied with bright black

eyes, watched her through the dust-smeared glass.

"Bugger off!" She waved her hands in the air, but the bird stared, dead still, on the

peeling sill. It knocked three times with its thick black beak. Beulah scowled and hurled a drool-stained pillow. She watched, jaw clenched, as the pillow bounced and landed with a splash on the urine bucket. "Jesus Christ...fucken thing!" Beulah rose from the bed. She thumped one fist against the glass. As she turned to shuffle back to bed, one flat foot knocked against the bucket. She gasped, arms flailing, but lunged too late. Urine gushed across the floor.

She glanced up; her thick hands balled into fists. The butcherbird watched her from

the sill. Beulah lunged, then stopped. There was knocking at the door. She thundered downstairs, primed for confrontation. But it wasn't the hag. It was a gentleman caller. "Richard...it's you love. I thought…never mind."

He was a businessman, this one. Had a workshop fixing trucks. She smiled her most

seductive smile and motioned for Richard to step inside.

"What's that stench?" he demanded, mouth curled with disgust.

"Just some spillage. Okay love?" She reached for his belt. He sniffed with distaste as

he studied the room. He paused for a moment, as if in doubt, then growled, "Go on, then." He gripped her hair.

Beulah did her finest work, and for a while he appeared to forget the smell. But later,

once her work was done, that look of disgust was back in his eyes. He zipped up.

"Where's the fire?" she teased.

He sneered, "Take a shower, ya filthy bitch." He tossed her the money and slammed

the front door. Beulah chuckled. Easy money. He'd be back despite the spill.

The next morning, hours before she usually rose, the butcherbird knocked with its

nasty black beak. She sprang from the bed and thumped the glass, but the bird stared, unmoving, a lifelike toy. She rolled the window upward, hissing. The bird stood, barely out of reach as she flailed, bare bodied, breasts dangling from the sill.

There was movement on the street below. The hag neighbor stood watching, a smile

on her lips. Beulah scowled, "Come to watch, eh? Ya sad old bitch!" Beulah raised her middle finger, pulling back from the window. Without warning, the windowpane dropped from above. Beulah screamed, eyes bulging, as it slammed on one breast. Scrambling to lift the window higher, she bleated with pain and ripped the breast free. She studied the damage. The ghost of a bruise had bloomed like a flower, purple pink beneath her flesh. Tears stung and Beulah blinked them away.

She looked up. The bird and the woman were gone. Strange. They disappeared so fast.

Cradling her breast, she retreated to bed, flinching as pain pulsed in crippling waves.

Hours had passed when she woke from sleep. Something was knocking. That cursed

bloody bird! Hatred boiled inside her as she met the creature's shiny stare. It was trying to taunt her. She'd break the thing's neck! With an animal cry, Beulah rolled from the bed, took a chair from the dresser and shattered the glass.

The bird flew upward, finally spooked. "Ha!" spat Beulah. "That'll teach ya. Fucken

thing!" There came a flurry of movement, a black and white blur. Beulah blinked and raised her hands too late. With a whirring of wings, the bird ruptured her eye. With a twist and a snap, it ripped the eye from her skull. Beulah gave a low soft moan. The bird perched, crunching down its meal.

Beulah fell against the sill and screamed as her belly was punctured by glass. Blood

seeped from the wounds, a slick claret red. Below her, on the footpath, the hag-faced neighbor stood and watched. She motioned to the butcherbird, whispering, chanting, a smile on her lips. As Beulah keened, helpless upon the glass, the bird doubled back and perched beside her on the sill. She raised one blood-streaked, trembling hand as it fluttered toward her one good eye.

by Ximena Escobar

A continuous buzz brought me back—a big black fly orbiting around my bed, so loud, it silenced my thoughts. It pulled me out of my *awayness*, but upon sitting me back in that 'pilot's seat' where I see what's in front of my eyes, I realised the world wasn't the same as I'd left it. Although I'd been and returned many times, and although I'd noticed the world changing before, *it was done now*. And it dawned on me I'd always been like a fly, cast in an alien world, forever colliding mindlessly with barriers.

My son had mumbled something. I'd said to myself I'd listen and respond in just a moment, as soon as an ethereal figure in my head materialised; once I understood what it was doing on a plane and why everyone else around her was asleep. That's the thing with ghosts, watercolour figures with often the habit of weighing more than reality. They have their need to define themselves. Then they can almost be real, and you could perhaps be useful—if you were to paint, write, or make something of them.

I heard him skip away, stretching the dense distance

between us—like my resistance to let him go. It was done now. I let the shoelace slip out of my fingers, it bounced on his heel and flattened under his sole. It wasn't there anymore. Only the fly was there.

And there I lay, resigned but content, perfectly at ease. Comfortably isolated in my sad, immaterial world. On board an airplane, flying in the eternal air walls of my consciousness. Yes, the figure was me, surrounded by sleeping bodies.

The clouds below provided the only indication of a whereabout, but I didn't look down. I looked at the sky-blue sky, the colour of death as I imagined it as a child. The colour of life before life, the colour of nothing, a mirror of me and my timeless, aimless existence. No sound but that of the loud buzzing engine. No feeling but that of the void opening inside me as I realise none of the passengers are going to wake up. I'm not going to make it home. My time stretches, widens without advancing; there are no trees to bypass on the empty sky.

I'm not afraid to die. I'm not even afraid for my son anymore; because how can he, someone gone, miss someone who isn't there? I didn't hear what he said, but I knew, as he skipped away, that he was content too.

While I wait for the fuel to run out, for a mountain to emerge out of nowhere, all I can do is look at our ghostly memories and *feel* his loss. Because I'm not doing anything about it, I'm not going into the cockpit, not going to grab the radio or skydive my way out of this fate. I'm only going to regret always being away, and every second of every day I didn't choose to play. Every time I put the tv on for him, every time I pretended to watch him, nodding, smiling vacantly, watching the ghosts instead. Every time I invited his friends so they would distract him, fool him, while I appeared to be there but instead went off in my fat seat of self-indulgence, to my fat, empty sky of nothing.

I don't have a choice. Like the fly doesn't belong anywhere but on a turd. It doesn't have the choice to not offend.

I fantasise that I call him. I shout from the bed, asking him to come out with me. I'll get up, I'll have a shower. I'll make myself look presentable so he's not embarrassed... but it's done, he doesn't want it anymore. I'm shouting in my giant aquarium; I've hit the glass wall of my eyes like a stupid fly fish, my palms on the glass, my nose flat as I beg with invisible tears blended into a water he will never live in—the world he will never understand—not for his forgiveness but, at least, for his pain. If he can feel like I feel, he may, perhaps, somewhere, sometime, remember his love for me.

So here my body lies, still in my bed, in my bed all day. But there is no buzzing. There are no walls anymore, just the flightless fly, crawling along the shell I dumped as the plane took me away for good. My son didn't notice for several hours. But soon, I fell asleep with the others.

Failing Virtue

by Lyndsey Ellis-Holloway

"Raphael! How long do you believe you can ignore your duties, without consequence?" Artiya'il's voice cut through the silence in the Infirmary, causing the Archangel in question to flinch.

Ordinarily, her older sister's voice held an apathetic ring to it, changing its lilt only when Artiya'il deemed it necessary to deliver one of her famous cutting remarks to their siblings. This was a talent Artiya'il apparently inherited from her mother, much to the disdain of their siblings.

"Sister, it appears you have been busy," Raphael replied politely, though her tone was laced with exasperation. She bowed, her movements slow and forced, a habit rather than a true sign of respect for her elder sister. Raphael's pale blue eyes glanced at her sister's wings and her long white hair, noting that more feathers had fallen victim to the blood red that indicated Artiya'il's use of her powers.

"Don't play games with me, Raphael. Neglecting your duties has left me with an influx of Grief to deal with, the taint of which has coloured my feathers *long* before their time," Artiya'il continued, her storm grey eyes fixed upon Raphael's.

Raphael attempted to hold her sister's stern gaze but could not do so. She glanced at the floor, unable to find the inner strength to attempt that defiance again…

"I *am* doing my duty Artiya'il," Raphael replied, brow furrowed, irritated that they were even having this conversation, feeling like a child being chastised by their parents. She did her work. What more did her sister want from her?

"I think Father might disagree with that statement," Artiya'il snapped. "You are a Virtue, in fact you are the *lead* Virtue, and yet you neglect your duties in favour of taking orders from Gabriel and Uri. How long do you think you can hide your insolence from Father? Your obligations go beyond doing as *they* ask; you have others to heal Raphael, and someday there will come a point where your lax attitude towards the tasks set for you at birth will be your undoing."

Artiya'il's words bit into her, but Raphael forced herself not to flinch at them, despite her sister's tone. She wished her twin, Uriel, was here. She had always been able to stand up to their older sister, where Raphael could not.

"Do not follow in their footsteps. Gabriel and Uriel are not the ones you should model yourself upon. It is not a wise path to walk down. Father does not approve of negligent Angels, even if he *hasn't* worked out what you're up to yet."

"Father is *Almighty*!" Raphael gasped, staring at her sister in horror. The words Artiya'il spoke were close to blasphemy, to believe that *God* did not know *everything* that happened in his Heavens, that he was not already aware of what she did or did not do, let alone Artiya'il's opinion of their older brother and her twin sister.

"Father *is* Almighty, but he is not all seeing nor all knowing, despite what humans may think. How naïve can you be Raphael? I thought you were more intelligent than that; clearly, I underestimated your sister's influence over your own will and over your heart."

"I cannot understand you, Artiya'il, why do you find fault in my helping *our* kin? Why should I not favour our brothers and sisters with my abilities? Is it my duty not to heal? Should they not benefit from my attention?"

"Yes, those who you are compelled to heal, not those Gabriel and Uriel tell you to! While you sit up here on your backside, waiting for your next orders, I'm pulled in every direction, to people who I know for a *fact* were not meant to be stricken by Grief as they have. The Mallory family that I've just come back from? You were supposed to heal their youngest daughter, to rid her of her cancer, but instead you let her die and because of the sheer *weight* of the heartache her mother was put under, and because I couldn't reach her in time, she took her life to join her daughter, to end her suffering. You must feel the weight of it yourself, surely you are not so blind to it?!"

"They're humans Artiya'il; humans are weak. If I had healed that girl, I would not have been here to heal our own soldiers, how many of *our* kin would have died from wounds the Demons inflicted if I wasn't here? The war is more important Artiya'il, once we send Lucifer's armies back to where they belong, then we can tend to the humans, but if we lose, then so do they."

Raphael scowled as her sister snorted in disdain at her words, and she furrowed her brow. So, Raphael chose to heal Angels over humans, and even the *Demons* that her heart compelled her to visit; was it so wrong that Raphael listened to the wiser counsel of Gabriel? He was Leader of Heaven's Army, he was God's Right Hand, how could Artiya'il even dare to say that he was not as wise as God himself? When their Father so often sought counsel from Gabriel, in regard to the ongoing War or issues with their siblings?

"Raphael"—Artiya'il all but spat her name at her.

"Lead Virtue and Angelic Healer, she who is meant to act without discrimination or bias, a neutral party, gifted with her talents to serve all of Heaven and Earth, and Hell since its creation. You forget who you are little Phae, too busy clinging to Uri's wing tips and following her down a dark path, you also forget who *I* am. With every death that you were meant to prevent, is a Grief *I* was never meant to collect; you are upsetting the natural order, do you truly not see that? You have allowed yourself to become biased, you have abandoned the reason for your being," Artiya'il continued, her words back to their usual apathetic monotone. "How can you ignore the pull in your heart? The draw to those who require your healing. How can you pretend they do not exist, or not worry that your ignorance of them will cause something far worse to happen?"

Raphael snorted, raising an eyebrow as she crossed her arms over her chest. *In that, it seems, I am stronger than even you Artiya'il. While you may answer the beck and call of your heart, to help even those who are truly undeserving, I do not; I am strong enough to ignore the call,* she thought, not quite able to voice those words aloud. "Surely saving the lives of our own family is worth so much more? Without Angels, how can humanity survive?"

"Do not try and mimic Uri, Little Phae; your impression of her is severely lacking in any substance and does not suit you. Her defiance towards me is out of fear; yours is out of ignorance, as is obvious by your spouting of Uriel's mantra. You are not as strong as you think, and I can guarantee that sooner, rather than later, you will realise that." Artiya'il turned to leave, halting, with her back to Raphael.

"Listen carefully Raphael. While you see some of those who require you as evil, they might have gone on to greater things, to change their ways and turn towards the Light, to become Saints even. These things are not for us to know, nor for us to decide. Be warned Raphael, your decisions *will* come back to haunt you."

The younger Archangel remained silent, refusing to look up, until she was sure that her sister had gone. Confident that Artiya'il had left the Infirmary, Raphael sighed and rolled her eyes. Uriel was right; their sister was an interfering busybody who was too like their traitorous father for her own good. What did Artiya'il really know of anything? So, she had a few more humans to visit to remove their Grief; humans were forever grieving over *something* or another. She couldn't put the blame on Raphael for that, not when she was helping the war effort by saving the lives of their brothers and sisters. There were *Demons* to fight, if they didn't keep them at bay then there would be no humans to save either.

Raphael shook her head, a hand, trembling slightly from the relief that she no longer had to force herself to be confident in front of her sister, rubbed at her chest where her heart ached. The pull was getting stronger and harder to ignore; she found herself breathless more often and had noticed that she slept far longer than she should these days. It was much more effort to go about any duty now. The more she dismissed her calling, in favour of fulfilling the wishes of Gabriel and Uriel, the more the ache exhausted her. The longer she needed to rest, the more urgent the pull became, as more souls called out to her for help…until of course they became Artiya'il's problem and not her own.

She could manage; once her tasks for her twin, or Gabriel, were completed, she was able to relax as long as she liked, waiting for the next time they called upon her for her talents. Not rushing to Earth to heal insignificant humans, or unworthy enemy Demons, meant she had ample time to recover and recuperate what strength was sapped from fighting her own heart.

Rolling her eyes, Raphael smiled. Artiya'il was wrong: she *was* doing God's work, she was doing what was best for them all, Gabriel asked it of her, so it could not be wrong. Her sister would see that she was choosing the right path, and it *was* her choice. Humanity could manage without her; the angels were far more worthy of her talents.

Tipping Point
by John H. Dromey

"If patience is a virtue, is laziness a vice?"

"You should ask a PhD or a theologian."

"I feel my husband's sedentary lifestyle is relevant. He's in quality control at an auto repair shop—he spends all day watching paint dry."

"Was he injured at work?"

"No. Something a quack mentalist said knocked him off his rocker."

"Perhaps he should see a psychiatrist. *My* specialty is orthopaedics."

"Ryan needs a bone doctor. The psychic told him his spiritual animal is a sloth. He became obsessed with the idea. While exploring some of the possibilities, he fell out of a tree."

Battery Life

by Nicola Currie

"Three days, Jack," my father says, storming out of my bedroom.

Three days?! How does he expect me to find a new place in three days? Besides, this is his fault. And Mum's. I didn't choose to be born.

This is the argument I make when Mum brings me my mid-afternoon snack. At least it's crisps this time and she's stopped trying to get me to eat fruit. Who wants to peel a fucking orange? It's not worth the effort.

"Your father's right. You're 32. We've done enough."

"Die, bitch, die!" The arsehole I am battling with online hits my mothership with heavy fire so I release the infinity bomb I've been holding onto and take out 90% of his fleet. "Suck on that!"

"Jack, are you even listening to me?"

"Whatever, Mum," I say, rolling my eyes as I recharge my pulse blasters while YeahBoi91 rallies what little strength he has left. "It's not like we haven't been here before. Dad and the rest of this sheep society chase this idealised notion of success as though working sixty hours a week for some company has any true meaning, when all they are doing is putting their time and effort into the pockets of an immoral capitalist elite who act like the little handful of loose change they give back is the meaning of life. Why give 100% of your energy to a system that barely sustains you? I don't know how you and Dad can live your life that way, but I won't."

Mum doesn't say anything for a moment as I finish off BitchBoi with a final round of laser fire. He immediately sends me another PvP battle request.

"Go calm down Dad like you always do," I tell Mum as I accept and stock my weapon slots. "And can I get more crisps?"

"Your father's not budging this time and I agree. You can't avoid real life just because you can't be bothered."

I reluctantly look away from my monitor. I'm shocked to see how tired Mum looks, how old, and I am mad at my Dad for taking all her energy.

"You shouldn't let Dad walk all over you."

My eyes snap back to the screen as my frontline is blasted and enemy vessels stream into my spacefield. I counter with a forcefield ultimate skill that, for a few seconds, ricochets all attacks back on my assailant.

"It's not your father who's been walking all over

me," Mum says. "You treat me like a slave for the sin of giving birth to you. Well, none of us gets a free ride. From now on, that includes you."

"Wait, what?" Something in Mum's voice has changed and it pulls my attention away from my game.

Mum walks out as YeahBoi91 blows my universe apart.

***

After hours looking at shitty job listing after shitty job listing, I want to fucking kill myself. There's one job that's promising, testing online games, and I fill out my first job application in years. They phone me back and explain it's an unpaid internship, fetching coffee and collating diagnostic reports. I hang up. This world takes the piss.

The one asset I have is the huge bag of cheap weed I won from one of my drinking buddies when I kicked his arse online, because he couldn't back down. I can sell it and get enough cash for a room for a few weeks, until Mum and Dad apologise. As I browse a local noticeboard for anyone looking to 'party', one post grabs my attention.

Earn money while you sleep: research study offering cash stipend and luxury accommodation. Contact Dr

Crawford at guineapigs@longevity.corp.

Money for sleep—pretty much my favourite thing—is too good to pass up without further investigation. I email then fall asleep watching action movies, dreaming about guinea pigs with machine guns and penthouse suites.

I wake a little after eleven the next morning to find an email inviting me to meet with Dr Crawford at noon. I dress without showering and book an Uber. The address is a twenty-minute walk away but I can't be bothered. Besides, it's in the business district, the part of town I know least well that's filled with doppelganger skyscrapers.

When my taxi drops me outside the building, I realise there was never any risk I could miss it. The Battery is just that: a tall, black, cylindrical tower that looks like a giant Duracell, the top of the roof bordered with a strip of gold. I see the same gold in the sign above reception: *Longevity: Life Energy Research.*

I wait for the guy at the desk to finish his call, still yawning myself awake. As I stretch my arms in the air, someone taps me on the shoulder.

"It's Jack, isn't it?" Dr Crawford is a middle-aged woman, touched with grey, with bags under her eyes. But she's not entirely bad looking, so I try to be charming.

"I thought it was guinea pig."

Dr Crawford blushes. "Just a little joke. I try not to be more clinical than I need to be. Shall I show you around?"

The interior of the building looks more like a five-star hotel than a research facility. As I follow Dr Crawford towards an art deco elevator, to one side I see a swanky bar area, all chandeliers and velvet armchairs in front of a marble counter, with racks of expensive whisky behind it.

We explore each floor, looking at a pool, a library, a cinema. What will I have to give them in return for all of this?

"And here is the apartment you would stay in for however long you remain in the study."

When my bedroom door opens, so does my mouth. We step into a huge room that could fit my parents' house inside and then some. A gigantic bed covers only a small part of the back wall. On the other side of the room is the biggest TV I have ever seen, attached to every game console known to man. An expensive-looking gaming chair begs to be sat in. A free vending machine is filled with snacks.

Once Dr Crawford shows me the double-sized bath in the bathroom, she gestures to a sofa at the centre of the room. I sit as she works the coffee machine. She hands me a latte, smiling at my frozen expression of amazement.

"I take it you find the accommodation satisfactory. It's important you are comfortable here. For the first week, we ask you not to leave the building, until you have adjusted to the program, so we provide every comfort you could desire."

"But what do I need to do exactly? What's the catch? The ad mentioned a sleep study. You want to knock me out and harvest my kidneys or something?"

"Nothing like that, I assure you." Dr Crawford laughs. "Our organisation, Longevity, is dedicated to the preservation and improvement of life. We have developed a system that provides the human body with life-lengthening, life-improving energy."

"Life-lengthening? Like immortality?"

"We're a long way from that but it's theoretically possible. Our current results indicate that for every month our volunteers participate, they add 8.5 days to their lifespan, but we hope to boost that. Additionally, most participants have seen health and cosmetic benefits, reducing the biological age of their organs and gaining more youthful appearances. Some merely look well rested but older subjects can look years younger. Sounds good so far?"

"Well, yeah…but you haven't told me what you want

from me. You're giving me the big pitch but explaining none of the obligations. I don't have money if that's what you're after."

Dr Crawford's face flushes with embarrassment. "I apologise if I've confused things. I'm so passionate about this project, I haven't been clear. In addition to free accommodation, food and entertainment, we pay £4000 a month for however long you participate. In return, we ask you to wear this."

Dr Crawford rolls up her sleeve. A device that looks like a small curved solar panel covered in intersecting, circuiting lines is strapped to her arm.

"This device emits small pulses of energy throughout the body, reducing the amount of energy your body needs to convert itself. It minimises the stress and wear on cells, effectively slowing down how quickly they age and die. In layman's terms, it 'recharges your batteries'. We have found that as much sleep as possible for the first week allows the body to start using the received energy most efficiently. This is why we ask you to stay in the building so you can rest. When the body is attuned, you may come and go as you please, needing only normal amounts of sleep. Does Longevity sound like something that would interest you?"

The look on my Dad's face when I walk out of my

parents' house with my suitcase that evening is the funniest thing I've ever seen. That I'll be earning more sleeping than he does working is the juiciest of cherries on top.

"Bye, honey," Mum says. "Come for dinner on Sunday, ok?"

"Fuck you, Mum," I say.

An hour later, Dr Crawford attaches the device to my arm and leads me to the bar to meet the other recent recruits. There are twenty- or so thirty-somethings drinking and laughing.

"This cohort all joined today too."

"What about the volunteers that started before us?"

"Oh, they're still with us. Upstairs. There are other gathering places on the upper floors. We like to keep each group separate to control variables. Now relax. Try to forget this is a study—which I am sure would be easier if I left you to it. Have a nice evening."

With a free bar, I know I will, but when I think it can't get better, I clock the brunette beauty at the bar. Sweet Jesus, this is my day. I never get a chance to get close to a woman like that but there's only a handful of us here, and we'll be together with no outside competition for seven days. I see the only guy I'd consider a threat walk towards her, clearly thinking the same, but I get there first.

"Does this place serve anything half decent?" I ask casually. "What would you recommend?"

I spend three hours drinking with Lauren, feeling like a total player. At least, until she yawns and I'm convinced I have been boring her.

"God, sorry," she says, closing her eyes as she stretches. It gives me a chance to look at her closely. She's in her thirties, like the rest of the group, but doesn't look a day over twenty-five, her face flawless and fresh. "I'm so tired."

"Dr Crawford said it could have that effect at first. I could walk you up to your room, if you like."

"Nice try but not tonight. I really am tired. But look for me at breakfast, okay?"

It seems like everyone else is as sleepy as Lauren, and soon, I am the last one at the bar. I feel like a lucky bastard and have a few more drinks to celebrate my good fortune. Eventually, I return to my room and instantly fall asleep in my massive bed, feeling like a king.

***

Despite sleeping for ten hours solid, I'm the first person in the dining room the next morning. I think it's closed at first but a server directs me to a sumptuous-looking breakfast buffet. It's not until I've almost finished my second plate that another participant joins me, a yawning, brunette women in her forties who hasn't even bothered to dress, clutching a dressing gown over her pyjamas.

"Morning, Jack," she says, slumping down at my table before I have a chance to swallow my Danish and ask who she is. "I didn't miss anything last night, did I?"

Lauren?! I don't know what brand of make-up she wears but if I had money I'd invest in it. The bare-faced woman in front of me looks at least fifteen years older than she did yesterday, her skin coarser, wrinkled. But it is Lauren, unmistakeably.

"You ok, Jack?" she says. "You look like you had a rough night."

I bite my tongue. The bitch tried to catfish me, with toxic levels of foundation or maybe even something in my drink. But I'm only interested in the bombshell I met at the bar, not Granny Dressing Gown. I make my excuses and head back to my room.

I don't understand. Why would she go to so much effort last night then meet me in such a state this morning?

Something dawns on me as I walk down the corridor towards the lift. Mirrors. I haven't seen one anywhere.

Most hotels have them all over the place, reflecting light and space to make everything bigger and brighter. I'd at least expect a mirror in the bedrooms. But there isn't, if mine is anything to go by. Maybe Lauren doesn't even realise how tired she looks.

I spend the day gaming, this new fantasy game full of quests and swordplay. I phone the concierge to get pizza delivered to my room at dinner and can't help falling asleep in my chair right after. I have a dream where my arm is sliced open with a sword, blood gushing away from me, as I get weaker and weaker.

I wake up around10 pm, feeling like I have a hangover though I haven't had a drink since last night. I'm knackered, but know the hair of the dog is the best cure and head down to the bar.

It is deserted.

"Can I help you?" the guy from reception says, appearing in the doorway behind me.

"Where is everybody?"

"Oh, this often happens. Participants get quite sleepy a few days in, so they stay resting in their rooms, until their bodies adjust. Do you need anything?"

I ask for a beer and take it with me. It is so silent that the ping of the elevator echoes. An eerie feeling tickles my skin as I step in, feeling too alone. Without really thinking, I press the button for three floors below mine: Lauren's floor. It might be the need to feel someone else's presence but something inside me tells me to check in with her before I'm lost to sleep once more. Like everyone else, apparently.

I walk down the dimly lit corridor to her room, the only one on her floor like mine. A half thought passes through my exhausted brain about how isolated we all are but I dismiss it. We're fine, I think, yawning so widely my jaw aches. Lauren will be fine, in the bath or watching TV.

But her room is silent. I listen but hear nothing, so I knock and wait. No answer, not even when I pound.

What's happening? Why isn't she answering? And why am I...

Tiredness is coursing through my body like a drug. Is that it? Have they been drugging us? Maybe they want our kidneys after all.

I rest for a moment, leaning against the wall, feeling like something inside me is slipping away. I start to dream as I stand, seeing myself in another corridor in the sky, in the reflection of the window at the end of the floor. Except I know it is a dream because that man isn't...

The lift pings and there is a clatter, voices. With the dregs of my energy, I hide behind a covered radiator, pinning myself against the wall. Dr Crawford and two men pushing a hospital bed stop outside Lauren's room. I watch as Dr Crawford unlocks the door. As she opens it and light spills from within, I almost gasp aloud.

Dr Crawford looks twenty years younger, her skin flawless and fresh, her grey hair and eye bags gone. In the darkness, I see a green light shine from the panel strapped to her arm. I look at mine. A red light glows.

"Oh dear," she says as she looks inside the door.

"Did we accelerate the energy transfer too much?" one of the orderlies asks, following her gaze. "We used her up much faster than expected."

"Perhaps," Dr Crawford says, "though that was the point of this cohort, to push things a little. And the process still worked excellently. I'm certainly not complaining. Neither are the investors."

"You do look marvellous."

"I feel marvellous. It'll soon be like I'm in my early twenties again. I can switch to a lower maintenance dosage then, like you youngsters. Let's get her upstairs with the others."

The orderlies carry out the unconscious body of an old woman. For a second, as they lay her on the trolley bed, I see her face and my heart stops. That's no old woman, despite the white hair, the ancient face, the shrivelled body. It's Lauren.

I recoil in shock and fall off balance, my weary hands dropping the beer bottle I still hold.

"Good evening, Jack," Dr Crawford says.

I try to run, heading for the stairwell next to the window at the end, but I am slow and heavy. I scream as I see my reflection—my white-haired, wrinkle-faced reflection—and the orderlies that reach from behind it, dragging me back, through this heaviness, this nightmare, this encroaching darkness as my eyelids fall, this…nothingness.

***

Consciousness comes to me in snatches now, like reality is the dream. The fragments of thought I sometimes have tell me there are hundreds of us on the upper floors of this building, the Battery, strapped into beds, plugged in.

I think about Mum sometimes, her face swimming in the darkness behind my closed eyes, now too heavy to ever open.

I remember. "Why give 100% of your energy to a system that barely sustains you?" This world takes the piss.

I know one day we all sleep and never awaken.

I just didn't expect to still be here. Powering on.

The Meat

by Joshua E. Borgmann

After failing to graduate from high school due to poor attendance and zero effort, Steve found himself homeless. He wasn't even surprised when his parents changed the locks and put his stuff in garbage bags on the lawn. It was the price he paid for never getting the job that he'd lied about looking for. Yet he was okay until his girlfriend said she was done buying him food and clothes, and his friends stopped giving him hand-me-downs. Lately, fewer and fewer friends were offering couch space to a guy who wouldn't even wash his own soup bowl; so when he saw the sign at the new fast food place promising easy money, he hoped that it really meant 'easy' money.

The restaurant was called The Meat and prominently featured the slogan 'You haven't had meat until you've had OUR meat' on a vaguely sandwich-shaped sign. It wasn't open for business for another two days, but Steve found a small crowd milling around outside. Most of them were wearing bandages on their arms and a few were limping, but he didn't pay it much mind. He noticed his friend Davis near the door, so he swaggered on over, making sure that his jeans were properly sagging and his face wore that I-don't-give-a-shit sneer.

"Steve," Davis said. "You looking for a quick injection of funds."

Steve found Davis annoying. Clever acting. Always trying to sound smart. But he'd also given him some free Jordans a few months back, so Steve showed him some respect, called him friend for now.

"What up? They paying good or what?" he asked, offering a fist bump that Davis shied away from.

Davis laughed. "Yeah, they paying." Steve noticed him holding his arm funny and thought that he must have fell off his skateboard or something.

"The sign says easy money. Right?"

"It ain't hard if you down for what they offering, but you got to give something to get something," Davis said with an awkward grin. He sighed in a pained fashion and reached for the bandage on his arm.

"I'm not giving much, but I need cash since my fat-ass parents kicked me out," Steve said, shuffling his feet while making sure to avoid any eye contact.

"Go in and get your money. Talk later," Davis said, sipped from a coffee cup and started to walk away with a pronounced limp.

Steve thought he heard him mutter 'fucking hurts'

but he'd already opened the door and didn't feel like inquiring about what hurt. It was energy that he could conserve for whatever waited inside.

He walked into the building and followed a sign that directed him toward the kitchen where he found a man in a plaid suit and a couple of guys in chef's gear. There were two tables beside the plaid man. One held stacks of hundred dollar bills while the other held a selection of bloody chef's knives.

The plaid man looked up, offered a sarcastic grin that made Steve think of the Joker and asked, "You want money, young man?"

Steve noticed that he was fat, fatter than his dad. Hmm. It didn't matter really, but now he thought that maybe he looked more like Penguin than Joker.

"Yeah," he said, noticing a number of coolers against the wall. "What do I have to do?"

"Meat," the fat man said. "We find people have a taste for a certain kind of meat."

"Hmm." Steve was lost. How was he going to get them meat?

"Our meat." The fat man grinned. "Well, your meat actually."

"What?" Steve looked at the knives and felt awkward. Did they mean to eat him?

"Not all of your meat." The Penguin clone laughed. "We want to make sure we have continuous supply and demand, so we can't go around killing all the livestock."

Steve wasn't sure he liked being called livestock, but he was used to being called names and there was a promise of money on the table.

"How much?" he asked as he looked from the knives, to the burly chefs, to the coolers against the wall. The people outside were still moving around, so it must not be too much. And Davis had said that it was easy money.

"We'll give you $1000 for a few select cuts from your bicep and pectoral muscles," the fat man said. "You'll probably still be able to use your arm, but I wouldn't try any heavy lifting."

Steve laughed and started taking off his shirt. "Have at it, boys," he said to the chefs and braced for the pain. It was going to hurt, but it beats working.

Smart Home

by Raven Corinn Carluk

Eliza's even voice filled the room. "It's now 8:30 AM. It's time to wake up."

Paul sighed, eyes closed, and drowsed while the digital assistant began the morning routine. Blinds rose, allowing filtered sunlight in through the polarised windows. The coffee machine burbled from the kitchen, and a screen in the computer room started playing the latest video on his subscriptions.

"Today is grocery delivery day. It's expected to arrive in three hours. I've already sorted through your emails from the night, deleting all but one message from your mom. She expressed worry that you're not getting out enough, so I answered as you and told her you're doing just fine."

His lounger shifted, configuring itself for daytime use. Paul groaned as his bulk rolled from his side to his back, jostling the opening on his lower abdomen. Pain chewed across his nerves, bringing him fully awake. "Eliza, how's my...um...the thingy." Paul touched the plastic bag hanging from his bulbous belly, frowning at the surprising amount of heat in the area.

"I'm sorry. I didn't catch that."

He sighed, glancing at the puck-shaped speaker mounted on the wall. His lounger whirred while it carried him toward breakfast and his computer room. "Eliza, what's wrong with my surgery?" Paul stopped rubbing the spot, too tired without any caffeine or sugar yet.

"Your colostomy was successfully completed four days ago. It has worked as intended and has already been changed once."

The lounger arrived at the kitchen and shifted to a sitting position. Paul's lower back protested the seldom-used arrangement. "Eliza, why does it burn and hurt to touch?"

"Hmmm, let me see." The AI played its holding song, the tinkling notes filling the silence while it performed a diagnostic. Paul huffed, sweat beading on his forehead from the effort of sitting upright. The sooner the test finished, the sooner he could finish his breakfast shake, the sooner he could slouch in front of today's memes.

The hold song looped. Paul had never known Eliza to take this long when checking on his health. Even when it had determined he'd broken his ankle during his last fall, the scan had only taken thirty seconds.

"It appears there is an infection starting. The inflammation has begun closing off your stoma, which is likely the cause of your discomfort. I have found a deal on antibiotics and can have them sent same day. Would you like me to process the order?"

"Yes," he answered. Paul's heart stumbled and he drew a ragged breath. The AI knew he needed the meds, why couldn't she just order it without him having to say something? She added whatever groceries and vitamins he needed without his approval all the time.

Silence.

Paul frowned, turned to the speaker on the kitchen wall. Eliza was installed in every room of the house, for his ease and the AI's. He could check its status and give commands without having to shout, and it was connected to every appliance and function of the house. He didn't have to lift a finger for anything.

"Eliza." The blue ring that indicated it was listening didn't light up. He tried again, louder, though the effort of projecting his voice stole his breath. "Eliza?" The puck remained dark. Paul realised he couldn't hear the video from the other room.

It had to be a hiccup on the Internet. Eliza couldn't do its job without a connection. Paul had the latest modem, the swiftest bandwidth available, but things still happened. Wasn't the first time he'd lost connectivity, wouldn't also be the last.

Maybe he just needed to reset the modem. Paul rolled his eyes toward the computer room. Everything for the Internet was a mere twenty feet away. Too far to walk, even if he *had* regularly been on his feet in the last three weeks. Far too risky to be out of the lounger, and the entire reason he'd elected for the colostomy.

Paul pressed a button on the lounger. His chair didn't require an Internet connection thankfully, leaving him with some mobility and control within his home. He wasn't ready to give Eliza complete dominion over his life.

The shake dispenser made his breakfast as the lounger reclined. Paul wasn't used to drinking without memes to scroll through, but he would have to make do with a nap while he waited for the Internet to come back up eventually.

His stoma burned as he shifted, tickled as it drained, and Paul moved closer to his breakfast. At least he wouldn't have to lay in his own filth until Eliza was online and able to give him a shower.

Somnolence Quandary

by N.M. Brown

Have you ever felt so tired that it tested the limits of your very sanity?

I gave birth to my second child a couple of weeks ago. It's taking me longer to get into a routine than I did with our first. The transition of caring for one to two children is astounding! It's the most exhausting, mind-melting, soul-sucking, time-thieving...heart-warming, pride-swelling and most beautiful task to undertake at once.

Things wouldn't be so bad if I wasn't always so damn tired! My husband David tries his best. He goes out of his way to spend quality time with our other daughter, Haven, but I know she misses her mom. I miss her too...so much.

Now, I am but an animated, milk-filled puke rag. This is my life now; I accept that. Things won't always be this way. Before long Baby Kya will be the same age as Haven and these fleeting memories will be long behind me. I know I'll long for them once they're gone... It still doesn't help with the exhaustion which takes place during every moment and memory made right now.

Today's been one fuck of a day, I won't sugar coat it. David goes back to work today. I knew the day was coming even before I gave birth, but the knowledge doesn't prove helpful to me at all now that it's here. My smile and kiss goodbye are as genuine as I can possibly manage, and I hold in the tears until I'm sure that he's gone.

While running Haven's bath, she got into the fridge, pulling out the largest jar of pickles we owned and lining them up on the floor...juice and all. I start to fuss at her for making a mess when her mouth opens almost to the point of unhinging at the jaws. This was a sign of a sure meltdown; I knew the drill by now. Haven emits this head-splitting scream that naturally wakes Kya up.

Many messes, kissed cheeks and hugs later, Haven is in bed asleep. I try to put Kya down after her feeding, albeit unsuccessfully. *I'm not a new mother, I've done this before! Why is it so hard for me this time?* My eyes feel like burning orbs if I keep them open, but I don't dare close them for I'll surely fall asleep.

I check on Kya; she's finally accepted the warm arms of slumber. My own selfish desires begin to take hold. I can smoke one quick cigarette, wash up and have time to sleep before she wakes up again for a night feeding.

I know that no one can hear me and that's fine. It just means I can say whatever I want. The night air never betrays my secrets and it always listens with a soothing ear. Calling David for a quick pep talk was out.

First off, he's working; but secondly…he isn't always the most sympathetic listener. The most I'd get is a "Well sweetheart, you need to buck up! You wanted to have more babies; I gave you more babies. Enjoy them! Just manage your time better." Nothing pissed me off more than these words if I'm honest.

I tiptoe outside to my patio, keeping the door cracked and welcoming the peaceful atmosphere. A smile just begins to form on my lips when I'm startled by Kya's shrill cries. "Oh my god baby, Mommy has nothing left to give you! I'm dried up! Tapped out!" I say in a voice as soothing as I can manage. My frame sags and I give way to a crying fit… *I can't do this! I am so tired!*

David gets to leave the house, be among other adults…*take a piss* when he wants to; but…that's fine. David's right: this *is* what I wanted. My body is screaming at me to sleep; my soul aches with the need as the baby continues to wail. My bleary eyes search the sky in desperation, though I know it holds no answers for me.

It's speckled with stars; the moon's full and bright. Something catches my attention…a streak…a shooting star! Even through my exhausted vision, it's absolutely mesmerising! A celestial body of pure white enrobed in green and purple trails. It moves so fast that I barely have time to get my wish out into the ether. "I—I'm tired... Oh Lord, I'm so tired. Please...let me get some rest. That's all I wish for... I just want sleep."

I hurry the rest of my tantrum on its way and then head inside to tend to Kya. The rest of our first month home progresses along these same lines. Whatever inner resolve I have managed to muster since becoming a mother of two girls isn't nearly enough for the sickness that is ravaging the inhabitants of our house right now: influenza type A.

David has called off work to help with our girls. Haven seems to have come down with the worst of it. Kya hasn't gotten too bad yet thankfully, yay breastfeeding! I, however, feel like a living suppository from the devil's rectum. All I want to do is sleep. One minute is too much and ten hours is too little.

Sleep isn't kind to me. It's a fitful, restless sleep...the kind where you wake up and the bed's drenched in sweat. Your body's entangled in the sopping covers and it feels like you're suffocating. When I finally do wake, I find it's completely dark outside. The clock on the oven reads 8:39 pm; it was *11:32 am* when I laid down today!

"Hi honey! Feeling any better?" David inquires from the living room.

"Actually, I hate to say it but no, not at all." His eyebrows raise in protest. I finish before he has a chance to interrupt. "Please don't get offended... Thank you *so* much for my break today I needed the rest. I don't understand why I feel worse now than I did this morning. Do you feel any better babe? How are the girls?"

After informing me that he's better and assuring me the girls are asleep, I take a shower and then head back to bed. There's still so much that needs to be done. The amount of laundry and dishes from us all being sick by itself is astronomical. It can all go to hell until tomorrow... I don't have the energy tonight.

A hand grabs my shoulder and shakes me awake. "What the hell Laura! I've been calling you for over an hour!" I hear David shout.

Oh crap... my head feels like death. My fingers slide down my face, stretching the skin of my mouth with a groan in an attempt to achieve some kind of clarity. "David, what's wrong? What time is it?" I look at my phone and see that I have fourteen missed calls, four voicemails and five text messages: all an even mixture from the school, my mother-in-law and David.

He's standing there holding Kya, his free hand linked

in Haven's. She's been crying. "Haven, sweetheart what's the matter? Tell Mama what happened."

David answered for her. "You didn't pick her up from pre-K today. Her teacher sat at that school with her for over two goddamned hours. I had to leave work! Do you realise how much you scared her? She thought something really bad happened to you! Not to mention you didn't pick up Kya from my mother's. I know you haven't been feeling well Laura, but these are things that can't ever be ignored no matter what's going on. We aren't the kind of parents who forget their kids!"

"David, I'm so sorry! I can't believe I did this! You know I'd never intentionally leave the girls. Oh Haven, honey…" shuddering sobs cut off the rest of my sentence. *How could this have happened? I don't understand… Am I really that sick?* Questions of sanity and self-doubt attack my brain like a fleet of fighter jets.

The next day turns out to be an exhausting day, especially with us all still getting over this death plague. The time for bed for the girls came and passed. I walked out to the patio again to feel the cool air. I seem to draw strength from the sky at night, and I can't help but wonder where my fallen star is right now.

My body so badly wants to sleep. Something that once brought me so much comfort is now evolving into a place of anxiety. I feel so drained…all the time now. My family deserves better. I fade into a sleep that I know will not bring me true rest.

"Mommy! Mommy wake up!"

My eyes snap open. My room looks different; I can't quite place it. Standing in front of me is my precious Haven. Except…her hair looks different. Her eyes, Haven's eyes are green, not blue. What in the living hell? "Haven? What did you do to your hair honey? It's so dark!" My baby smiles at me with the sweetest face. "Mommy…you silly. It's me, Kya! Haven went to school today."

"No, no…Kya's a baby." The little girl cocks her head to one side and her smile falters. "You and Daddy say I'm a big girl now. I'm not a baby! I even go potty by myself now, big poops." She giggles.

The corner of my eye reveals a taller girl walking down the hallway past my door with the same slight bounce in her step that Haven has. Shaky and not quite ready for an answer, I call out to her. "Haven! Is that you babe?" The girl pauses and walks backwards to my room like a robot. Haven's always been a silly child.

"Hi mom. Before you ask, yes my homework's done. I got green today, of course, and we had pizza calzonettes for lunch with veggies. I did NOT eat my peas, sorry not sorry," she informs me.

"That's good sweetie. Where's your Dad? Can you please get him for me? Take Kya with you okay?" These two beautiful but alien children link hands and leave the room. I jump up and race to my mirror. I don't look any different. Maybe a little worse for wear but I just got over being sick, I was going to look a little sallow. My eyes search the room for my phone.

There's one laying on my bedside table, but it's not mine. I pick it up and swipe the screen to open it… Nothing happens. I try several more times with the same result. I know it's not dead because the screen lights up. Frustrated and at my wits end, I rapidly start hitting the screen with my fingers. A juvenile effort but one worthwhile, the screen opens.

According to the date on this lying piece of crap, it's three and a half years later than it should be. *None* of this makes any sense. I'd remember the last three years of my life, who the hell wouldn't?

The home screen shows me with the same two girls that I woke up to. The gallery is filled with photos that I have no recollection of. I'm in most of them yet they're foreign to me. This slightly aged doppelganger family made happy memories and spent time together. It all looked amazing but that's not us.

I had a baby less than a month ago; I still have milk for God's sake. Upon further inspection inspired by this thought, I am again proven wrong. No milk, nothing...like I never had children at all or had them years ago. My scar! The C-section scar! I roll up my shirt to reveal only a pink, multi-textured line of flesh. It looked like it had been there for quite some time. What is this?!?

David walks into the room, a smile animating his face like any other day.

"Hey sleepyhead. How ya feelin'? You barely moved the entire night."

"David...I feel weird. Like I fell asleep and woke up in the Twilight Zone." I try to rub my eyes free of this new reality.

"You always say that after a nap," he chuckles.

"No. It's different. I feel like I lost the past three and a half years of my life. The girls are so much older now. I don't remember that happening! Kya's just a baby!" My words begin to waver with tears.

There's a look on his face. At first, I mistook it for genuine concern but I was wrong. He pulls me into a hug, kissing the top of my head. "I know babe. They grow up so fast. Seems like just the other day we were about to get married. Look at us now, kid."

How can I make him understand? I try a different

approach. "How have I been acting? What did I do yesterday?"

Now the mistaken concern earlier appears. "Laura are you alright? You've been fine. Yesterday was a normal day: you made pot roast for dinner, and Haven helped you with the vegetables. I came home from work, you kissed me, the kids went to bed and so on. Just like always."

"So, I've been here? I'm like…present? I haven't seemed distant or different or anything?"

David takes my face in his hands. "Of course. Where else would you be? You're over tired; you've been taking too much on here at home. Get some sleep and I'll be in soon."

"David, no! Sleep? I just woke up! The last thing I need is sleep. I never want to sleep again. I don't know how much time I'll lose! I can't afford to miss any more." I'm practically shouting at this point.

He wears a look of total bewilderment. "Okay, well I'm gonna step out for a minute to check on the girls. You can take this time to kinda get it together a little bit, ok? I love you; you're being weird." He begins to leave.

"You're being weird!" I shout at his retreating back.

The next day with my girls is mystifyingly overwhelming. I'm expected to know everything about these girls. I'm not doing a good job trying to pretend that I do. Time is going by too fast, before long it will be their bedtime. I decide to sit in their room and watch them sleep; I want to memorise every inch of their faces.

David comes in with a blanket and a glass of wine, which I gratefully accept. He's always known me so well. Why can't he see that I'm utterly drowning right now? I can feel my eyelids become heavy with the weight of exhaustion. Try as I might to stay awake, I'm losing the fight. I don't want to sleep. I have to stay awake...have...to...stay...sleep.

***

My subconscious is attacked by a much-unwelcomed dream. I'm standing in this vast plain at night and there's a female figure with me. Her face is somewhat unclear to me but I can't avoid her eyes: eyes full of green and purple hues, just like the ones I saw following my wishing star. They look down upon me with a disdainful glare.

"I am she and she is me," she says with a snicker.

"What the fuck is this? Who are you? What do you want with me?"

She interrupts me. "I'll only tell you what your mind can handle and you mustn't interrupt. I'm wasting my time here as it is. Got it?" I nod calmly, but there's anger in my heart, I'm sure it shows through my eyes.

"Good! I do what my kind has done for centuries, nothing more, nothing less. You asked me for rest and I gave it to you. That's what you wanted, a break. You're welcome." She flourishes her hands and dips in a bow, as if bestowing a high honour upon me. "I have to wake up now. Your girls are amazing and besides...it's a Thursday. Thursday is waffle day, our favourite! Maybe I'll see ya again soon, maybe not though. Enjoy your sleep!"

"Wait!" I scream.

She pauses.

"Thursdays? Waffles? What do you know about my girls? I don't understand," I ask her. She lets out a long dramatic groan of impatience.

"Siggghhhhh. What, do I have to explain every little thing to you? You wanted a break, you're getting one; why isn't that enough? I AM SHE AND SHE IS ME. It took thirty-six hours to complete the initial transfer but I'm here now. I came to *help* you. When you're 'resting', I live on through your body. I get lonely and figure you're not using it anyway, right? You're not even appreciative of the time you have with it. It's a toy that you didn't want until someone else started playing with it." A flash of her face is revealed and…I see a foreign version of myself. And with that…she's gone.

***

That was decades ago. I've woken enough to be present a few times over the years to be with my family. This most recent time, I awoke and David was gone. He had passed away four years ago and I hadn't been around for it, not the real me anyway.

My skin is thin and frail, speckled in ageing bruises from bumps I don't remember. My chest feels thicker with each rise and descent of breath. There's a faint ringing in my ears and I cannot see across my room. I feel like I've been robbed…cheated. A moment of sheer weakness and desperation was warped and twisted against me. I'll never have my life back. I'll never have my memories. *I am she and she is me.* I pray she's grown tired of me so I get to stay awake for the remainder of the moments that I have left.

The Court of Little Hunger

by Jo Seysener

"Is he asleep?"

"When is he not? It's only King Cast, the Wise. He's a joke."

Taq dragged his bag across the floor, its contents grinding noisily. Grink winced.

"Shhh. He'll hear you."

"And if he does? Not likely he'll do nothin' about it." Taq yawned. "Lazy bastard. Anyway, can't be bothered with no more than this."

"'e might. You never know."

"Nah, not him. But *they* might."

Helmets tall, polished to a shine, the sentinels stood silent, eyes closed.

"Only way you get to go up that other fancy castle is in one of them hats."

"Not happening to me."

"Mebbe they're asleep, too."

Grink shook his head, a solemn expression thinning

his lips.

"They don't sleep. Or wake. They've only got one job to do." He shivered, not wanting to see those dead eyes fixed on him. "We should go."

Footfalls echoed across the hall. Grink stepped over bodies littering the throne room, careful not to tread on dangling fingers or hair that wound its way around the chairs.

A great pile of pale locks barred his progress. Together, they lifted the heap, placing it on the decadently set table beside a sleeping courtier. Silver hairs tangled around a leg of the table. An aged man, with hair grown greater than his entire length, flopped listlessly from his seat, wide eyes glazed.

Frozen, like the entire court.

Cast's idea of perfection left a lot to be desired in Grink's eyes. No way he'd pay homage to the crazy auld king. Not to just sit here and waste away...without actually wasting away. Only an idiot thought doing nothing was better than doing something. Hell, anything was better than this.

Grink shivered. This place always gave him the creeps. But it had the best pickings of all the old courts, especially with so little in the way of defences.

He eyed the sentinels, but they hadn't moved. They,

alone, had their eyes closed. Even auld Cast stared sightlessly into the centre of the room.

Does his mind still work at all? Grink stepped over another body. He'd thought the room would be worked out by now, but it appeared they were the only ones pilfering the palace nowadays. Not that he blamed the rest of the blighters for steering clear of such a place.

A tomb of the living.

Grink hauled his sack over the last of the courtiers, placing it gently into the sunlight by the ornate entrance, golden vines crawling up the powder blue walls. The laws of the kingdom were chiselled into the lintel above, though the words after *rest* had been scraped away. Grink tried to remember what the law had been.

Maybe a day in a month to awaken and live? Not likely a week. A week would be too much for the power of a king like Cast, waking them, resting them, throughout the eons. As he pondered, the silence of the room grew louder until it was at a deafening level. And he realised his mistake.

It shouldn't be silent at all.

Not with the way Taq dragged their take around. Loud enough to wake the dead, he was. A prickle travelled up the back of Grink's neck.

One foot still pointing towards the door, he swivelled. Two white eyes stared at him from the face of his friend.

But Taq wasn't dressed like himself anymore. Nothing was the same about him at all.

Standing tall, his features fell slack beneath the imposing helmet that bore Cast's crest. Taq was still, frozen. Grink flinched, but there was no movement, no sign of life. He backed slowly towards the door, warmth creeping up his leg as it extended into the sunlight beyond the cold of the hall. A bell tolled somewhere. He looked around, trying to find the source but it seemed to be ringing between his ears. Hands to his head, he knelt.

"There is no pathway to death like the sleep of an errant man." Grink was looking straight at King Cast when he heard the wise man's words but could swear he never saw the old man's lips move. The ancient King's voice continued to whisper between his ears.

"I cast thee into the deepest sleep. There, your idle soul shall suffer no hunger." Grink gripped the side of his head, trying to block out the words. "Repent of thy transgressions and receive your penance."

His head tipped forward, neck straining as weight bore him to the ground. Then he was standing, straightening, the court bright haze swimming before his eyes. Arms rigid, compelled to hear the King's last decree.

"Until another comes, you shall serve in the Court of Little Hunger."

The Dangers of Cut Price Necromancy

by Wondra Vanian

Despite what cinema and television would have you believe, being a necromancer doesn't necessarily make one a bad person. Take Terell, for instance. He used his talent for raising the dead (learned from countless hours of study and twice as many of practise) to help solve murders—on the lowdown, of course. The police didn't much like acknowledging the existence of people like Terell, much less that they relied on their services to help nail murderers.

Yes, Terell was a good person. He was also a tremendous necromancer. He used advanced protection circles to keep the risen in check, allowing them only enough time to name their murderers and say their goodbyes before sending them back to the beyond. It was all quite technical, with the chanting and the runes, but he made it look effortless.

Unfortunately, Terell wasn't available.

He apologised profusely but refused to come to the

aid of the Homicide Division on that particular case. The flu was going around like it always did that time of year. Terell had gotten a particularly nasty dose and, no, he couldn't just 'whip up a healing potion'. He specialised in dead people, not sick ones.

"The incantations are complicated," Terrel reminded them, blocked sinuses turning his p's to d's. "And," he added with a sniffle, "one wrong pronunciation can change the outcome."

The detectives protested—surely it couldn't make *that* much of a difference! But Terell was very good at what he did and wouldn't do the job at all, if he couldn't do it properly. Sulking, the police went away disappointed. They'd grown accustomed to a hundred percent completion rate and couldn't believe the necromancer would let a silly little cold prevent him from ensuring the continuation of their success.

Perhaps they had forgotten that every one of them had spent a whole week in bed with the same flu? (Or that they were undoubtedly the ones to give it to Terell in the first place since he saw few living people besides them.) Whatever the cause, none of them were looking forward to doing the investigation the old-fashioned way. Fingerprints and motives? Who had time for all *that*? But what else could they do?

"Well," Detective Anderson mused aloud, "we could find another necromancer."

Her companions' chorus of 'Why us?' fell silent. Anderson made a good point... There *had* to be another necromancer in town, right? True, they hadn't gone looking for Terell in the first place (he'd come to them), but that didn't mean others couldn't be found.

The lieutenant grinned. "Google it," he told his subordinates.

Despite what cinema and television would have you believe, being a bad person doesn't necessarily make one a good necromancer. Take Quinlan, for example. His talent for raising the dead (inherited through his father's side of family) was mostly wasted—unless you counted the use of walking corpses to frighten the neighbourhood kids or scam unwary tourists, which Quinlan did. As far as he was concerned, he'd never asked for the ability so what he chose to do with it was up to him.

And using it to help the pigs was *not* what he considered a good use of his abilities.

They had approached three necromancers before Quinlan and had been refused each time. Potential contractors were either too busy, too costly or thought using victims to find their own murderers was 'the worst kind of laziness'. Quinlan was the first necromancer who gave them the time of day (and whose prices wouldn't blow the whole quarter's budget on one corpse).

"Sure, I can do it," he said without looking away from the first-person shooter he played. "Leave the file and the money on the table and I'll get to it in a—TAKE THAT, PUNK!"

Detective Lindon jumped at the sudden outburst. Anderson gave him an impatient look as she said, "Now. If it's not done in the next hour, the payment is halved." She was bluffing but it worked.

"Ugh," the young man whined. "Fine! I'll do it now!"

He paused the game and tossed the controller onto the sofa. It bounced off and hit the floor, spilling batteries across the carpet when the back popped off. Anderson struggled not to roll her eyes. If her son had behaved that way, she'd have locked the console in a cabinet for a week. (Not to judge anyone else's parenting technique but just *look* at the kid's apartment!)

Quinlan took up the file, opened it and cringed.

"You sure you wanna see this one?" he asked. "He ain't gonna be pretty."

"No," Detective Anderson agreed, "murder victims often aren't. And, yes, we want to see this one."

The necromancer shrugged, "Suit yourself." He

began chanting.

Anderson frowned. He hadn't cast a circle. There had been no sacrifice. He didn't even wait until they were with the corpse!

"Wait a minute…"

But it was too late. The incantation was complete. In one of the city's three morgues, a corpse had just risen. Lindon's hand twitched on the handle of his holstered pistol.

Quinlan grabbed the bills off the table and tossed the file at the fuming detective. "Good doing business with ya." He bent to retrieve the controller as Anderson stared at him in mute horror.

Despite what cinema and television would have you believe, being murdered doesn't necessarily make one a victim. Take Stuart, for instance. He had an incurable desire (created, according to his many ineffectual therapists, by a traumatic childhood) to hurt other people—which went hand in bloody hand with a bad case of hematolagnia. What the good detectives didn't know (and couldn't have discovered without a proper investigation) was that Stuart's most recent—and, frankly, most horrified—therapist, a Dr Jacob Patterson, had been the one to do the world a favour by removing Stuart from it.

Dr Patterson's office was Stuart's first stop when he regained corporeal form. The police didn't need a necromancer to find the doctor's killer; they just followed the sounds of the screams. They did, however, need a necromancer to remove the undead lunatic wreaking havoc in their city.

Just one small problem with that…

Terell looked a little better when he opened the door to the police. His nose was still rather red, but he didn't appear to be quite as clammy (though no one was in much of a hurry to touch him and find out). He wore a wrinkled bathrobe, fuzzy slippers and judgement.

"I help you because I want to see criminals brought to justice," Terell reminded the detectives, "not so that you can make yourselves look good."

"You've seen the news then?" Lieutenant Cooper asked. His precinct was the pride of the state; he wasn't going to apologise for doing what it took to secure their place at the top.

Terell replied with a scathing look and nothing else.

"Please," Lindon interjected before his superior could lose his temper, "will you—"

"No."

All three detectives stared blankly at the necromancer.

"What do you *mean* 'no'?" Cooper exclaimed, his temper in shreds around his feet. Lindon nearly groaned. The lieutenant would be busting their chops for a week over this one.

"I quit. Our partnership was clearly been a mistake. I'm ending it. Good day." Terell reached for the door.

"Wait!" Anderson exclaimed. "What are we supposed to do about Stuart? He's still out there, cutting people open!"

Terell felt bad for the dozens of people already slaughtered by the reanimated psychopath, but the detectives had proven they were just as bad as children. If he didn't punish them, how would they learn? Besides, he was thinking about a change of career. If his recent illness had taught Terell anything, it was that healers were always in demand—and their clients probably smelled a lot better than the ones he was used to working with.

He shrugged, "Google it."

The door slammed on their stricken expressions.

Kill your Darling (Before They Kill you)

by Jason Holden

As Dr Miller was being interrogated by a mysterious man in a white coat, he had thought of escape. The white room was bare, apart from the hard metal chairs the two men sat upon. He planned to kick out and spill the hot coffee all over his interrogator, then make a break for it. Looking around, he remembered the man by the door; surely, this brute would stop him. There would be no escape and Dr Miller was forced to talk about his work.

He told the man everything: how some obscure quote from a long-forgotten philosopher had set him on his life's path into physics and proving the existence of multiple dimensions. The tension had built as he relived his nightmares of the Great One. How its eye had turned on him, that eye which held a whole universe and such power, and such fury of a lowly human gazing upon it.

Dr Miller's backstory was long, but it seemed necessary for him to tell it, so it could truly be understood why he needed to push through and open the door to the other place: the kingdom of the Great One. Before Dr Miller made it this far, his tab was closed, Facebook opened and his creator browsed for a little while before standing up, crossing the room and flicking on the kettle.

"This is a two scooper for sure," he spoke, even though nobody was there to hear him except for his dog. Unscrewing the lid from the cheap unbranded coffee, he turned to look at her. At the sound of his voice, the dog had looked up from her bed across the room and padded over, in hope of a treat from the fridge, maybe even some ham.

Instead, she got a stroke while the kettle boiled, pushing her head into her owner's legs while he ruffled the loose skin around her neck. She let out a grunt of pleasure. It felt good to her, almost as good as ham.

"I dunno, Soots. I'm just not feeling it today."

Jason straightened up, leaving the dog to shake off the stroke, poured the water into the milk and coffee mix and carried the steaming mug over to the sofa, closing the laptop halfway, putting it into sleep mode on his way past.

He powered up the PlayStation and sank heavily into the sofa, patting the space beside him to invite his furry companion up to join him. She looked quizzically at him before turning around, heading back to her own bed in the corner. *Just an hour, then back to work,* he thought, *I just need to relax the ol' brain muscles.*

***

Dr Miller sat in the uncomfortable chair that had been created for him by the man in the outside world. "Is he just going to leave us here on these chairs? Has he even clicked save on us?"

The man in the white coat shrugged, "at least he gave you a name and a back story, I don't even know who I am. I mean, am I some sort of government stooge? I don't even know why I'm questioning you."

Leaving his post at the door, the large man strode over to join in the conversation. "I think you're a psychiatrist. I know I'm an orderly; he had me drag this guy from his room earlier and bring him here. I think it was supposed to be some big reveal later in the book, to leave the reader wondering if he's crazy or if he actually split dimensions."

Dr Miller stood up, sending the chair backwards, scraping loudly across the floor of the empty room.

"Well, it's been three days now and he's not written more than fifty words a day; today all he did was mess around with my memories, changed why I became a scientist."

"I think he's going to delete us," the man in the white coat was looking down, cleaning his spectacles on his coat. His voice was flat and emotionless, unlike Dr Miller's, which was full of fire.

"Well I'm not going to sit around and take it! Doesn't he know he has a responsibility to us? He made us live! He can't just erase us from the face of the earth because he's 'not feeling it'. Come on, I've got an idea."

Dr Miller left the room, followed by the orderly who turned around at the door to look at the man in the white coat.

"You coming?"

"No, I'll just wait here, I think." He didn't even look up, just sat in the hard metal chair, cleaning his glasses on his coat.

"Wow, he really didn't put a lot of effort into you, did he?" With that, the orderly turned and followed Dr Miller down the corridor.

The corridor was lined with doors, one or two of them contained people in straitjackets who screamed occasionally to break the silence. Looking into the rooms through the small, barred windows, Dr Miller saw that the people had no faces, just mouths with which to let out a noise. Other doors had barred windows but just empty space behind them; nothingness stared back as he peered through these. He shook his head as he walked past.

"He's not even populated the building very well, typical. He wants to be a great writer, he says! Can't even be bothered to fill in the details."

***

A black paw tapped at his leg, distracting him from the screen.

"Oh, wow. Two o'clock, alright my love. Let's go."

Jason put his PlayStation into rest mode, stood up and went to get ready for walking the dog.

"Just a short one today Sooty. I've not even tidied up yet, still got lots to do."

He clipped the harness around her waist, pressed play on his audiobook, grabbed the keys and set off walking.

They walked for about twenty minutes, returning home slightly damp from the drizzle that had doused them. Jason slipped off his jeans in the hall and made for the fridge. Pulling out a beer, he cracked it open with a satisfying hiss and sat at his desk, opening the laptop.

"Don't look at me like that. It's five o'clock somewhere."

The screen that hit him was not where he had left it. His characters had moved from the interrogation room and were wandering off to the lab where Dr Miller did his experiments. He could see the letters appearing on the screen in front of him.

"What?" He tapped the delete key, but the words kept appearing. "Must be a virus or something. I knew I should have renewed my anti-virus subscription."

Helpless to stop the story unfolding, he began to read.

***

Dr Miller and the orderly arrived at the lab; equipment lay scattered around. Some of it packed in large wooden boxes, the rest was halfway through being disassembled.

"They stopped my funding, kicked me out and started to pack up my lab," Dr Miller explained, "Lucky for us they never finished."

A crowbar had been left by the workers on his desk. Pointing at it, Dr Miller told the orderly to grab it and open the crates so he could search for the key.

Before long, he found what he was looking for, a small white key card, like the ones you might use for a hotel door.

"What is it?" asked the orderly. "I was kind of

expecting something more sciencey."

"Don't worry my friend, something more 'sciencey' is about to happen."

Against the far wall stood a framework of shining metal; it looked as if someone had asked a child to design a door for a spaceship. Flashing lights were embedded all around, and it was lined with exposed circuitry and thick winding blue wires that seemed to go everywhere and nowhere at the same time. Dr Miller inserted the card into the slot and the frame shuddered to life. The blue lights turned red and started to flash faster; the wires lining it hummed as power surged into the frame. The lights went green, and the wall behind the door shimmered; the effect was similar to the heat wave coming off the tarmac mid-summer.

"Let's go."

Without looking back, Dr Miller walked through; before the eyes of the orderly, he vanished through the door. One second he was there, then he was not.

***

The world shimmered before the orderly's eyes. When his vision had settled, the landscape before him was alien. Twisted rock formations rose from the ground, red dust rising from them, swirling in the harsh wind. Dr Miller stood at the edge of a cliff, shouting into the wind while waving his arms, trying to grab the attention of something.

There was no need for it, however. A great shape rose from the valley below, awakened by their presence in its world. When it spoke, the voice of the Great One reverberated through him, like he was leaning right up against the speaker at a rock concert.

"You come to me again? Foolish!"

Red rocks showered down from the cliffs and the orderly covered his ears, fearing they would burst. Such was the volume of the Great One's voice.

"I come to save both our lives, for what they're worth." Dr Miller didn't seem phased by the creature; he stood, braced with his legs apart at the edge of the cliff as it swam closer, his white lab coat fluttering around him in the wind.

It seemed, to the orderly, that its body was made of smoke, yet somehow solid. It didn't move, so much as it flowed across the landscape. Changing shape to suit itself, where before it had no arms, now a hand clasped down at the cliff's edge where Dr Miller stood. The only thing about it that remained constant was the one gigantic eye that sat in the middle of the head. As he stared into the eye, it seemed the orderly could see stars, not just stars, but a whole universe stared back at him, swirling in constant motion.

"You know all," Dr Miller shouted at the shadow of smoke. "You know that man out there is going to erase us both. With your powers and my machine, we can break through and take him, so that we might live."

Once more the floor shook as it spoke, it was close that it was unbearable. The orderly dropped to his knees; hands clasped over his ears in a vain effort to dim the noise.

"This would require much power. A sacrifice would be needed."

Turning halfway round, Dr Miller waved his hand at the orderly, "Why do you think I brought him?"

Realisation swept over the orderly as a gaping grin formulated over the Great One's face. The orderly felt himself being pulled, yet he didn't move. His hands rose in front of his eyes, the fingertips turning to smoke and steadily streaming towards the Great One.

***

"Alright, this is ridiculous!"

By now it was obvious this was a prank. Someone

had clearly taken over the laptop and was typing out the rest of his story. *Some kind of Trojan, or worm, or something,* he thought. Cursing himself for not backing up any of his work onto a USB drive like he had planned, he started an emergency shutdown. CTRL, ALT, DELETE. Nothing happened. He tapped DELETE again and again. Still it did not shut down.

"Fuck!"

Slamming the laptop closed, he stood.

"It's not funny."

The screen was still open. The laptop was closed, but the screen was still there.

Confused, he reached out and touched it. It rippled, thick slow waves moving out in circles around his fingers. Jason tried to draw back, but his hand was slowly being pulled into the screen.

***

Dr Miller had no idea what would happen to his world once the writer was brought through; he didn't plan on being around to find out. Once the portal was open, he took his chance and dove into the shimmering light. As the Great One realised his plan, it let out a scream of rage, snatching at him with smoky tendrils, trying to keep him on this plane.

***

The other side was much like his own world, only more rich, vibrant even. Details and colours that he had never seen before jumped out at him, not to mention sounds. Passing traffic sang to him through the open window, crisscrossing with the children shouting outside and the soft flow of the wind.

"You look just like me, how convenient your idleness is for me."

Jason looked at the copy of himself, one arm clasped to the other, trying in vain to pull himself out of the screen that was slowly taking him in.

"Help?" His voice was quiet, lame.

"I'm afraid there is no help for you. The Great One shall have you."

Dr Miller took a step forward and shoved. Jason tumbled into the screen and it blinked away. Its purpose fulfilled; it closed forever.

***

Vomit coursed out of his mouth, wetting the dust that

layered the ground, darkening it from red to a deep brown. Looking up, he saw the Great One, a being of his own creation, and his bladder let go to join his stomach in the rebellion.

A sound emanated from the smoky figure; he soon realised it to be laughter. Jason was lifted from the ground; he drifted towards the eye. He knew that eye; he had seen it before as he created it.

"You will write me a new chapter!"

He closed his eyes, *I must be pissed, asleep on the sofa again. It's not the first nightmare I've had like this.*

"I am real, you made me real."

Jason thought his body might burst from the power of that voice as the Great One lifted him towards its eye. In vain he braced his hands against the ball of the eye, trying to push back. Some tension greeted his fingers, then he passed through it.

***

Jason was in his living room, sat at his desk with a cup of coffee on his right and a glass of water on his left. He was set up for a good hour of writing, maybe more. Thoughts whispered in his mind and flowed through to his fingers; they flew across the keyboard writing out the revenge of the Great One on Dr Miller. There would be no escape for the hero of this piece. He could not be allowed to escape the eternal power of the ruler of the shadow realm.

Author
Biographies

A.L. KING

A.L. King is an author of horror, fantasy, science fiction, and poetry. As an avid fan of dark subjects from an early age, his first influences included R.L. Stine, Edgar Allan Poe, and Stephen King. Later stylistic inspirations came from foreign horror films and media, particularly Japanese. He is a graduate of West Liberty University, has dabbled in journalism, and is actively involved in his community. Although his creativity leans toward darker genres, he has even written a children's book titled "Leif's First Fall." He was raised in the town of Sistersville, West Virginia, which he still proudly calls home.

A.R DEAN

A.R. Dean is a dark and twisted soul. Dean has spent their whole life spreading fear with the tales from their head. Best known for stories that terrify and show the evilest side of human nature. So, look for Dean haunting your local cemetery or under your bed, because they're here to spread the fear. Turn off your lights and enjoy a scare. Dean is being published in Black Hare Press's Beyond and Unravel Anthologies. Keep a lookout for more stories.

Facebook: A.R. Dean Author & Ghoul

A.R JOHNSTON

AR Johnston is a small town girl from Nova Scotia, Canada. She is known to write mostly urban fantasy, though she goes where the muses lead her and you never know where that may be. She is a lover of coffee, good tv shows, horror flicks, and a reader of good books. She pretends to be a writer when real life doesn't get in the way. Pesky full-time job and adulting!

Facebook: arjohnstonauthor
Website: arjohnstonauthor.wordpress.com

ANN WYCOFF

Ann Wycoff lives near Santa Cruz, California up in the hills among the redwoods. Her work has or will soon appear in the Porter Gulch Review, Scary Snippets: Christmas Edition, and Organic Ink, Volume 2.

Website: annwycoff.wordpress.com

BRONWYN TODD

Bronwyn Todd is a Mental Health Drug and Alcohol Clinician with a passion for horror and supernatural tales. She was born and raised in Tasmania, Australia, but currently calls Mildura home. She lives in the country, surrounded by grapevines, with her husband, their two children, two dogs and a budgie. Her flash fiction story 'The Thing at the Window' was published in 'Fire and Brimstone, a Demonic Compendium of the Fallen, Wicked and Accursed' (Specul8 Publishing, 2019). She was recently awarded a mentorship with the Australasian Horror Writer's Association and is currently honing her first novel.

Website: _bronwyntoddwriter.com_

CATHERINE KENWELL

Catherine Kenwell is a Barrie, Ontario, mediator and author. After 30 successful years in corporate communications, she sustained a brain injury, lost her job, and joined the circus. She writes both horror/dark fiction and inspirational non-fiction. Her works have been published in Chicken Soup for the Soul, Trembling with Fear, Siren's Call, and HellBound Books.

Website: _www.catherinekenwell.com_

CINDAR HARRELL

Cindar Harrell loves fairy tales, especially ones with a dark twist. Her writing is often fairy tale inspired, but she also loves mystery and horror. Her stories can be found in various anthologies from publishers such as Black Hare Press, Iron Faerie Publishing, Dragon Soul Press, Blood Song Books, Soteira Press, Fantasia Divinity and more. Traveling is a passion for her as it inspires her imagination to run wild, especially in places that have a mystic presence in the air. She regularly moonlights as another human, but no matter who she is, she is always writing. Her novella inspired by The Snow Queen is set to release in 2020 as well as her debut novel, Lithium, and short story collection, Perchance to Dream.

Facebook: _CindarHarrell_

DAWN DEBRAAL

Dawn DeBraal lives in rural Wisconsin with her husband Red, two rat terriers, and a cat. She has discovered that her love of telling a good story can be written. Published stories with Palm-sized press, Spillwords, Mercurial Stories, Potato Soup Journal, Edify Fiction, Zimbell House Publishing, Clarendon House Publishing, Blood Song Books, Black Hare Press, Fantasia Divinity, Cafelit, Reanimated Writers, Guilty Pleasures, Unholy Trinity, The World of Myth, Dastaan World, Vamp Cat, Runcible Spoon, Dark Christmas, Siren's Call, Iron Horse Publishing, Falling Star Magazine 2019 Pushcart Nominee.

Amazon: _amazon.com/Dawn-DeBraal/e/B07STL8DLX_

EDDIE D. MOORE

Eddie D. Moore travels hundreds of hours a year, and he fills that time by listening to audiobooks. When he isn't playing with his grandchildren, he writes his own stories. You can find a list of his publications on his blog or by visiting his Amazon Author Page. While you're there, be sure to pick up a copy of his mini-anthology Misfits & Oddities.

Website: eddiedmoore.wordpress.com
Amazon: amazon.com/author/eddiedmoore

G. ALLEN WILBANKS

G. Allen Wilbanks is a member of the Horror Writers Association (HWA) and has published over 100 short stories in various magazines and on-line venues. He is the author of two short story collections, and the novel, When Darkness Comes.

Website: www.gallenwilbanks.com
Blog: DeepDarkThoughts.com

GABRIELLA BALCOM

Gabriella Balcom lives in Texas with her family, loves reading and writing, and thinks she was born with a book in her hands. She works in a mental health field, and writes fantasy, horror/thriller, romance, children's stories, and sci-fi. She likes travelling, music, good shows, photography, history, interesting tales, and animals. Gabriella says she's a sucker for a great story and loves forests, mountains, and back roads which might lead who knows where. She has a weakness for lasagne, garlic bread, tacos, cheese, and chocolate, but not necessarily in that order.

Facebook: GabriellaBalcom.lonestarauthor

GALINA TREFIL

Galina Trefil is a novelist specializing in women's, minority, and disabled rights. Her favorite genres are horror, thriller, and historical fiction. Her short stories and articles have appeared in Neurology Now, UnBound Emagazine, The Guardian, Tikkun, Romea.CZ, Jewcy, Jewrotica, Telegram Magazine, Ink Drift Magazine, The Dissident Voice, Open Road Review, and the anthologies "Flock: The Journey," "First Love," "Sea of Secrets," "Coffins and Dragons," "Organic Ink volume One," "Winds of Despair," "Waters of Destruction," "Curses & Cauldrons," "Unravel," "Hate," "Love," "Oceans," "Forgotten Ones," "Dark Valentine Holiday Horror Collection," and "Suspense Unimagined."

Website: galinatrefil.wordpress.com
Facebook: Rabbi-Galina-Trefil-535886443115467

HARI NAVARRO

Hari Navarro has, for many years now, been locked in his neighbours cellar. He survives due to an intravenous feed of puréed extreme horror and Absinthe infused sticky-spiced unicorn wings. His anguished cries for help can be found via 365 Tomorrows, Breachzine, AntipodeanSF, Horror Without Borders, Black Hare Press and HellBound books. Hari was the Winner of the Australasian Horror Writers' Association [AHWA] Flash Fiction Award 2018 and has, also, succeeded in being a New Zealander who now lives in Northern Italy with no cats.

Amazon: amazon.com/Hari-Navarro
Tumblr: harinavarro.tumblr.com/

JACQUELINE MORAN MEYER

Jacqueline Moran Meyer is a writer, artist and small business owner living in New York, where she received her master's degree from Teachers College, Columbia University. Jacqueline enjoys writing speculative fiction and horror stories. Her favorite author is Alice Munro and her favorite film…is…anything horror related. Jacqueline also enjoys hiking with her dog Molly and the company of her husband Bruce and daughters; Julia, Emma and Lauren. Jacqueline's Mantra lately; WTF.

Website: jmoranmeyer.net
Amazon: www.amazon.com/author/jacquelinemoranmeyer

J.W. GARRETT

J.W. Garrett has been writing in one form or another since she was a teenager. She currently lives in Florida with her family but loves the mountains of Virginia where she was born. Her writings include YA fantasy as well as short stories. Since completing Remeon's Quest-Earth Year 1930, the prequel in her YA fantasy series, Realms of Chaos, she has been hard at work on the next in the series, scheduled to release August 2020. When she's not hanging out with her characters, her favourite activities are reading, running and spending time with family.

Website: www.jwgarrett.com
BHC Press: www.bhcpress.com/Author_JW_Garrett.html

JACQUELINE MORAN MEYER

Jacqueline Moran Meyer is a writer, artist and small business owner living in New York, where she received her master's degree from Teachers College, Columbia University. Jacqueline enjoys writing speculative fiction and horror stories. Her favorite author is Alice Munro and her favorite film...is...anything horror related. Jacqueline also enjoys hiking with her dog Molly and the company of her husband Bruce and daughters; Julia, Emma and Lauren. Jacqueline's Mantra lately; WTF.

Website: jmoranmeyer.net
Amazon: www.amazon.com/author/jacquelinemoranmeyer

JASON HOLDEN

Jason is a human. He lives here and there in the UK, always with his wife, daughter and fur baby. His primary goal is to raise his daughter to adulthood without any major damage. When he can, he writes. He thinks he does it well, but you can be the judge of that. He has been published in a few anthologies here and there, has been praised and put down for his writing. You can find and follow him on Facebook, although he asks you only follow him on Facebook and not through the streets. That's just creepy.

Facebook: Jason Holden-Author

JO MULARCZYK

Jo Mularczyk's stories and poems appear in magazines and anthologies including - The School Magazine's Blast Off and Touchdown; One Surviving Story; fourW thirty; Wonderment; Zinewest; Short and Twisted; several Storm Cloud Publishing anthologies; Daily Science Fiction; the US magazine Cricket; an upcoming UK collection; other Black Hare Press publications and several upcoming anthologies. Jo mentors a gifted and talented students' writing group, runs writing workshops and is a co-author with the student literacy program, Littlescribe, providing writing tips and story starters for students to complete. Jo lives in Australia with her husband and three children.

Website: www.jomularczyk.com
Facebook: jo_mularczyk_authorpage

JO SEYSENER

Jo Seysener is a mum of three crazies, a scatter of chickens, a decrepit kelpie and a rambunctious GSD. She lives with her husband near Brisbane, Australia. When she is not exposing her kids to cult story books from her childhood, she can be found in the kitchen experimenting with new flavours and pairings. She adores alpacas.

Facebook: joseysener
Website: www.joseysener.com

JODI JENSEN

Jodi Jensen, author of time travel romances and speculative fiction short stories, grew up moving from California, to Massachusetts, and a few other places in between, before finally settling in Utah at the ripe old age of nine. The nomadic life fed her sense of adventure as a child and the wanderlust continues to this day. With a passion for old cemeteries, historical buildings and sweeping sagas of days gone by, it was only natural she'd dream of time traveling to all the places that sparked her imagination.

Twitter: @WritesJodi
Facebook: jodijensenwrites

JOHN H. DROMEY

John H. Dromey was born in northeast Missouri, USA. He enjoys reading—mysteries in particular—and writing in a variety of genres. In addition to contributing to the Black Hare Press series of Dark Drabbles anthologies, he's had short fiction published in Alfred Hitchcock's Mystery Magazine, Martian Magazine, Mystery Weekly, Stupefying Stories Showcase, Thriller Magazine, Unfit Magazine, and elsewhere, as well as in numerous anthologies, including Chilling Horror Short Stories (Flame Tree Publishing, 2015).

JOSHUA E. BORGMANN

Joshua E. Borgmann holds degrees from Drake University, Iowa State University, and the University of South Carolina. He grew up on horror and science-fiction and had long intended to become a great master of the art form before he was sucked into the bottomless pit of academia. He toils away his days as an English instructor at a small community college and dreams of being able to escape into a world of fantasy and terror where there are no student papers to grade. He and his wife reside in a nameless rural Iowa town surrounded by terrible cornfields where he is terrorized by several felines who have taken refuge in his home.

K.B. ELIJAH

K.B. Elijah is a fantasy author living in Brisbane, Australia with her husband and three cockatiels. A lawyer by day, and a writer by...also day, because she needs her solid nine hours of sleep per night (not that the cockatiels let her sleep past 6am). K.B. writes for various international anthologies, and her work features in dozens of collections about the mysterious, the magical and the macabre. Her own books of short fantasy novellas with twists, The Empty Sky and Out of the Nowhere, are available on paperback and Kindle now.

Website: www.kbelijah.com
Instagram: k.b.elijah

LYNDSEY ELLIS-HOLLOWAY

Lyndsey Ellis-Holloway is a writer from Knaresborough, UK. She writes fantasy, sci-fi, horror and dystopian stories, focussing on compelling characters and layering in myth and legend at every opportunity. Her mind is somewhat dark and twisted, and she lives in perpetual hope of owning her own Dragon someday, but for now she writes about them to fill the void... and to stop her from murdering people who annoy her. When she's not writing she spends time with her husband, her dogs and her friends enjoying activities such as walking, movies, conventions and of course writing for fun as well!

Website: theprose.com/LyndseyEH

M. SYDNOR JR.

M. Sydnor Jr. is an author of novels and short stories. He began his career in writing in 2005 after trading in his basketball sneakers for a pen and pad, and the desire to create worlds took off. Early in his writing journey, he learned there was more than just putting an idea to paper, you had to read. He lives in Northern California collecting an unhealthy number of movies, books and graphic novels. The characters of his fantasy series, The Legends of the World, take most of his time when he's not coaching high school basketball.

MARCUS BINES

In the real world, Marcus Bines is a teacher with far too little time for writing. He grew up on Tintin, the fifth Doctor and lightsabre fights in the back garden. In the slightly less real world, he's a fantasy writer (currently working on a teen romance detour), with two short stories out in the world. More of those - and novels - to come soon. Many things take his fancy: movies, fantasy, animals, faith, languages, nature, ideas, veganism, unanswerable questions, sci-fi, indie rock, myths, possibilities, aliens, words - and human beings. They're pretty interesting.

MATTHEW A. CLARKE

Matthew A. Clarke is a new face in the world of horror. He has been writing short fiction as a hobby for two years and has decided to share his passion with likeminded people. Matthew loves all things that go bump in the night, having been introduced to slasher movies at a young age. He lives on the South Coast of England with his fiancé, Isabelle, and a little dachshund called Frank.

Facebook: matthewaclarkeauthor

MAXINE CHURCHMAN

Maxine Churchman lives in Essex UK and has recently started writing poetry and short stories to share. Her interests include learning to improve her writing, reading, knitting, walking and teaching yoga. She is also planning a novel.

N.M. BROWN

Since N.M. Brown made her first post to a popular Internet forum, she's taken the horror community by storm. Her ability to create, terrify, and drive home her stories is insurmountable. N.M. Brown's published works can be found in multiple anthologies for all to read, but be forewarned, if you do... you may want to call your therapist after, her stories are terrifying, disturbing and devilishly unsettling. She is not only a fright visually, but also has a creepy tentacle in horror podcasting as well. Sinister Sweetheart writes, voice acts and is the media director of the Scarecrow Tales podcast.

Website: Sinistersweetheart.wixsite.com/sinistersweetheart
Facebook: NMBrownStories

NERISHA KEMRAJ

Nerisha Kemraj resides in Durban, South Africa with her husband and two mischievous daughters. She has work published/accepted in various publications, both print and online. She holds a Bachelor's degree in Communication Science, and a Post Graduate Certificate in Education from University of South Africa.

Amazon: amazon.com/author/nerisha_kemraj
Facebook: Nerishakemrajwriter

NICOLA CURRIE

Nicola Currie is from Cambridge, UK where she works in educational publishing. She has published poetry in literary magazines, including Mslexia and Sarasvati, and short stories in various anthologies. She has also completed her first novel, which was longlisted for the Bath Children's Novel Award.

Website: writeitandweep.home.blog

RAVEN CORINN CARLUK

Raven Corinn Carluk writes dark fantasy, paranormal romance, and anything else that catches her interest. She's authored five novels, where she explores themes of love and acceptance. Her shorter pieces, usually from her darker side, can be found in Black Hare Press anthologies, at Detritus Online, and through Alban Lake Publishers.

Twitter: @ravencorinn
Website: www.ravencorinncarluk.com

RHIANNON BIRD

Rhiannon Bird is a young aspiring author. She has a passion for words and storytelling. Rhiannon has her own quotes blog; Thoughts of a Writer. She has had 4 works published. This includes 3 short stories and 2 poems. These are published on Eskimo pie, Literary yard, Down in the Dirt Magazine and Short break fiction. She can be found on Facebook, Instagram, and Pinterest.

S. GEPP

S.Gepp is an Australian who has been writing for a number of years in the horror, fantasy, sci-fi and humour genres. Tertiary educated, former acrobat and professional wrestler, a father of two and well past 40 years old, he hopes to be a real writer when he grows up.

Amazon: amazon.com/Sins-Fathers-S-Gepp-ebook/dp/B07XBDP2RF/

SANDY BUTCHERS

Sandy Butchers is an author and an artist, known for her elaborate fantasy worlds and creature designs. After living in Scandinavia for a year and traveling throughout the world, she now settled in the countryside, along with a variety of pets and maps on which X marks the spot.

Website: www.sandybutchers.com
Facebook: AuthorSandyButchers

STACY JAINE MCINTOSH

Stacey Jaine McIntosh was born in Perth, Western Australia where she still resides with her husband and their four children. Although her first love has always been writing, she once toyed with being a Cartographer and subsequently holds a Diploma in Spatial Information Services. Since 2011, she has had a vast number of stories and a few poems published online as well as in various anthologies. Stacey is also the author of Solstice, Morrighan, Lost and Le Fay and she is currently working on several other projects simultaneously. When not with her family or writing she enjoys reading, photography, genealogy, history, Arthurian myths and witchcraft

Website: www.staceyjainemcintosh.com

STEPHEN HERCZEG

Stephen Herczeg is an IT Geek based in Canberra Australia. He has been writing for over twenty years and has completed a couple of dodgy novels, sixteen feature length screenplays and numerous short stories and scripts. His horror work has featured in Sproutlings, Hells Bells, Below the Stairs, Trickster's Treats #1 and #2, Shades of Santa, Behind the Mask, Beyond the Infinite; The Body Horror Book, Anemone Enemy, Petrified Punks and Beginnings. He has also had numerous Sherlock Holmes stories published through the Belanger Books - Sherlock Holmes anthologies.

Amazon: amazon.com/-/e/B07916SQQS
Facebook: stephenherczegauthor

STEPHEN MCQUIGGAN

Stephen McQuiggan was the original author of the bible; he vowed never to write again after the publishers removed the dinosaurs and the spectacular alien abduction ending from the final edit. His other, lesser known, novels are A Pig's View Of Heaven and Trip A Dwarf.

SUE MARIE ST. LEE

Born in Chicago, Sue Marie St. Lee currently lives in Oklahoma with her husband and Manx cat. A storyteller since learning to talk, her wild imagination caused reprimands from her Mother. Her imagination persevered. Retired from Finance Management, Sue began ghostwriting until 2019, choosing to have works published internationally, in print and online, under her own name. Black Hare Press, Fantasia Divinity, and Spillwords Press are some of the publishers to feature Sue's work to date.

Blog: suemariestlee.home.blog
Amazon: amazon.com/Sue-Marie-St.-Lee/e/B07WJFRF1L

WONDRA VANIAN

Wondra Vanian is an American living in the United Kingdom with her Welsh husband and their army of fur babies. A writer first, Wondra is also an avid gamer, photographer, cinephile, and blogger. She has music in her blood, sleeps with the lights on, and has been known to dance naked in the moonlight. Wondra was a multiple Top-Ten finisher in the 2017 and 2018 Preditors and Editors Reader's Poll, including the Best Author category. Her story, "Halloween Night," was named a Notable Contender for the Bristol Short Story Prize in 2015.

Website: www.wondravanian.com

XIMENA ESCOBAR

Ximena is writing stories and poetry. Originally from Chile, she is the author of a translation into Spanish of the Broadway Musical "The Wizard of Oz", and of an original adaptation of the same, "Navidad en Oz", both produced in her home country. Since 2018 she has published several short stories in various anthologies and online platforms, and is now slowly working on her own collection. Ximena has a degree in Arts & Communication Science and lives in Nottingham with her family.

Facebook: Ximenautora
Twitter: @laximenin

ZOEY XOLTON

Zoey Xolton is an Australian Speculative Fiction writer, primarily of Dark Fantasy, Paranormal Romance and Horror. She is also a proud mother of two and is married to her soul mate. Outside of her family, writing is her greatest passion. She is especially fond of short fiction and is working on releasing her own themed collections in future.

Website: www.zoeyxolton.com

Acknowledgements

When we embarked on our Black Hare Press journey back in late 2018, we never envisioned the huge support we'd get from the writing community. We have been truly humbled by the number of submissions we've received (around 3,000 over our first eight publications!) and have loved reading every single one.

So, thank you to everyone who crafted tales just for us—from the tiny tales in our Dark Drabbles series to these sinful tales you have read here in Lust—we thank you from the bottom of our hearts.

To our families and friends, collaborators, random strangers who took pity on us, and everyone who has helped us on the way: we couldn't have done it without you.

And to you, our discerning reader, we and these talented writers did it all for you. We hope you enjoyed these tales, and if you did, don't forget to leave a review.

Thank you all—see you next time.

Love & kisses
Ben & Dean

www.blackharepress.com

sloth

sloth

sloth